I HESITATED.

At the depths of the mind is a great unconscious mindstream. It was into this that the futuretellers dipped for their predictions. Without training it was possible for a mind to literally dissolve. I was already deeper than I had ever gone before.

I braced myself. Fighting an irresistible urge to rise, I pushed my mind fraction by fraction into the depths. All at once the void seemed to brighten and, below, I was aware of the shining silver rush of the mindstream.

"I have come," I grated.

"Deeper," Maruman urged. "Must come deeper."

BOOKS BY
ISOBELLE CARMODY

◆

THE OBERNEWTYN CHRONICLES

Obernewtyn
The Farseekers
Ashling
The Keeping Place
Wavesong
The Stone Key
The Sending
Red Queen

◆

THE GATEWAY TRILOGY

Night Gate
Winter Door

◆

LITTLE FUR

The Legend Begins
A Fox Called Sorrow
A Mystery of Wolves
Riddle of Green

ISOBELLE CARMODY

THE FARSEEKERS

Random House 🏠 New York

Copyright © 1990 by Isobelle Carmody
Cover art copyright © 2007 by Penguin Group (Australia)
Map copyright © 2008 by Penguin Group (Australia)

All rights reserved.
Published in the United States by Random House Children's Books,
a division of Random House, Inc., New York.

Random House and colophon are registered trademarks of Random House, Inc.

The text of this work was originally published by Penguin Books Australia Ltd,
Camberwell, in 1990. Published here by arrangement with Penguin Group
(Australia), a division of Pearson Australia Group Pty Ltd.

Visit us on the Web!
www.randomhouse.com/teens

Educators and librarians, for a variety of teaching tools, visit us at
www.randomhouse.com/teachers

Library of Congress Cataloging-in-Publication Data
Carmody, Isobelle.
The farseekers / Isobelle Carmody. — 1st Random House ed.
   p. cm. — (Obernewtyn Chronicles ; bk. 2)
Summary: When Elspeth and others undertake a dangerous journey to rescue a
powerful psychic and find an enormous book trove, the fate of the Obernewtyn
colony hangs in the balance.
ISBN 978-0-375-85768-3 (pbk.) — ISBN 978-0-375-95768-0 (lib. bdg.)
[1. Voyages and travels—Fiction. 2. Persecution—Fiction. 3. Human-animal
communication—Fiction. 4. Extrasensory perception—Fiction. 5. Friendship—
Fiction. 6. Science fiction.] I. Title.
PZ7.C2176Far 2008   [Fic]—dc22   2008018503

Cover and map design by Cathy Larsen
Cover background artwork by Les Petersen
Cover photographs by Getty Images

Printed in the United States of America
10 9 8 7 6 5 4 3 2
First Random House Edition

for Shane

✦ THE GUILDS OF OBERNEWTYN ✦

Rushton, Master of Obernewtyn

The Beastspeaking Guild
Guildmaster: Alad
Guilders include Lina, Zarak, and Louis Larkin

The Coercer Guild
Guildmaster: Gevan
Guilden: Miryum
Ward: Domick

The Empath Guild
Guildmaster: Dameon
Guilden: Miky & Angina

The Farseek Guild
Guildmistress: Elspeth
Guilden: Ceirwan
Ward: Matthew

The Futuretell Guild
Guildmistress: Maryon
Guilden: Christa
Ward: Dell

The Healer Guild
Guildmaster: Roland
Ward: Kella

The Teknoguild
Guildmaster: Garth
Ward: Pavo

PART I

✦

REFUGE

✦ 1 ✦

ROLAND SHOOK HIS head decisively. "I can do nothing to hasten the healing, Elspeth. If you rested them more often . . ."

I sighed and rubbed the tender soles of my feet. "Kella said a warmer climate might help."

Roland nodded absently, returning satchels of herbs to his carryall. "It's true that cold doesn't help the healing process, but whatever miracles we healers can do, changing the weather to suit our patient is not among them."

I was startled at the unexpected touch of humor from the dour Healer guildmaster. Hefting the weighty bag onto his shoulder, Roland gave me a piercing look. "If you would stay in your room in wintertime with banked fires instead of wandering around the drafty halls—and beyond . . ."

"I *am* mistress of a guild," I said.

Roland was unsympathetic. "Garth finds no difficulty in remaining in his caves, and the Teknoguild works do not crumble because of its master's inactivity," he said with faint asperity.

The Teknoguild was concerned with studying the Beforetime and researching the effects—past, present, and future—of the Great White. I had little interest in such things, but I had met secretly with Garth only that morning. I wondered if Roland knew.

"Garth . . . is Garth," I said with a smile. Roland's lip twitched.

There was a knock at the door, and Kella entered, carrying a jug.

Roland waved his ward in impatiently as he addressed me. "Soak in that, then rub some of the salve into the soles. And stay off your feet!" he growled, slamming the door behind him.

Kella poured the liquid in a flat pan, smiling ruefully. "He's angry with himself, because your feet aren't healing properly."

I lowered my feet gingerly into the shallow pannikin. A sweet scent rose from the water. "Herb lore?" I guessed.

Kella nodded. "A recipe given to us by the Master of Obernewtyn himself."

I smiled, never quite able to accept Rushton's grandiose title. When I had first met him, he was an enigmatic farm overseer only a few years older than myself. No one had been more astonished than I to discover he was the legal owner of Obernewtyn.

Kella was staring into the fire, its orange glow playing over her cheeks. "Rushton has not come back yet from the highlands," she said, a faint line of worry between her brows. I wondered idly if the healer was attracted to Rushton. It would be a pity for her. His brooding singleness of purpose made him blind to anything but his complicated plans for the future. I smiled wryly.

"It's good to see you smile," Kella said. The old fear of revealing myself caused me a moment of panic, then

I consciously relaxed. The need for hiding my expressions was past, at least at Obernewtyn.

"Yet there is not much to smile at, even here," I said somberly.

Kella's look sharpened. "You spoke to the newcomers?"

I nodded. "Their news is worrying. When I was in the orphan homes, torture was nothing more than a rumor."

Kella's face was pale. The deliberate infliction of pain was an anathema to any healer, but torture was doubly dreadful, involving as it did both mental and physical pain forged into one. She disliked even the mind-bending activities of the Coercer guild, and this was far worse.

As if reading my thoughts, she said, "Miryum claims there are times when the end justifies the means, but even a coercer could not condone torture."

Tactless Miryum was guilden of the aggressive Coercer guild, whose function was to defend Obernewtyn and prepare for battle with the Council, if it should come to that. There was a growing rift between the Healer and Coercer guilds. The members of each, along with futuretellers, could descend into the unconscious mind—we called it *deep probing*. But no two guilds used the ability to deep-probe in the same manner. The mind of a coercer was a weapon to suborn the will of other minds. By contrast, the healer used a probe, honed tendril-thin, for healing. It was little wonder the two guilds were at loggerheads—they used the same ability to opposing ends.

"Anyone would think you were a futureteller," Kella said resignedly, clearly referring to the habit futuretellers had of drifting into a dream in the middle of conversations.

I laughed. "It might be pleasant. You would never be surprised by anything."

"Not for me," Kella said. "I prefer to live in the present. I don't want to know the future."

Without warning, the door was flung open by a wild-eyed Matthew. Seeing me, his anxious expression dissolved. "Here ye are! I've been searchin' all over for ye!" he said accusingly.

I blinked at him. "Oh? I must have forgotten to say where I was going."

Kella snorted, knowing I disliked the lack of privacy that went with being a guildmistress and often evaded such formalities as making my whereabouts known.

Forgetting his frustration, Matthew hurried over. "Rushton has just come back! An' he's called a guildmerge."

"When?" I asked.

"Now!" Matthew said.

My heart jumped. Rushton often traveled outside the mountains, for there was no danger to the legal Master of Obernewtyn doing so. But something serious must have happened for him to call a guildmerge so abruptly.

"Did he say why?" I asked. I dried my feet quickly and slipped on my boots.

"Nowt a word," Matthew answered, handing me my walking stick. "He was investigatin' a rumor that th' Council meant to establish a soldierguard camp in th' highlands. Do ye suppose . . . ?" he began, aghast at the thought of a camp so close to Obernewtyn. It had been bad enough when a soldierguard training camp was set up just below the lower ranges. If the Council meant to put a camp in the highlands, it could only be because they intended to tighten their control of the high country.

"It might be no more than gossip," I said.

Ceirwan would know what had happened, since he had gone with Rushton. As guilden of the farseekers, he would normally have reported to me at once, but Rushton's call for an immediate guildmerge had clearly made that impossible.

I wondered if any of the guilds would use the unexpected meeting to make requests. I had had no time to prepare a submission since meeting with Garth, but Pavo would be at the meeting and might fill in the gaps. If Matthew's speculations were right, it was important to act quickly in case Rushton decided to suspend all expeditions.

I shivered as we exited the outer doors of the Healer hall. As ever in the mountains, there was a chilly underbite to the air, and the old burn scars on my feet and lower legs ached. Roland had promised they would heal in time, but two years had passed and they still hurt at the first sign of cold weather.

My eyes went beyond the gray stone walls that surrounded Obernewtyn and its fields and farms to the horizon and the jagged line of the western mountains separating us from the highlands. Those mountains were our best protection, especially if soldierguards did set up camp in the highlands. In winter, snow cut us off from the highlands entirely, and even in the mildest season, the road to Obernewtyn was difficult.

The mountains kept us safe, yet the sight of them never failed to disturb me in some deep, incomprehensible way.

Long ago, in one of his queer fits, Maruman had told me my destiny lay in the mountains. Battered and half mad, the old cat had been my first friend and had followed me to Obernewtyn. Expecting a grim existence there, perhaps a horrible death, I had found friends and learned I was not alone in my mutant abilities. Once Rushton had taken control of Obernewtyn from his defective half brother, who had been manipulated by the wicked Alexi and Madam Vega, I had accepted his offer of refuge and stayed on. Alexi and Madam Vega had been killed in their battle to keep control of Obernewtyn, and their young accomplice Ariel had fled to his death in the bitter mountain winter. I could hardly recall Alexi's face or even Madam Vega's, but Ariel remained a vivid nightmare image. Of them all, he had left an impression, for his cruelty and his manipulative lust for power, hidden behind his angelic beauty, were evidence that evil might wear its own face.

To my surprise, I had been happy at Obernewtyn. Apart from his periodic wandering, Maruman also made Obernewtyn his home.

Yet I had the sudden chill premonition that the long time of healing and peace was drawing to an end.

"What is it?" Matthew asked.

"I was thinking of the past," I said. "Everything that happened in the caves with Alexi and Madam Vega, the Zebkrahn machine exploding, these . . ." I touched my scarred legs. "It all seems so long ago."

Matthew nodded grimly. "Sometimes I dream of Ariel an' I . . ." He shook his head. "I wish I had killed him. If he had nowt died in th' storm . . ."

I looked up, surprised at his vehemence.

When I had first met him, Matthew had been thin and frail-looking, with a pronounced limp and hungry, intelligent eyes. The limp had been long since healed with a reset bone, and Matthew now stood a head taller than I, with strong, wiry limbs. He had proven more than capable in his role as Farseeker ward. Ceirwan was convinced he was developing deep-probe ability, saying he often seemed to know our thoughts before we sent them. I had dismissed that, thinking it no more than the natural result of our closeness. But it might be so. There was so much about our abilities we had yet to understand.

Farseekers could converse mind to mind over varying distances, an ability that involved conscious rather than unconscious thought. I had believed myself the only farseeker also able to deep-probe. Yet multiTalents were not uncommon among us, and assignment to a guild was based on the dominant ability. In rare cases, two abilities were of equal strength.

As if to confirm his ability to know my private thoughts, Matthew said, "Maybe we should use this guildmerge to raise th' matter of Zarak changin' guilds."

Zarak had a strong Talent for communicating with animals, like his father, and he had chosen the Beastspeaking guild, only to discover that he had equally strong farseeking abilities. This had resulted in the desire to transfer to the Farseekers.

I shook my head decisively. "Now is not the time. Besides, I think that matter can be better resolved on a personal level. But something will have to be done soon, I agree. Zarak is proving to be a disturbing influence in the wrong guild."

Matthew nodded fervently. "Not that Lina isn't capable of gannin' up to mischief on her own. . . ." He trailed off as we approached the front steps to Obernewtyn.

The new doors were less imposing than the old, being too plain to complement the ornate stone scrolling of the entrance. I had a fleeting memory of watching the original doors burn, and with them the concealed maps that I alone knew showed a route to the Beforetime weaponmachines that had caused the Great White. To the others, the burning had been simply the easiest way to get at the inlaid gold we had used to make armbands for the guildmasters. That had been my suggestion, and Rushton had agreed. Perhaps my wounds had led him to humor me. He had been very kind and attentive then, I thought pensively.

As if conjured up by my thoughts, Rushton was waiting for us in the circular entrance hall.

He looked tired, and it was clear from his clothes that he had not bothered to change. I felt a rush of gladness at the sight of him, for though Obernewtyn ran smoothly even in his absence, I never felt as safe as when he was there.

He met my look with an ambivalent stare. It was almost a challenge. Before I could speak, he sent Matthew to find representatives from the Futuretell guild; then he ushered me toward the guildmerge, matching his steps to my own limping progress.

"What has happened?" I asked.

Rushton turned to look at me. "The Council is showing renewed interest in us. Two men were in the highlands asking questions about Obernewtyn."

"You think they were from the Council?"

He shrugged angrily. "I know nothing, except that I am tired of my ignorance. Do you remember when I went to claim Obernewtyn in Sutrium?" he asked.

I remembered. Sutrium was the center of Council activities. It had not been easy for him to convince everyone to wait for his return. Many had wanted to leave, fearing his trip would lead to their capture and burning. That we had chosen to wait had been an act of faith in Rushton. We had never regretted it.

"I remember," I murmured.

"I thought the Council had trusted me when I'd told them that Obernewtyn had been badly damaged in a firestorm but that I meant to rebuild slowly, using those who had survived for labor. I thought they would lose interest in us. Maybe I was wrong. With farseeker or coercer help, I could have made sure. But now . . ."

"Now?" I echoed.

Rushton looked at me, his green eyes glowing with sudden excitement, as if he had resolved some inner doubt. "It's time we found out what the Council is up to. Time we made a move into *their* territory."

"Sutrium?" I whispered.

"Sutrium," he echoed.

✦ 2 ✦

As USUAL, GUILDMERGE was held in the circular room that had once served as the doctor's work chamber and library, but all of the tables and benches that had filled it were gone. Only the enormous fireplace and the enormous hinged bookshelf dividing the chamber remained, though the bookshelf was pushed back to allow for the enormous table and the chairs surrounding it.

The tunnel concealed by the pivoting fireplace was now used only for easy wintertime transport of firewood into the meeting hall and as a swift, hidden route to the complex of caves where the Teknoguilders worked. Like other hidden passages at Obernewtyn, it was no longer a secret, although the incorrigibly curious Lina was convinced there were others and was forever to be found tapping the walls and listening for telltale hollowness.

Obernewtyn's first master, the reclusive Lukas Seraphim, had been a morose and secretive man, and the great gray buildings reflected his personality.

Louis Larkin, the eldest of our number, had known the man who had carved Obernewtyn out of the wilderness on what was then the very fringe of the Blacklands. He said Lukas had possessed a mind that was as much a labyrinth as the greenthorn maze separating the main house from the farms.

As its current master, Rushton had made many changes to the main building to provide clear paths and better access to all parts of the rambling wings and levels. It had been his idea that each guild be allocated a certain section of Obernewtyn as its base and that the guild members make changes to their areas as they desired.

Though cavernous, the domed meeting room was kept warm by an enormous fire, and I seated myself in a chair near it, surreptitiously toasting my sore feet.

The buzz of talk was louder than usual, partly because of the abrupt way Rushton had called the meeting and partly because it was a full guildmerge, with almost all wards, guildens, and guildleaders present. Even the irascible Garth had come, though he looked impatient and bored.

On the other side of the table sat Ceirwan, guilden of my own guild, still clad in riding clothes. I felt momentarily irritated by the guildmerge rule restricting communication during meetings to the spoken word, but I did not try to reach him.

Matthew took a seat opposite me and next to Dameon, the blind Empath guildmaster, who smiled at me unerringly, sensing my attention. Empaths could read emotions the way farseekers read thoughts, though few were actually able to converse mentally. Some empaths, like Dameon, could also transmit emotion. The twin Empath guilden, Miky and her brother, Angina, sat beside him, deep in animated discussion.

Rushton had walked to the head of the table and

was talking to Domick, the Coercer ward. Next to him, Maryon sat staring into the distance, a slight smile on her lips. No one could mistake her for anything but a futureteller. She had come in with Matthew, but the seat between her and the Futuretell ward was empty. I wondered what was important enough to keep the guilden, Christa, away.

Roland was alone in representing his guild. This was not unusual. The healers put their patients before anything else. Next, and completing the table, were the three members of the Beastspeaking guild—the master, Alad, looking unusually grim.

I was conscious of an expectant atmosphere among us as Rushton rose to speak, formally commencing the guildmerge. He invited those with business to raise their hand. Traditionally, Rushton spoke last. This meant that whatever had prompted the sudden guild-merge must wait until all other matters had been dealt with. His eyes widened speculatively at my hand among those few to rise.

Alad rose to speak, again raising the need for animals to be represented in guildmerge by one of their own. As before, no one could agree which animal should represent all animals and whether the animals should propose their own candidate. The increasing dominance of the volatile younger horses' attitude was raised. With a hint of impatience, Rushton suggested the matter be addressed at the next guildmerge.

The Beastspeaking guildmaster frowned. "This is the third time it's been put off. It's time we dealt with this once and for all."

"It will be dealt with. Next time," Rushton said tersely.

"The animals themselves requested a decision one way or the other. There will be trouble if it is left any longer," Alad said coldly.

Rushton lifted his brows questioningly. "Threats, Alad?"

The guildmaster shook his head. "Just a warning, Rushton. They have the right."

Rushton said nothing, and Alad sat, looking disgruntled. I was surprised at his persistence. Everyone knew it was only a matter of time until the animals had a representative. But the mention of trouble from the horses made me decide it was time I visited the farms again.

The Coercer guild then proposed a competition, a contest of coercer skills, pitting one against another until a champion could be announced. Master, guilden, and ward would be excluded. This resulted in a heated discussion about the value of competitiveness. The Futuretell ward, Dell, argued persuasively against it, saying it would produce antisocial and aggressive tendencies in an already aggressive guild.

"The aim of Obernewtyn is to have all minds working together for a common goal, not to isolate winners from losers and devalue those whose skills are less violent," she said.

Roland was even more seriously opposed. Rushton interrupted what looked to be erupting into an argument to suggest the coercers draw up a complete plan for their proposed tournament. This would then be voted on by a full guildmerge.

At last he nodded to me, and I stood. "I request that the ban on Teknoguild expeditions be lifted," I said.

Rushton frowned. He did not like anyone to step

outside the procedures that governed guildmerge and made it run smoothly. "This is a strange request for the Farseeker guildmistress to make, Elspeth," he said. "Surely it's up to Garth, especially since he graces us with his presence today."

There was a titter of humor, since everyone knew of the Teknoguild master's reluctance to leave his laboratory. Garth scowled.

"This request also concerns my guild," I said quietly.

Rushton's eyes bored into mine. "What interest could you have in the Teknoguild expeditions? If I recall, you were among those to vote for the ban."

I took a deep breath. "If the ban was lifted, I would propose a joint expedition."

Rushton shook his head emphatically. "If I refuse to let teknoguilders kill themselves roaming on poisoned Blackland fringes, I would hardly let farseekers replace them!" he said with impatient sarcasm.

The death toll among teknoguilders had always been high. The ban had been enforced after a disastrous Teknoguild expedition in which Henry Druid's people and the teknoguilders clashed over a newly discovered ruin on the edge of the Blackland. The argument had ended in a mysterious explosion that killed most of both parties. Either the Druids, as Henry Druid's men named themselves, had deliberately set off a forbidden weapon, or some ancient device hidden in the ruins had been accidentally triggered. Either way, there had been no further Teknoguild expeditions, and no more had been seen of Henry Druid or his followers.

Henry Druid had been a Herder novice until he had opposed the Council's book-burning laws. Cast out by the fanatical priests of the Herder Faction, the Druid had fled to exile in the high country and was assumed dead by most. And yet he lived. Rushton had even been befriended by the old ex-Herder, and for a time, their paths had matched. But the old man's fierce hatred of the Council was exceeded only by his hatred of mutations, and in the end, it had become too dangerous to continue the connection.

Sometimes it made me uneasy that we had not heard anything of the Druid for so long. Like Alexi and Madam Vega, the renegade Herder had wanted power in the form of Beforetime weaponmachines. What if he were to discover the machines that could set off another Great White?

I choked off that train of thought. "The expedition we propose will not be to Blackland fringes."

Rushton looked puzzled. "Then I don't see any difficulty. Teknoguild expeditions were banned because they never want to go anywhere but the fringes. But that still doesn't explain your interest. I would be surprised to find you had any aim in common with the Teknoguild."

It was true I had often opposed their interests. Of all those at Obernewtyn, the abilities of Teknoguilders were hardest to define, being little more than a vague empathy for inanimate things, a slight power to move things by will alone, and a passionate interest in the past. The Teknoguild was the only one that had established its base outside Obernewtyn because the caves that housed it were the remains of a Beforetime establishment and contained a number of ancient machines.

Pavo's request that I visit the cave network had been unexpected and unnerving. I had not been there since

Alexi had tortured me with the Zebkrahn machine in his effort to force me to use my powers to locate an Oldtime weapons cache. In the end, I had gone, as much to lay my fears to rest as out of respect for Pavo, who was more concerned with understanding the Beforetimers than unearthing their mechanical secrets.

Also, I had been curious.

Returning to the cave had been a disturbing experience. The past had seemed to lie tangibly beneath the present, despite all that had changed. The passage into the cave network was now littered with boxes and sacks of Beforetime papers, books, and other relics unearthed in previous expeditions. The passage was well lit by candles set in sconces at regular intervals.

Coming from the sloping passage with its strangely smooth walls into the main cave, I had been forced to stifle a gasp, having forgotten how big it all was and how bright the Beforetime sphere of light that lit the area. High up in the shadows, stalactites still hung, poised like spears. Yet it was also very different than I remembered. Woven rugs and thick mats softened cold floors, and the walls were almost covered with paper, scrawled with lists and notes and diagrams. Tables and chairs were occupied by busy teknoguilders, who barely registered my entrance.

Only the Zebkrahn machine had looked the same, though I knew it could no longer be used to coerce and torture, having long since been modified. Now it served as nothing more than an enhancer, enabling farseekers to double their normal range. Even so, my skin had risen to gooseflesh at the sight of it.

I thought of all this as I stood before the guildmerge. "Pavo asked me to come to the Teknoguild cave network this morning," I began in answer to Rushton's puzzlement.

The guilden gave a dry cough and rose. "It might be better if I explain, Guildmistress," the Teknoguild ward offered diffidently.

As in the cave that morning, I was struck anew by his pallor.

"I did not know Elspeth would raise this matter today, and so I have not brought my notes; therefore, you will have to take my word on some matters," Pavo said. "A while back, we uncovered evidence of an enormous book storage, which we believe might be untouched since the Beforetime. However, because of the ban, we set this matter reluctantly aside. Meanwhile, we succeeded in getting the Zebkrahn machine to penetrate the blocking static over tainted ground." He paused to remind everyone that the machine, like farseekers, had been unable to project through Blackland wastes; even the tainted ground at the borders of the Blacklands produced a static that limited our range to just beyond the mountains that surrounded Obernewtyn.

"It still only *locates* Talents—it won't help us to communicate with them. But the machine is now able to monitor areas previously out of reach even to farseekers as strong as Elspeth, whose range is otherwise better than that of the machine," Pavo said. "I thought it was necessary for Elspeth to see the machine—not to admire the new modification but so that she could see what it revealed." Pavo looked at me, and all eyes swung expectantly my way.

I said obligingly, "The Zebkrahn was registering a Talent at its outermost limit."

"But . . . that's impossible. Th' machine has to be focused through a farseeker," Matthew objected.

Pavo shook his head eagerly. "Only to detect ordinary or weak Talents. That is to say, in most cases. But the Zebkrahn would need no farseeker focusing to register, for instance, Elspeth."

"But . . . that means this Talent the Zebkrahn registers mun be as strong as she . . . ," Matthew said.

"Perhaps stronger," Pavo corrected gently.

"Such a Talent would be worth rescuing," interjected Gevan, guildmaster of the coercers.

"The two—the new Talent and the book storage Pavo told you about—are in the same region, and since it is so far away, we thought of a joint expedition," I said.

There was a buzz of excited talk, but Rushton ignored it. "'So far away' . . ." he repeated coldly. "Exactly how far?"

My mouth felt suddenly dry. "Somewhere between Aborium and Murmroth."

There was silence, then someone sighed heavily. Aborium was on the west coast. The only known way to get there was to travel the main coast road, passing soldierguard camps and all the main towns, not to mention passing through Sutrium to reach the ferry that plied the Lower Suggredoon. And any expedition would be cut off from contact with Obernewtyn, as it would be far beyond the outer limits of even the most powerful farseekers.

Rushton's face was tight with anger; he must have realized his brief words to me before the guildmerge had prompted me to propose the expedition. He knew that he could not dismiss my proposal when he meant to propose his own equally dangerous expedition.

"That would mean traveling through Sutrium and crossing the river by ferry," Roland said brusquely. "A crazy, dangerous idea. Our false Certificates would not deceive the soldierguards for a moment."

Pavo coughed again. "It is not necessary to journey through Sutrium." He pulled one of the maps on the table toward him and spread it out. "I have a better map, but"—he pointed to the red circle denoting Obernewtyn—"the expedition would travel out of Obernewtyn and down the main road but would turn off to cut directly across the White Valley, then through an Olden pass between Tor and Aran Craggie in the lower mountain ranges and down to the lowlands. From there, it would be an easy trip across the Ford of Rangorn and down to the coast."

Rushton examined the route. "You are sure this mountain pass exists? I have never heard of it."

The teknoguilder nodded.

"T'would mean winterin' outside maybe, unless an expedition were to leave at once," Matthew said tentatively.

"It would be best to act at once," Pavo said anxiously. "Think of what we might learn from an untouched collection of Beforetime books. And who knows what ability this Talent will bring to us."

Rushton nodded for us to resume our seats, his expression inscrutable. His eyes swept the assembled faces. "Well," he said at last, "I called this guildmerge for a particular reason, but Guildmistress Elspeth has preempted me. I, too, meant to propose an expedition.

While in the high country these last few days, I heard rumors of men asking questions about Obernewtyn. Strangers—perhaps Councilmen, perhaps not. They were asking questions about the damage caused by the firestorm, wanting to speak to anyone who had actually seen Obernewtyn. This means the Council may know I lied about the storm. If so, we will be investigated, probably after the next thaw."

There was a muffled howl of dismay.

"Or," Rushton went on, "it may mean nothing. The problem is that we have no idea what they know. Up until now, we have striven to avoid any contact with the Council, to hide and grow in strength until we were powerful enough to confront them. We are not yet strong enough for that battle, or any sort of open confrontation, but it is time we moved on to the next stage of our plans.

"I called this meeting to propose an expedition to Sutrium, with the aim of finding out if we are in danger and if the Council has any real knowledge of our existence. We can no longer hide in the dark, shivering. We must look, in the next year, to establishing a safe house in the lowlands, preferably right in Sutrium."

"What is a safe house?" Miryum asked.

"A refuge that will form the nexus of our inner defense. It means we can move with more confidence among the lowlanders. Most important, it means we will be in a better position to know what the Council is up to."

"What if someone is caught and . . . tortured into giving up its location or, worse, to tell th' truth about us and Obernewtyn?" Matthew asked. A few nodded fearfully at this.

"Don't you understand that we are no safer hiding up here?" Rushton demanded. "Even if the rumors are just gossip, the soldierguards will come to hear of it, especially if they set up camp in the high country. The question is, do we wait until the Council descends on us before we act, or do we act now, while we can still move with relative freedom?"

A thoughtful silence greeted his words.

"Then, do you propose two expeditions to the lowlands?" Roland asked.

Rushton smiled slightly. "I vote that we accept the expedition proposed by Elspeth, with the addition of another person, whom I will choose, who will leave the main party after Rangorn and venture into Sutrium to investigate the possibility of establishing a safe house. An expedition that can have two purposes can as easily have three. Now we will vote on the expedition with its threefold purpose, and on the establishment of a safe house in Sutrium. Yes, first." He lifted his own hand.

I raised mine, hiding a reluctant smile. Rushton was as sly as ever. He knew Garth would never have agreed to the move on Sutrium without the lure of the coveted library. In the end, the vote was unanimous. Perhaps all felt that the time had come, whether we liked it or not, for a less passive strategy. At any rate, no one liked the idea of waiting like a lamb to be slaughtered.

Rushton rose to close the meeting but was interrupted by a commotion outside the doors.

Christa entered, her face betraying her worry.

Seeing me, the Futuretell guilden beckoned urgently. "Elspeth, it's Maruman. He's returned but is unconscious, and we cannot waken him. You had better come quickly."

◆ 3 ◆

MARUMAN HAD BEEN taken to the Healer hall. As usual after days of wandering, often on tainted ground, his fur was filthy and singed in places; dried blood matted the fur on one paw. But he looked no worse than he had on any other return. The wan afternoon light slanted obliquely from a high, slitlike window to lie across his body, making it seem insubstantial, while candles burning all around the hall gave the room a ghostly orange tinge.

In the bed alongside the old cat's was a girl, heavily bandaged. She had been literally wrested from the Herders' purifying flame and had been unconscious since her arrival. One of Christa's fellow futuretellers sat beside her, sunk in deep concentration.

I looked up to see Alad come through the door.

"He looks like he's asleep," I said.

Christa shook her head, then gestured at the meditating futureteller. "She can hardly think for Maruman's emanations. I don't understand how you can't feel them," she added.

"I have my shield up," I explained. I dissolved the protective mental barrier and almost staggered beneath the force of gibberish flowing from Maruman's mind. "I see what you mean."

I saw from Alad's expression that he had lowered his own shield. "Usually I find the flow of beast thought soothing," he said ruefully.

"He was lying outside the Futuretell wing when we found him. It looked as if he had dragged himself there," Christa said.

"Can you reach his mind to find out what he's been doing?" I asked.

She looked down at the old cat. "The truth is, his mind is generally such a mess that it is a wonder he can think straight even some of the time. I can't imagine what caused the damage in the first place—perhaps a traumatic birth. For the most part, his mind seems to have adapted itself amazingly well. There are the most extraordinary links and bypasses—somehow it all functions. The fits he occasionally has are the result of some sort of upward leak in his mind, where material from the deepest unconscious levels rises to distort his everyday thinking, hence the wild futuretelling, but this . . ."

"What do you make of it?" I asked Alad.

He sighed. "I'm a simple beastspeaker. This is beyond me. I've sent for one of the few strong beastspeakers with a small Talent for deep probing. Christa suggested it since Maruman will not allow her to enter his unconscious mind. Perhaps he will permit a beastspeaker to deep-probe."

"I can deep-probe," I said.

Christa raised her brows, then she looked at the cat pensively. "You could try. He's less likely to oppose you. I'm afraid if it goes on much longer, he'll die of exhaustion. He looks calm enough, but this is pulling him apart."

I stared down at the battle-scarred old cat, tears pricking my eyes. He looked so vulnerable. He would have hated that. I stroked him, fighting for control.

"Is there no healer free to ease him?" I asked gruffly.

Christa shook her head. "They have done all they can. He's in no pain."

"What can I do?" I asked.

"Go into his mind," she answered. "See what you can find out. Make him wake if you can."

"I've never tried to deep-probe him before. What if he resists? I might hurt him."

Alad broke in impatiently. "He'll die if we can't help him. He is more wild than tame, and you know as well as I that the wild ones are hardest to reach, even in a normal communication. But you must try."

With a feeling of dread, I sat on the chair beside the bed. I stroked Maruman's coarse fur gently, willing him to wake. I was repelled by the idea of entering my old friend's most private mind. I could not have borne such an intrusion myself.

Alad squeezed my shoulder. I bit my lip, then closed my eyes. Loosing a deep-probe tendril gently into the first level, I forced myself to ignore the screaming babble that assaulted me. For a moment, I was swept along like a leaf in the dizzy maelstrom of Maruman's unconscious mind. I had a fleeting temptation to let myself go but concentrated on Alad's hand on my shoulder, forcing myself to the next level.

I slipped through effortlessly. Maruman was letting me in.

I drifted deeper, concentrating to avoid the forgetfulness that was one of the greatest dangers inherent to entering an unconscious mind.

Deeper still and suddenly the clamor of the upper levels ceased. It was very quiet and still.

"Maruman," I whispered. "Maruman?"

I sensed a ripple in the fabric of the cat's unconscious mind. In a sense, I knew I was inside his dreams. I went deeper still. Again I whispered his name.

This time he responded. "ElspethInnle . . ."

"Come with me," I invited, hoping to draw him to the upper levels and wakefulness. I was buffeted gently by his refusal.

"Cannot. Must wait," he responded.

I was puzzled. "Wait for what?"

"Must wait until Seeker comes."

This was a name Maruman sometimes called me. More confused than ever, I said, "I am the Seeker."

"Deeper. Must come deeper," Maruman responded instantly.

"Why must?" I asked.

"The oldOne wishes it."

I shivered violently, becoming suddenly conscious of my physical presence in the Healer hall. I forced myself to concentrate, but I was unnerved. It struck me that Maruman had let me in easily, because he had wanted me to enter his deepest mind. Why? I could only know that by slipping deeper, but I was almost at my limit. The desire to rise was powerful, and my energy was running out quickly. Before long, I would have no choice. I would not have the strength to remain. If I wanted to go deeper, I had to do it immediately.

Yet I hesitated.

At the depths of the mind is a great unconscious mindstream. It was into this that the futuretellers dipped for their predictions. Without training, it was possible for a mind to literally dissolve at that depth. And I was already deeper than I had ever gone before.

I braced myself. Fighting an irresistible urge to rise, I pushed my mind lower, fraction by fraction. All at once, the void seemed to brighten, and below, I was aware of the shining silver rush of the mindstream.

Now I felt an opposite tug from the stream, a siren call to merge. My innate fear of losing myself gave me the strength to resist.

"I have come," I grated.

"Deeper," Maruman urged. "Must come deeper."

I was truly frightened now, for it was possible Maruman did not realize the danger. I hesitated and felt myself begin to rise. Then I clamped on my probe and forced it deeper. I could feel the wind of the stream and its incredible cyclonic energy below. It seemed to sing my name in an indescribably lovely voice, willing me to join. Again fear helped me to resist. Then, suddenly, the pull to join the stream and the pull to rise equalized exactly, and I floated motionless.

I was on a high mountain in the highest ranges, the air around me filled with cold gusts of wind. I was inside the body of Maruman. I felt the wind ruffle his/my fur.

An illusion, but real as life.

He/I licked a paw and passed it over one ear.

Then I felt the calling. It was not a voice so much as an inner compulsion. Maruman/I rose at once and began to walk, balancing with easy grace on the jagged spines of rock leading to a higher peak. It was there, I sensed, that the calling originated.

Then I heard my own name, but the voice was not Maruman's.

I was so astonished that the mountain illusion wavered, and for a moment I saw the Healer hall overlay the mountain.

"Do you know me?" I ventured.

"I have always known you," came the response.

"Who are you? What are you?"

"I/We are the Agyllian," it answered in a tone a mother might use when speaking to a small child. "I have used the yelloweyes to communicate with you, ElspethInnle. The strangeness of his mind and his pain make him receptive to us and allow us to use him. He is weary to death, and it would be kind to let him join the stream, but he is not ready to go yet, and nor, I think, are you ready to let him go."

"So it's you who is making him sick," I said indignantly.

"Be at ease. He will suffer no harm, though he cannot sustain us much longer. I come only to warn you that your tasks have not ended, and to remind you of your promise. The deathmachines slumber, waiting to be wakened. While they survive, the world is in danger. When the time is right for you to seek out the machines, you must be ready to act swiftly and without doubt. You must not allow the concerns of your friends or your own needs to sway you. When the time for the dark journey is near, you must come to us, and we will provide you with help."

"Journey? What journey?" I cried, but I was alone.

The mountains dissolved, and I used the last of my strength to rise to where the upward drift would carry me to the surface of Maruman's mind. I was vaguely aware that the upper levels were now quiet.

"Are you all right?" Alad asked tensely as I opened

my eyes. I was slumped in the chair, soaked with perspiration and vaguely amazed to find it was dark outside.

He reached out and touched Maruman gently. "He'll recover. He's sleeping normally now. What did you do?"

I was too tired to answer. Seeing I was nearly asleep in the chair, Alad and one of the healers helped me to my room.

Yet lying in bed, I found myself unable to sleep, so disturbed was I by what I'd experienced in Maruman's mind.

I told myself that my visit to the Teknoguild caves had a caused a deep probe illusion based on the memory of the misfit Cameo, who had died there some years before, after she whispered to me that it was my destiny to destroy the weaponmachines that had caused the Great White. Or more likely, the dream was simply the product of Maruman's distorted mind, for he believed that I was a figure in beast mythology named Innle, or "the Seeker," destined to save what remained of the world.

It was foolish to dwell on what had happened as if it were real, yet the voice that had spoken to me had felt so real. And I knew, as no one else did, that the weaponmachines that had destroyed the Beforetimers were intact and might be used again.

The next morning, I came across Dameon and Matthew making their way toward the kitchen. I watched them approach, wondering what kept Dameon from running into things. His empath ability could not help him see, yet he was never clumsy.

"Elspeth?" he said unexpectedly in his soft, well-spoken voice. His father had been a member of the Council before his death, and Dameon had been a product of that privileged class before a cousin had arranged to have him judged Misfit in order to claim the deceased's estate. For the Council, one of the beauties of the Misfit charge was that it could not be absolutely proven or disproven.

"Are ye sure ye canna see?" Matthew asked the empath.

Dameon smiled sweetly. "I possess neither sight nor the wondrous magic of your precious Oldtimers," he teased. "I knew Elspeth was there because of your reaction to her."

"You empaths!" Matthew exploded. "I thought I had th' shield in place then. Ye'd think emotions at least ought to be private."

"You need to perfect that shield," Dameon admonished. "Do you think I want to be privy to your emotional turmoils, entertaining though they are?"

Matthew blushed to the roots of his hair. "One canna always be screenin' every thought," he muttered.

I bit my lip to conceal my amusement, but Dameon laughed aloud. He smiled in my direction. There was a touch of sadness in his face that had not always been there. Even as I wondered what had caused it, I caught Matthew's knowing look, as if he knew something I did not. I was tempted to deep-probe him when Dameon said pointedly that we ought to go into the kitchen before midmeal became nightmeal. He could not read my mind, yet I felt a flush rise to my cheeks.

Rushton always called the empath his conscience, and suddenly I understood why.

Dameon took my arm and said, with a smile in Matthew's direction, "I hear young Lina has been up to her tricks again."

Matthew scowled blackly. "That girl an' her pranks. She had me so flustered at nightmeal that I accidentally sat next to Miryum, who has as much grace an' wit as a lump of stone."

"Yet she is guilden," Dameon said with faint reproach.

Matthew looked put out. "She has Talent, I grant ye. But all she ever thinks about is the latest way to make people do things they dinna want to do."

The sound of cutlery clinking and laughter flowed down the hall from the kitchen to meet us. There had long been vague plans to open up another room as a separate dining area, but somehow the alcoves adjoining the kitchen remained the main eating area.

Guilds had gotten into the habit of sitting together for meals, but most of the guildleaders and some others sat at the table by the door with Rushton, who treated meals as another kind of strategy meeting. But Dameon went to join his guild members.

Though empath guildmaster, Dameon spent most of his time working with Rushton, and he had offered to forgo his place as master of the Empath guild to make way for Miky and Angina. The twins had refused emphatically, and their refusal had been echoed by the rest of the guild. No other guild had quite the same love for their master as the empaths. They made little official demand on Dameon's time, but at social occasions they were possessive.

Rushton and Domick were both absorbed in something Gevan was saying, and I noticed that Rushton's soup was untouched. I sighed and wondered if he ever noticed anything he ate or enjoyed a conversation just because it was fun.

I saw Louis Larkin hovering just inside the kitchen courtyard door, peering about nearsightedly. He hated coming up to the house, and I wondered what had been important enough to bring him up through the maze.

I sent a probe to Matthew, telling him to find out what Louis wanted. "He says he must talk with you," Matthew sent after a moment. "Ye'll have to come. I can't crack grouchy bugger's shield."

I sighed. Louis was just as hard to get along with as he had always been. His white hair stuck out like coils of wire on each side of his head but was sparse on top. His cheeks and nose were red with cold, but he insisted I come out into the maze courtyard before he would talk. Matthew came with us, closing the door behind him. It was growing colder, and my breath came out in little puffs of cloud.

"What is it, Louis?" I asked tersely.

"Hmph," Louis grumped. "I'm surprised ye've any time to spare for a beastspeaker." Though himself an unTalent, Louis had a natural affinity for animals and held an honorary place in the guild. He regarded my decision to lead the farseekers rather than the beast-speakers as the worst sort of traitorous defection.

"What is it, Louis?" I asked resignedly. Sometimes he reminded me of Maruman at his most difficult.

"No need to snap my head off," Louis said smugly. "T'were a bit of gossip I heard I thought might interest ye."

Louis was a remarkable source of odd bits of information. He hardly ever left Obernewtyn, but he always seemed to know what was going on in the highlands. And he knew everything that went on at Obernewtyn.

"I heard ye were wonderin' if th' Druid has left th' high country," Louis said, looking over his shoulder as if he thought someone might be listening. I was never sure how much of his eccentric behavior was affected and how much was genuine.

"Have you heard anything?" I asked.

He nodded. "Th' word is that th' Druid has nowt left th' high country. No one has seen a sign of his people in many a long day, but now an' then there are disappearances."

"That could be our fault," Matthew said. "Them missin' could be Misfits we rescue, despite th' trouble we gan to to make the disappearances seem natural."

"Ye'd be right, of course! It could nowt be that th' Druid is doin' his own recruitin'. 'Tis nowt possible the disappearances are the reason th' Council takes an interest in th' high country!" Louis huffed sarcastically.

"But if the Druid is taking people, where is he? An why haven't we been able to locate his camp in farseeking searches?" I asked.

The outrage on the old man's face melted into genuine puzzlement. " 'Tis strange enow. I would have said th' Druid had gone. But if he's nowt away from th' White Valley, yer expedition route mun be more dangerous than goin' th' main way."

"Have you mentioned this to Rushton?" I asked.

Louis gave me a look of sly entreaty. "Fact is, I only just heard it. Ought to tell th' master, but I've a yen to go on this expedition. I'd like to see th' lowlands once afore I die," he added. "Ye could put in a word for me."

"Ridiculous," Matthew said. "Ye'll live forever, ye ol' fake!"

"I will speak to Rushton," I said.

Louis's eyes were fixed on my face, and whatever he saw there made him smile sourly. "Ye do that," he said.

After he had gone, Matthew looked at me incredulously. "Why did ye let him bluff ye? Rushton'll nivver agree!"

"Because if Rushton heard this, he would be bound to cancel the expedition or at least delay it. And Louis knows it. Besides, he might . . ."

"What th' devil?" Matthew muttered, hearing a wild yell from the courtyard behind us.

Zarak and Lina of the Beastspeaking guild ran up to us. Both were white-faced.

"Guildmistress, we have to talk to you!" Lina gasped.

"Well?" I snapped, in no mood for their antics. Then Zarak looked up, his eyes miserable and frightened, and suddenly I was filled with apprehension. "What is it?"

Lina answered, "We were sitting in the kitchen garden, and Zarak was . . ." She trailed off and glared at Zarak, who was now staring at his feet. I restrained an urge to shake him.

He burst out, "I know I'm not supposed to farseek, Guildmistress, but you don't know what it's like—being able to make your mind fly and not being allowed to do it. I only meant to go a little way, but it felt so wonderful. Then I bumped into someone. A stranger!"

I stared at him coldly. "You know even farseeker

novices do not farseek beyond the mountains." He nodded. "Do you know why we have this rule?" He nodded again. "Tell me," I snapped.

"Because they might bump into a wild Talent . . . and not be able to shield well enough to stop them . . . tracing back to Obernewtyn," he mumbled. "But I swear it was someone as untrained as I am. He couldn't have traced me. He thought I was an evil spirit."

I felt a sneaking sympathy for Zarak, who was in the wrong guild because his father was a beastspeaker. But I showed none of these thoughts on my face. Zarak had to learn to curb his curiosity, for all our sakes.

"Then since you know the rules, it is not a matter of ignorance but of deliberate disobedience," I said coldly. Zarak hung his head, flushing. "You will go at once to Javo and tell him you will be available for heavy kitchen work until I say otherwise. You will be suspended from the Beastspeaking guild for the same period. I will speak to Alad and your father. Or do you want to lodge an appeal at the next guildmerge?"

Zarak shook his head.

Matthew nodded approvingly. "A fool who knows he is a fool is near to becomin' wise."

Lina fidgeted and looked at Zarak. "You'd better tell them everything," she advised.

Zarak bit his lip. "I might be wrong. It was so quick," he said, then floundered to a halt.

"What now?" Matthew asked.

Zarak said nothing.

"The person Zarak bumped into," Lina said with a sigh. "He thinks it was a Herder."

❖ 4 ❖

"Do ye think it were truly a Herder?" Matthew asked dubiously when the Farseeker guild met the following day.

"I don't know," I said. "Misfits have come to us from almost every walk of life. Why not from the Herder cloisters?"

Matthew frowned. "But would nowt they just burn any Misfit they found among themselves? They have th' right to do it."

I shook my head. "I don't know. The Council might, but the Herders are subtle enough to think of using a Misfit for their own purposes."

"You think this accidental meeting was no accident?" asked an older farseeker.

I shrugged. "Accidental on Zarak's part."

"Maybe Zarak was wrong about not being traced," Ceirwan said.

I shook my head. "I think he would have been able to tell, but we'll have to make sure, pending Rushton's approval. Have you traced the path from Zarak's memory?"

Ceirwan nodded. "Whoever he touched minds with was in a cloister, all right—in Darthnor, of all places."

"Darthnor. A town full of pro-Herder bigots and fanatics. Wonderful," Matthew said darkly.

Later that day, I went down to the farms. Ostensibly, I wanted to organize wagons for the expedition to the lowlands. But I was also curious to talk to Alad about the horses. The Beastspeaking guildmaster was nowhere to be seen, but I noticed a dark stallion grazing nearby.

He looked up warily at my approach. "Greetings, funaga."

I was surprised at his guarded tone. "Greetings, equine," I sent. "Do you know where Alad Beastspeaking guildmaster is?"

The horse looked at me measuringly. "Who knows where the funaga go?" he sent coolly.

All at once, I realized whom I was talking to.

Alad had encountered the black horse in the town of Guanette. Half starved, he had been trying to pull a cart loaded with furniture, five plump children, and a fat, dirty gypsy man cursing and lashing out with a whip. Alad had told me the horse's imaginative mental curses had attracted his attention—that and his strength of mental projection.

The beastspeaker had ended up buying the horse from the gypsy troupe and bringing him to Obernewtyn. Despite a deep hatred of humans, the horse had chosen to remain, becoming almost at once the spokesman for his kind. He had arrived a dusty, bedraggled bag of bones. Now he was lean and muscled, his coat gleaming and sleek. Only his eyes were unchanged, still filled with anger and suspicion. Suddenly I was sure this equine was behind Alad's difficulties with the horses.

"I remember when you came to Obernewtyn," I sent gently.

The horse tossed his head, nostrils flared wide. "I was brought here a slave. I did not choose to come."

Taken aback, I sent, "We had to do it that way. It would have looked odd to buy a horse and set it free. But you chose to stay."

"That is so, for there is no place in the world not infected by the funaga. Here is the same as anywhere else."

From the corner of my eye, I saw Alad approaching.

"We are not like the people who owned you before," I sent. "Here, all work together. We are equals."

The horse snorted savagely. "You talk like a fool. We have no place in the funaga conclaves."

"It's only a matter of time—" I began, but the horse cut me off with his own thought.

"Alad-gahltha asked that we be treated as true equals. Again this was set aside. 'Wait,' they say. We have waited long enough. Now we are tired of waiting. From now on, we work only for our food and shelter. We will carry no funaga, and we will pull no cart beyond these mountains. We will not risk our lives to help the funaga. We will not fight the funaga's battles unless they are also ours."

There was no doubt in my mind that the proud, bitter horse meant what he said.

"That won't make anyone like you or take—"

He snorted violently in my face. "Like! I care nothing for the likes and hates of the funaga. Allies we will be, or nothing. I have heard the funaga plan a journey to the lowlands. We will see how they fare with no equine to draw their carts or carry them in the dark lands."

I blinked. "But we're not going to the Blacklands."

"The places where the funaga-li dwell are dark," the horse sent bleakly.

"I tried to warn Rushton. And it's not just the horses," Alad said from behind.

I ignored this and addressed the horse again. I knew as well as Alad that no expedition could be undertaken on foot, especially one so far and through such terrain. We needed the horses. "What if the journey were a test—to see if your kind and mine could really be allies, working together, trusting one another?"

The black horse stood very still, but he did not respond.

"A way to find out if your kind and mine can work in accord," I went on softly. "A test in which we funaga must pretend to have no special abilities, and equines must pull carts, be ridden by funaga, and reined."

The horse reared violently, and Alad started swearing. I had expected the reaction, knowing the younger horses would not even tolerate a modified rein and would only work with beastspeakers.

For long moments he bucked and reared, driving bladelike hooves deep into the ground. At last he calmed and turned to face me, his coat dark with sweat. "What if all who journeyed were slain? What if this journey fails?"

"If the equines do their part faithfully, the test will be judged a success—regardless of the outcome. And one of your kind will sit at guildmerge."

I knew I was offering what I had no right to offer, but I had no doubt Rushton would concur. He knew we needed the horses.

"It shall be as you have stated, funaga," the horse

sent finally. "I will find those to draw your cart for this testing. But I will join your expedition also. Not to draw a cart, but to bear *you*. Then we will see whose kind is best fitted to lead."

"Elspeth, you can't!" Alad cried aloud. "A guild-mistress on an expedition? Rushton would have a fit!"

The black horse did not take his eyes from mine, and there was challenge and cold amusement in his look. He was daring me to agree, certain I would refuse.

I took a deep breath, ignoring the horrified Beast-speaking guildmaster. "It will be as you say, equine. Together we will deceive the lowlanders into thinking I am your master."

The horse neighed his laughter.

✦ 5 ✦

"WHO ARE YOU? Where are you? I know you're there. I feel you."

The probe was clumsy, its movements graceless and badly focused. "He's young," I assured Ceirwan. Even so, I was surprised he had sensed my presence, since I was tightly shielded. I let my probe brush against his fleetingly, testing.

His mind stabbed out in fright. "Are you the demon?"

Even while he grappled with my shielded probe, I entered him at a deeper level, deep-probing to find trace memories of his encounter with Zarak. The meeting had made a huge impact on his mind, for he thought Zarak a minor demon come to test his faith.

I decided to risk outright contact. If he reacted by calling out to his masters, I would stun him, and Domick would manufacture a coercive block.

Rushton had insisted Domick monitor the attempt after being reluctantly convinced we had to establish whether Zarak's probe had been traced back to Obernewtyn. I suspected Domick had orders to cripple the boy's mind if there was any risk of the Herders using him.

"Do your elders know of us?" I sent.

The boy's mind recoiled from my mental blast. I had deliberately made it harsh and even slightly painful. While the boy believed he was dealing with demons, we were in no real danger.

"It is the way of a priest to undergo his tests in silence, demon. My master has warned me your kind would try to shake my faith," the young Herder sent proudly.

I had read from his thoughts that he was a novice, or apprentice, priest. After his initial training in the main cloister in Sutrium, he had been sent to Darthnor's cloister to serve out his apprenticeship in the highlands. It was only the town's proximity to Obernewtyn that had made it possible for Zarak to stumble upon the novice's thoughts. Ironically, he had become aware of his powers under the rigorous mental training of the priesthood. But Herder teachings said that anything outside normal abilities was a mutation. The boy had tried to refuse his abilities, refusing to accept that he might be a Misfit.

Despite all his reactions, he was no hardened fanatic. And the Herder boy's youth was a mark in his favor. We rescued few older folk, since most were unable to accept that their mutant abilities might not be evil. Those we encountered whom we judged a bad risk, we simply blocked, making it impossible for them to use their powers. This horrified the healers, but, in truth, the Misfits were happier to seem normal. Many believed Lud had cured them.

It was this boy's youth that stopped me from simply having Domick expunge the memory and block his mutant powers. That and an instinct that told me he was worth rescuing. But because he was a Herder, I had to be sure he would respond the right way. I had promised Rushton I would do nothing until I was certain he could be trusted.

"How do you know I am a demon?" I asked, curious to see how much dogma he had swallowed.

The response was immediate. "You are a greater demon. The other was a lesser novice. Only demons can talk inside a man's head. My master says many are driven mad by such things, but you will not find me easy to break."

I sensed Ceirwan's amusement. "A puppy," he sent in ardent relief.

"If we can bring him in, we would have an insight into the Herders' world," I said. "It's always possible those men asking questions about Obernewtyn were from the Herder Faction."

Ceirwan looked unconvinced. "He is a novice, unlikely to know their inner secrets."

"He is one of us," I insisted stubbornly. "If we leave him, the Herders might end up finding out what he is anyway, sooner or later. Then he might betray us at their behest. He is not fully committed to their way, and I believe he would do well among us."

"A rescue would have to be completely foolproof," Ceirwan warned.

"Are you still there, demon?" the boy sent.

The wistful inquiry in his voice reminded me of my own long-ago loneliness, thinking myself a freak, living in fear of disclosure.

"Do others of your kind speak to demons?" I asked.

There was a significant hesitation in his mind before he answered evasively. "Demons test many priests."

"They do, but I have not encountered any other human who could communicate with me," I sent, trying to sound like a demon.

Still probing his lower mind, I thought again of my childhood in the orphan home system. I had not known at once that I was a Misfit, but some instinct of self-protection had kept me silent about my developing abilities. My brother, Jes, had been even more frightened. His hatred of my mutant abilities had warred with his love for me. He had spent a lifetime suppressing, even from himself, the fact that he, too, was a Misfit. In the end, he had been killed trying to escape from an orphan home after I was sent to Obernewtyn.

"I want to bring him out," I told Ceirwan aloud.

The memory of Jes made me determined to rescue the boy before leaving for the lowlands. With this in mind, I contacted him for several consecutive nights, working on his buried fears. At last he broke down, confessing that he was a Misfit—and his fear that his masters had begun to suspect him.

"Surely such a small mutation would not matter," I said, at the same time evoking an old nightmare in the boy's mind based on a burning he had once witnessed.

I was startled at the strength of his reaction. He screamed.

The noise brought an older Herder. Fearing the worst, Domick struck to wipe the boy's mind clean. I deflected his blow with an ease that made him glare at me suspiciously.

"I said I'll handle this," I hissed aloud.

I was relieved to hear the Herder boy tell his master he had been dreaming, and I injected my own calm control over his outward expressions. The priest departed with a final hard stare. My own heart was thudding, reacting to the boy's fear.

"He knows," he sent forlornly. I had not meant to make an approach so soon, but the desperation I sensed in his thoughts decided me.

"You could run away," I suggested.

"Where could I go that they wouldn't find me?" he asked miserably. "If they suspect, they won't let me get away. They are interested in Misfits. They don't send them to the Council." I saw a fleeting thought that confirmed the rumors of the Herder interrogation methods and shuddered. What would happen to the boy if they guessed the truth?

"You know I am no demon," I sent gently, after a moment.

"Yes," the boy sent simply.

"Once, I was an orphan. Like you, I was different. I didn't fit in, and I was afraid of being found out and burned or sent to the farms. Now I live free, with others like me."

"Misfits," he sent, using the hated word.

"Other people like you," I sent. "You could join us," I added lightly.

Hope flared, swamped by a sudden regressive fear that I might, after all, be a demon tempting him to the loss of his soul. "The other one. The first one I met. Is he there?"

I called Zarak and shielded his beam while they talked. In the end, the young Herder agreed to join us.

"He wants to know if he can bring his dog," Zarak asked with a grin.

❖ ❖ ❖

Zarak, Matthew, and Ceirwan brought him out. Officially, Zarak was still in Coventry, but the Herder boy trusted him and had insisted he be present.

Over a matter of days, the boy gradually gave his Herder masters the impression he was becoming increasingly homesick. He talked constantly about his family and refused to eat. He let his masters think he was having trouble with the mental disciplines of the priesthood. When he escaped, it was made to appear as if he had run away with his dog and had drowned trying to cross the Suggredoon.

It was a good scenario, one of the best we had designed. It had to be, or Rushton would never have approved it. It was artfully managed, even to the point of having clothes washed up on the bank and beastspeaking scavenger birds to hover ominously about the spot when the Herder search party arrived. It was one of the few rescues that had gone off without a single hitch.

The boy proved not only to be a powerful farseeker, which we had known already, but also a strong empath, which explained how he had sensed my presence when I was shielded. The joint ability was unusual. There were only two other farseekers among us with weak empath Talent. To my regret, the boy chose the Empath guild—little wonder, since Dameon had taken him gently in hand from the start. Within days, he had developed the empaths' traditional adoration for their gentle leader.

His name was Jik.

The expedition was due to depart in only a week when I met with Rushton to discuss the final plan. Discovering my name on the list of those to go, Rushton had exploded. He was furious to hear of my agreement with the black horse and even angrier that I had not spoken of it to him sooner.

"I won't be threatened," he said.

"It is an agreement," I said calmly. "We really don't have any choice. We need the horses. And I am the strongest farseeker and a perfectly good candidate for this expedition."

Rushton shook his head. "I will agree to this test in principle, but you won't be the one riding the black horse. I won't risk a guildleader on an expedition."

Using Alad as translator, Rushton argued with the black horse, but it was useless. "He asks why the equines should risk their leader if the funaga will not," Alad explained. "He says a test should involve leaders."

"Then offer *me* as his rider," Rushton said grimly.

The horse agreed this would be a fair exchange, but guildmerge outvoted Rushton, saying he was more valuable than any other at Obernewtyn, being the legal master. Incensed, Rushton found his own rule, permitting a unanimous guildmerge to outweigh his lone vote, used against him.

I was taken aback at his reaction. I understood his reluctance to risk a guildleader, but to offer himself as a replacement was senseless. Even he must see he was more important to Obernewtyn than I.

Ceirwan, along with two other farseekers, was to run the Farseeker guild in my absence, since Matthew had also been appointed to the expedition. Unspoken was the knowledge that Ceirwan would become guildmaster if I failed to return.

Rounding out the final list were Pavo, Kella, and

Louis Larkin, with the Coercer ward Domick as Rushton's choice for our spy in Sutrium. The expedition was to be disguised as a gypsy troupe. The carts had been built by the Teknoguild.

The black horse snorted his loathing at the sight of the gypsy rig. He had appointed two older horses to draw the carts. "Finer horses will encourage robbers," he sent in terse explanation.

"What about you?" I asked.

The horse pricked his ears forward. "They will not find me desirable," he sent cryptically.

The night before we were to leave, Rushton came to my turret chamber, which had been his own room in his time as farm overseer. He had collected our false Normalcy Certificates. Written on old discolored parchment, they were good forgeries, but I hoped we would not need them.

"It's done, then," Rushton said. He stared into the fire. There was a drawn-out silence, and the fire crackled as if the lack of sound made it uneasy.

"Is something wrong?" I asked.

"Are you afraid?" he asked unexpectedly. I had a sudden vivid memory of him asking me the same question in that room when it had been his.

This time, I nodded soberly. "It will be dangerous, despite bypassing Sutrium and the main ways."

Rushton turned to face me, his green eyes troubled. "Don't . . . risk too much for this Talent," he said. "Whoever it is might not even want to join us. You . . . are perceptive, but you don't always see what is in front of your eyes."

I had the notion he had meant to say something else and shifted uncomfortably. I had never felt really at ease with him since the awkward intimacy of being forced into a mindbond with him two years earlier.

Rushton stood abruptly, shook his head, and walked across to open the window shutters, breathing deeply as if the air in the turret room were too thin. He turned, leaning back against the open window, his face in shadow. "You . . . are important to Obernewtyn. We can't afford to lose a guildmistress. Even now it is not too late to change your mind. . . ."

I shook my head. "I want to go. Besides, I promised."

"You belong here," Rushton said sternly.

I wished he would come back into the room so I could see his face. There was an odd note in his voice that puzzled me.

"Have you been so unhappy here?" he asked.

I laughed. "I've never been more content in my life. But I am glad to go away for a while. It's as if I'm too safe and comfortable—like an old house cat. As Maruman would put it, I'm being tamed by comfort."

"And look at *him*," Rushton said darkly. "Someday you will have to come out of your ivory tower."

I shrugged, not understanding the reference. "Alad said Maruman is recovering, though he still sleeps."

Rushton nodded. "He will miss you."

Before I could answer, there was a knock at the door.

I was surprised to find Dameon and Maryon outside. Their eyes went beyond me to Rushton.

"What is it?" he asked brusquely.

"I have futuretold th' expedition," the Futuretell guildmistress announced in her soft highland accent.

"What have you seen?" Rushton demanded. "Will it be a success? Will those who travel return?"

I held my breath.

Maryon merely want on, looking grave and serene. "I have seen that th' boy Jik mun travel with th' expedition. If he does nowt go, many, perhaps all th' rest, will nowt return."

"Surely another, more experienced empath?" Rushton said.

Maryon shook her head. "The prediction deals specifically wi' th' boy, but it is unclear. I dinna see any direct action on his part. It is my belief that he matters in some obscure manner—perhaps something he will do or say will offer a turning point for the journey."

"That settles it; the expedition will have to be put off until Maryon can clarify the prediction," Rushton said.

Again the Futuretell guildmistress shook her head. "The boy was only part of the foreseeing. Th' fate of Obernewtyn hangs in th' balance of this journey, an' it mun proceed as planned. The expedition mun return to th' mountains wi' their prizes before winter freezes th' pass, else we will fall to our enemies."

Rushton shook his head. "I don't know what to make of this."

"You need not fear Jik will betray us," Dameon said.

Rushton looked taken aback. "I don't doubt his loyalty if you vouch for him. But he's a boy! It's bad enough . . ." His eyes darted momentarily in my direction.

"I don't think we have any choice," Dameon said. "For some reason or other, Jik has to go on the expedition. There is no time to wait for clarification."

"Which might never come," Maryon added.

Rushton ran a hand through his hair and sighed. "I felt it was time to end our isolation, but I little thought what that would cost." He turned and nodded at the stack of Normalcy papers. "Jik will have to use the blank one I had made for the Talent you hope to find. It's too late to make another."

When they were gone, I went to the window and breathed in the cool night air, thinking how strangely things came about. A fortnight before, Jik had been a Herder novice. Now, suddenly, he was vital to Obernewtyn's future. If Zarak had not disobeyed me . . .

I shook my head. One could go mad thinking of alternate possibilities. Kella was right. The present was enough to deal with.

✦ 6 ✦

THE DAY OF the departure dawned, grim and unseasonably cold.

Gray clouds scudded across a metallic autumn sky. Wind blustered and rain fell in short, violent flurries.

I shivered, staring out over the gardens from my window. In that moment, I could imagine vividly the mountain valley blanketed in ice and snow, the mournful sound of wolves echoing across the frozen wastes. The lowlands would be much warmer than the mountains, even in wintertime. Perhaps at last the scars on my feet would have the chance to heal completely. I had avoided speaking to Roland about my feet for fear Rushton would hear of it and use them as reason to ban me from the expedition. Fortunately, Kella understood and had been treating me without telling Roland.

Thinking of the healer made me remember Maruman. I had gone to see him before firstmeal, but, though conscious, he was still dazed and barely coherent. I had wanted desperately to talk to him about the vision I had seen in his unconscious mind, but it was impossible.

As with all expeditions, no amount of forethought

could avoid the last-minute rush as remembered necessities were rounded up. Feeling harassed with preparations, I looked up with relief to see Ceirwan and Matthew approach.

"See, I've been practicin'," Matthew sent on a tightly shielded probe. The momentary mischief in his eyes faded as he looked around.

"Until today, it hardly seemed such an important thing to be doin'," he said pensively.

Those who were part of the expedition knew we carried the fate of Obernewtyn on our backs, though the general population of Obernewtyn knew nothing of Maryon's prophecy. And Dameon had requested I tell no one, including Jik, of the part of the prophecy that concerned Jik. "It would not be fair to the boy," he insisted.

Jik was even younger than Lina and Zarak but was more serious and quieter of nature. He seemed bemused by the news that he was to be part of the expedition, though it seemed he would prove useful, for he had been to Sutrium more recently than any of us and would give Domick some idea of the present shape and disposition of the town as we traveled.

Jik had insisted that his companion, Darga, accompany us as well. A nondescript short-haired dog with a ferociously ugly face, he was one of a breed used by the Herders to guard the cloisters. Darga had been a miscolored runt in his litter, expected to die when Jik had volunteered to nurse him. No one had any objections to the dog's inclusion.

Zarak and Lina stood beside Jik, their faces openly envious.

The three horses to travel with us had been supplemented by another. I would ride the stallion, who had told Alad haughtily that he would answer to the title Gahltha, meaning leader. Domick would ride a newcomer, a small, wheat-colored mountain pony with doelike eyes. Named Avra, she had been brought wild to Obernewtyn the previous wintertime, having injured herself in a fall. Alad told me she was the black stallion's chosen mate. The two mares to pull the carts were Mira and Lo.

The horses stood together as Alad harnessed and installed the hated bit and bridles. Privately, Alad had warned me Gahltha had chosen horses that were completely loyal to him. It was clear where their allegiance would lie if it came to a choice between equine and funaga aims. They would follow me as leader of the expedition only under instructions from the black horse.

None of the equines seemed inclined to closer acquaintance, and I hoped I had not made a mistake in choosing Louis over a full Beastspeaking guilder. I could beastspeak, of course, but the animals were more receptive to those of the Beastspeaking guild.

With Kella, Jik, and Darga in one cart and Matthew, Pavo, and Louis in the other, the caravans were authentically crowded. Gypsies traveled traditionally in extended family groups, singing and dancing for money and providing amusing and impromptu plays. The descendants of those who had originally refused Council affiliation, they were little liked or trusted for all their variety of skills. In some ways, it was a dangerous disguise, but it was one of the few ways a number of us could travel about without drawing attention. Travel was not undertaken lightly, for people everywhere were suspicious of strangers in their midst.

To complete our disguise, we were unnaturally tanned and wore the layers of colored clothing favored by gypsies. The dark skin was the result of a powerful berry-based dye. I doubted anyone would have the slightest suspicion we were anything but a motley gypsy troupe.

Rushton stressed the need to maintain our disguise at all costs. We had all set up coercive blocks that would erase our memories in an emergency. These were Obernewtyn's safeguard in case one of us was caught and tortured. Only Jik had been unable to prepare a block, being too untrained. Domick or I could wipe his memory should it come to that.

Rushton adjured us to work together and not to forget that each of the three aims in the expedition was equally important.

At the last, he wished us good fortune. "This journey is the beginning of a new stage for us. I wish you success, for your sake and ours." If anyone else noticed the slightly ominous note in his final words, it was not apparent.

All Obernewtyn turned out to see us go, but the festival air did not last long. We had barely finished preparations when it began to rain heavily.

I climbed awkwardly into Gahltha's saddle, ignoring his derisive whinny. He might not want to be ridden, but he knew an incompetent rider when he had one.

Wrapping an oiled cape about my head and shoulders, I nodded to Domick. We had decided he would ride in front of the carts and I at the rear, at least until we left the main road.

The rain had sent everyone running inside, but looking back, I had a final glimpse of Rushton standing alone on the top step, apparently oblivious to the downpour.

Even at that distance, I could see the same odd tension in his stance that had puzzled me in the turret room.

I wondered what he was thinking and impulsively lifted a hand to wave.

Instantly, he responded, raising his own hand. I stared over my shoulder until the gray curtain of rain came between us.

I felt an unexpected regret at the thought that I would not see him again for a long time, perhaps many months if we failed to make it back before the pass froze.

PART II

✦

THE LOWLANDS

✦ 7 ✦

I HAD BEEN nervous about riding and found it only slightly less traumatic than I had expected.

Gahltha began instructing me the moment we left Obernewtyn. Under his terse instructions, I tied the reins to the saddle. When I did not know what to do with my hands, I clutched at the saddle, hanging on for dear life. Gahltha forbade this, saying I must learn to ride by balance before we reached the lowlands. A gypsy did not rely on hands or stirrups. This seemed impossible enough, until he warned me that I would also have to be able to ride without a saddle, since gypsies rarely used them. And no gypsy would be so inept a rider as me.

It took great concentration to coordinate all the contortions Gahltha seemed to feel riding required.

"Heels out so you do not jab me in the ribs, or I may forget and buck you off," he sent. "Knees tight or you will be off the first time I stumble."

The first hours were punctuated by the horse's staccato instructions. He made no comment to me except to give me orders. I had the feeling he was enjoying every minute of my discomfort.

I noticed Domick casually slouched in his saddle

as if it were an armchair and envied his skill and confidence.

The rain continued throughout the remainder of the day, drumming steadily on my oiled coat and on the roofs of the caravans. The weather was so bleak that we traversed the tainted and storm-wracked pass almost without noticing. The last time I had gone over the stretch of tainted grounds, I had been journeying to Obernewtyn for the first time, filled with apprehension for the future. Now I was leaving, still full of apprehension.

We passed the area without mishap and soon after left the main road for the White Valley. Fortunately, the floor of the valley was flat, and there was little undergrowth beneath the trees, else the carts would have been useless.

I felt Jik clumsily seeking entrance into my thoughts. "Will the caravans be able to go through the Olden way?" he asked.

"Pavo thinks so. He believes it was once an important Beforetime thoroughfare," I sent.

"Why doesn't anyone else know about it?" he wondered. "I never heard any of the priests in the Darthnor cloister here mention it, and I never saw it on any of the maps."

The question had also occurred to me. "Pavo says it is probably because there has been no need of it, what with the main road. And no one much uses the White Valley. The highlanders believe it to be haunted."

When night fell, it was still raining. After a hasty conferral, we decided to go on as long as we could, since it would be impossible to make a proper camp or cook in the sodden valley.

In the end, Gahltha was the one to call a halt, saying the horses pulling the cart needed to rest. I was surprised at his consideration, then reminded myself his concern was for the horses, not the humans. But I was glad to stop just the same. Climbing down from his back stiffly, I was convinced every bone in my body was fractured and wondered if it could possibly be any worse to ride bareback.

Relieved of the hated trappings, the horses wandered off to graze, untroubled by the rain. Domick and I hung our soaking oil cloaks under an eben tree in the hope that they would dry by morning.

We all climbed into one carriage to talk. Darga had jumped out the moment the cart stopped; even so, it was too cramped to change my damp clothes, so I wrapped a blanket around my shoulders.

"We might as well close th' flaps an' keep out th' night air," Matthew said, tying the strings.

Kella had lit two candles in shielded sconces, and the interior of the van glowed dimly in the flickering light. It warmed up quickly with the flaps closed, and I felt myself drifting off to sleep watching Jik and the healer prepare a simple nightmeal. I felt so tired, it was an effort to eat, but Kella insisted.

I tried to shift my position, but my legs seemed to have set in their riding stance. Laughing, Kella produced a strongly scented green paste that she promised would ease the muscle strain.

I sighed regretfully and imagined sinking into my favorite chair in front of the turret-room fire when Jik interrupted my weary daydream to ask why he had been included on the expedition.

I had imagined Dameon would have provided some

plausible reason, but it appeared he had left it to me. Trying to give myself time to think, I asked Jik why he had not asked Dameon himself.

He shrugged diffidently. "I thought somebody would tell me why eventually."

I nodded, deciding that I could not burden him with the true reason. "Your knowledge of Herder lore will be useful to us. We know so little about the practices of the priesthood or of their ambitions. They seem to be growing stronger and more powerful. And, of course, there is your knowledge of Sutrium."

Jik frowned. "I was taken by the priests when I was very young. I hardly remember it. I don't know any more about Sutrium than you," he concluded in a troubled voice.

I patted his arm reassuringly. "Don't worry about why you're here. Just concentrate on remembering everything you can about Sutrium and the Herder Faction."

I heard squelching noises outside just as Gahltha's cold probe slid into my mind.

I pulled aside the flap and looked into his dark, wet face, almost invisible in the night. Directly behind him, Avra was a pale blur.

"What is it?" I sent, matching his brevity.

"Avra found fresh equine tracks nearby, less than a day old. Funaga rode the equines," Gahltha sent. "They traveled the opposite way to us, making for the main road."

"Maybe someone else knows about the Olden way," Domick said when I told the others.

I sent a questing thought to Avra. "Do you know how many funaga there were?"

64

"More than here—two times more than here," Avra sent, as shy as Gahltha was arrogant. I bit my lip.

We had been incredibly lucky to miss the riders, but that did not solve the question of where they had come from. There were no mapped villages in the White Valley. But Louis said the highlands were full of small settlements unknown to Council mapmakers, made up of people who wanted to be free of Council domination without openly opposing it.

"Perhaps the riders came from such a settlement," he offered without conviction.

"Perhaps they were hunting," Domick said.

I weighed the options. "We'll stay the night here and leave at dawn."

I asked Gahltha to warn Darga and the other horses to keep an eye out for any sign of funaga that might give us a clue about why they had been in the White Valley. Then I dropped the flap, shutting out the bleak night.

"He doesn't like you," Jik said in puzzled wonder.

I nodded wryly. "Gahltha was badly abused by his old masters. I don't think he likes any human."

"But it's different at Obernewtyn. No one would hurt him there," Jik said indignantly. "It's not fair for him to blame us."

I smiled gently at his loyalty to his adopted home. "Not much in life is fair."

I realized Jik had not been able to hear Gahltha but had sensed the horse's dislike. Such sensitivity to a beast's emotions seemed to be a new use of empathising, or perhaps a new Talent altogether. I made a mental note to discuss it with Dameon when we returned.

"What do you think those people were doing here?" Kella asked.

"I don't know," I said. "But if they are in hiding, they won't want to see us any more than we want to stumble into their midst. I'm going to farsense the way ahead. If there is any sign of a settlement, we'll change course and bypass it." I closed my eyes.

For a moment, I was half mesmerized by my own exhaustion and the monotonous sound of rain on the canvas roof of the caravan. I had forgotten how storms could affect my range. Pavo's theory was that rain occasionally contained some sort of mild taint to which humans had adapted but which nevertheless acted upon Misfit abilities.

I forced myself to concentrate, and then my probe was flying swift and low along the path we had planned to take. I touched briefly on the minds of various nocturnal creatures but found no human mind. At one point, I was startled when a cloud of shadowy birds rose, flittering and shrieking indignantly, disturbed by my scrying. Finding nothing, I came back along the same path, swinging out on both sides.

My probe brushed briefly along the static barrier on the fringe of the Blacklands; then I went farther ahead, along the banks of the Suggredoon. I was surprised to realize we were less than an hour's ride from the river. We planned to follow the Suggredoon down to where it disappeared underground at the foot of the Gelfort Range. Not far from there, we would find the Olden way.

Making a last sweep of the area, I encountered a blank spot. I tried to penetrate it, but it was like trying to see in a blinding snowstorm.

Defeated, I withdrew and opened my eyes.

"Are ye all right?" Matthew asked.

"Did you find anything?" Domick asked.

I told them the result of my farsensing. "It sounds like Blackland static," Matthew said.

"It was like that but denser and cloudier," I said. "Maybe it was tainted water."

"But no settlement," Domick persisted.

"I couldn't sense even a single person, let alone a settlement," I said, feeling relieved. "Maybe it was a hunting party."

Matthew looked doubtful. "I dinna think anyone would come here to hunt. T'would be like takin' mid-meal in a graveyard. Maybe it were soldierguards lookin' for escapees or robbers?"

I chewed my lip. "It wouldn't be possible to have a machine that would create that kind of blocking static, would it?" I asked.

Pavo looked thoughtful. "That would mean someone had found a way to modify another Beforetime machine. The Zebkrahn took years to modify—first Marisa Seraphim, then Alexi, and then the Teknoguild worked to change what seems to have been no more than a thing originally devised to measure brain waves. Besides, I think you would know if it was a machine."

"It must be some sort of taint, then," Domick said dismissively.

It was a cold night. I slept restlessly, dreamed of running through dark tunnels, and woke with the feeling that I had forgotten something important. After racking my brain, I pushed the nagging feeling to the back of my thoughts.

Pulling the flap aside, I was delighted to find sun streaming through the treetops. The others stirred in the blaze of light, blinking and groaning. The ground was soaking wet, and there was no question of lighting a fire, but it was lovely to stretch our legs and walk around. I was very stiff but suspected I would have been worse without Kella's healer wizardry.

Gahltha and the other horses emerged from the trees as we were finishing a scratch firstmeal. Darga accepted a bowl of milk with a polite flap of his tail. We tied the oilskins, which were still wet, on top of the caravans and washed our faces in a streamlet. Domick worried that the water might be tainted, but Darga pronounced it safe. He had an acute sense of smell and could tell when water was bad.

We set off far more cheerfully than the previous day. I felt happier despite Gahltha's insistence at my riding bareback. Mounting him was an awkward debacle, because my legs were too stiff to flex easily. But once up, I felt more comfortable than I had on the saddle, though less secure.

The sun shone in a golden autumn way, and Jik played a jaunty harvest song on his gita, accompanying himself in a surprisingly sweet singing voice. Even grim Domick appeared to enjoy the impromptu concert, and the horses perked their ears as if they liked the sound.

Later, I listened to a communication between Darga and Avra about funaga. I was amused to hear their interpretation of human parenting, but Gahltha snorted loudly at Avra's observation that the children of funaga seemed less dangerous than grown funaga.

"You do not know anything about the funaga and their ways," he told her icily. "They are all the same. I have been beaten savagely by a funaga child who

68

laughed at my pain and jeered when I bled. Like poisoned ground, funaga bear poisoned fruit."

I shivered at the venom in his voice.

Gahltha's pace quickened after that. On a flat stretch, he broke into a trot without warning, and I fell. My only consolation was that the wet ground was soft. My anger made no impression on Gahltha, who insisted that I would not have fallen if I had been gripping with my knees the way I was supposed to. Louis laughed uproariously, and though the others restrained their amusement, my next fall sent them all into gales of laughter.

I kept my temper with difficulty, realizing Gahltha sought to goad me. And I knew he was right, however sarcastic he was. I had been sitting lazily.

By the time we stopped for midmeal, I was covered in mud. It was not worth changing, so I merely washed my hands and face to eat. The afternoon was worse than the morning, despite my forlorn hope for an easy walking pace. Gahltha decided I must advance to riding at a gallop. Only stubborn pride kept me from protesting that he was progressing too quickly.

So we cantered and galloped, and when the wagons moved too slowly for Gahltha, he would ride ahead, then turn and ride back. By late afternoon, I was beginning to feel the rhythm of his movements. Once or twice I even found myself enjoying the speed.

We had been traveling parallel to the Suggredoon most of the day, but soon after midmeal, the river broadened suddenly, swollen from the night's rain. The undergrowth thickened, too, slowing the caravans to a walking pace. Avra went slightly ahead with Domick, seeking the easiest path for the caravans. Later, Gahltha and I took over, leaving Domick free to range farther ahead.

We hoped to reach the foot of the mountains before nightfall, but Domick returned just as the sun fell behind the mountains. One look at his grim expression told us his news was bad.

"I found the place where the Suggredoon goes under the mountains, but I couldn't find any pass. We went a fair way up from the river, but there was nothing," he reported glumly.

"The distances on the map might be wrongly drawn, or the entrance to the pass might be sharply aslant so that you would have to be coming from the other way to see it," Pavo said.

"I hope you're right," Domick said. "But that's not all the bad news. Just ahead, there are great patches of swamp and wetlands. The wagons won't have a hope of going through, and it will take days to go round."

There seemed no point in pushing on in the darkness. We decided to make camp on a high, grassy knoll beside the Suggredoon.

Louis, Jik, and Matthew went to forage for dry wood while Kella organized nightmeal. Domick unharnessed the horses and checked the wooden wheels for stress cracks. Pavo sat near the wagons and pored over his maps.

I went to bathe in the river, but just as I reached the edge of the clearing, I heard Kella and Domick begin a heated argument. Sighing, I turned back. The last thing we needed was guild rivalry.

Before I could intervene, Pavo broke into a violent fit of coughing. Kella stared at him for a moment, then went over and commanded him to open his mouth.

"I swallowed a fly." He laughed and waved her away. But Kella's face was deadly serious.

"What is it?" Domick asked her.

The healer ignored him and laid a hand over Pavo's thin chest. The smile faded from his face, and suddenly I felt frightened.

"Why didn't you tell anyone?" Kella asked in a subdued voice.

Pavo smiled sadly. "What good would it have done, eh? I don't need a healer to tell me what the matter is."

"Rushton would never have let you come if he had known," Kella said.

Pavo turned away abruptly. "Don't you think I know that?"

"What is it?" I asked, coming back into the clearing.

Kella looked at me bleakly. "The rotting sickness. It's in his breathing."

"Are you sure?" Domick asked.

"It's not hard to feel, once you know. And the coughing is always a sign. There's nothing I can do for him. Nothing," she said flatly.

Pavo still had his back to us, rigidly unmoving.

"You'll have to . . . ," I began.

"No!" The usually mild teknoguilder whirled, eyes ablaze. "I won't go back." He turned to Kella. "You said yourself there's nothing to be done. I accept that, but I'll go the way I want. I won't be a problem. Tell them."

She nodded. "He'll cough, and there will be bouts of pain. He won't be affected badly until near the end—three or four months, maybe less . . ."

I gaped. Pavo stared back, his eyes pleading and determined at the same time. "You will need me to get to the library."

71

I wished Rushton were there to decide. After a long moment, I nodded, and Pavo's shoulders slumped visibly as if he had been holding his breath.

"Thank you," he said.

I felt tears in my eyes and was relieved to see Matthew and Jik arrive, laden with dry wood. Jik froze and looked about, sensing the tangle of emotions. I sent a quick shielded instruction to Matthew, and he began to make a fire, diverting Jik's attention.

We slept inside the caravans again because of the sodden ground but left the flaps open for fresh air. Obernewtyn seemed very far away.

Near dawn, I was jolted awake by Domick poking his head into the wagon.

"Quick, there are people coming. Men," he hissed urgently.

I farsensed the area and almost fainted with horror. There were at least a dozen men approaching the clearing. "It's too late to escape," I told him. "You get away. I'll send the horses away and contact you once I find out what this is all about. Quickly," I whispered.

He nodded, then melted silently into the gray predawn shadows.

My heart thundering, I farsent the group, warning them to let me do any talking. Then I urged the horses away.

Our only hope, I knew, was to be taken for the gypsies we appeared to be. I cursed my stupidity at not taking better precautions after Avra had found the tracks.

"Ho. What have we here?" called a gruff voice. I leaned out of the caravan. Three men stood in the open, illuminated by the dying embers of our fire. Behind them, the dark sky showed pink and gray traces of the dawn. I sensed the other men waiting in the bushes.

"Who are you? What do you want?" I shouted.

"Gypsies," sneered one, a fat, bristle-bearded man with a great pouting stomach and pale, glistening eyes.

"Perhaps," said the voice that had first hailed us. It belonged to a muscular young giant with ginger hair.

The third man appeared frail and was clad in a long, fine woolen gown much like the garb worn by Herder priests. I was terrified that we might have fallen into Herder hands. I prayed the priest would not recognize Jik and hurriedly warned him not to draw attention to himself. With his dark skin, dyed hair, and gypsy clothing, he did not look much like the Herder boy we had rescued.

"Who are you to be waking us in the middle of the night?" I demanded. Gypsies were not known for their manners.

"Get out of those wagons, all of you!" snarled the black-bearded man.

"This is a funny time to want your palm read," I grumbled. "If you mean to rob us, you'll be disappointed." I climbed out and put my hands on my hips as the others gathered behind me. I watched the man in the robe closely, but he did not seem to recognize Jik. "Well, you have us all out. Now what?" I asked.

The ginger-haired woodsman quirked his brow speculatively. "Is this all of you?"

"Enough for you," I said cheekily.

"Are you the leader of these people?" asked the man in the robe. He had a curiously colorless voice and very cold eyes.

"For now," I answered after swift thought. "My

73

father is the leader of our troupe. We are to meet up with him in Arandelft." I nodded at Pavo. "My cousin here fell sick, and our party split in two. Though I don't know what business it is of yours," I added rudely.

"What are you doing here if you are headed for Arandelft?" asked the white-robed man.

My heart jumped. "We heard there was an Olden way through the mountains," I said. The best lies are the ones that are mostly true, Louis always told us. He was glaring belligerently at the men, and I hoped he would keep his mouth shut.

"There is no such pass." The robed man stepped forward, and I resisted the urge to step away. "Enough of this. We will bring them back to camp."

More men stepped out of the trees. I pretended to look surprised. "Find the horses and bring these vans."

"Where are you taking us?" I demanded.

The robed man did not answer, but the ginger-bearded woodsman grinned over his shoulder. "You are to meet the great man himself. The Druid."

♦ 8 ♦

THROUGH THE TREES, I could see a settlement. I realized we were headed for the blank area I had been unable to penetrate the night before. This and the knowledge that we had been captured by Henry Druid filled me with apprehension. We could hardly have gotten into a worse mess deliberately.

But more disturbing, as soon as we entered the area of blankness, my powers were useless. I could not even reach Matthew, who was directly behind me.

Mindbound for the first time in my life, I was nearly overcome with panic and the feeling of being trapped. Glancing over one shoulder, the look of rigid terror on Jik's face acted like a bucket of cold water on my own fear. I made myself smile reassuringly, and the stark tension in his movements subsided. Then I concentrated on calming myself. I had to find a way to free us, and that would only be possible with a cool head. Methodically, I tried reaching all the others, including Darga, who padded along quietly beside Jik. I could not sense a single thought. Then I tried to farseek outside the area—Domick, then Gahltha.

Nothing.

No wonder the Druids had seemed to disappear so completely. The block had to be a machine, modified like the Zebkrahn. There was something mindless about the static.

I was deeply concerned by what such a block must mean. We had long heard rumors of Council and Herder interest in Misfits with special abilities, but to most of the Land we were thought to be harmless defectives who might occasionally have a meaningful dream. The Druid must know otherwise.

Somehow, Rushton had to be warned that he had mind weapons. What would happen if the rogue Herder discovered we were Misfits?

Or did he already know that, too?

Behind, Louis grunted in astonishment at the size of the walled encampment visible through the trees. The wall itself was no more than a barrier of thin, dark-stained striplings set upright in the ground, reaching high enough to obscure all but the tops of thatch-roofed buildings and a number of gently smoking chimneys.

Rounding the outer wall, we came to a wide gateway that was firmly bolted. A ruddy face appeared at an opening in answer to the red-haired woodsman's call. "Who is that wi' ye, Gilbert? I diven't know them faces."

Gilbert gestured impatiently at the door. "Open up, Relward."

"Bain't he a gypsy?" Relward inquired, staring doltishly into my face. He chewed his lip ponderously, then, unlatching the gate, planted himself firmly in the gap.

"Step aside, fool! You try my patience," Gilbert snapped.

Relward shook his head. "I canna let strangers in. Take him"—he nodded at me—"an' them others to th' compound. Her can come in," he added, nodding at

Kella. Despite the seriousness of our situation, I felt indignant at being taken for a boy.

"I'll decide where they will be taken, Relward," Gilbert said through gritted teeth. "But I'm not sure we should have a gatekeeper too blind to know the difference between man and maid."

The bumpkin's eyes widened. He stared at me accusingly, as if I had deliberately transformed myself to confound him. Then he gaped, seeing the robed man. "Master," he bleated. "I dinna know ye was there." He tripped over his feet in an effort to get out of the way. The robed man ignored him and swept into the camp.

Gilbert grinned covertly over his shoulder at me. "Do not think we are all such fools as that—or so blind," he murmured in a low voice.

There was nothing makeshift about what lay within the walls. It was a complete and settled village with graveled streets and stores. There was even a blacksmith and extensive holding yards and stables for horses.

People came out into the street to watch us pass, their eyes curious. Almost everyone seemed to wear arms, including the women and older children. The prospect of escape seemed dim.

At the very center of the settlement was a wide green expanse and garden beds. I was oddly reassured to see children playing on a swing, though they stopped their game to watch us pass.

Only one building edged on the square, a big stone house that reminded me vaguely of the main Councilcourt in Sutrium. Broad stone steps led up to the entrance, and double wooden doors like those at Obernewtyn stood open, revealing a long hall with a shining timber floor and a high sloped ceiling. Two young men emerged from one of the many doors leading off the hall. They smiled at Gilbert, but their good humor faded when they saw the rest of us.

"Gypsies," one spat. Gilbert frowned but made no comment, shepherding us through a door into an unadorned room.

The other men continued farther into the building, leaving us alone except for Gilbert. I tried again to breach the block but with no success. It was incredible to think such mental blindness was considered normal.

"Gypsies, eh?" Gilbert said, leaning against the door. "Where were you really headed? The main road would be much quicker than any so-called Olden way."

I stepped up to him boldly. "I told you already, or are you as deaf as that gatewarden was blind? We are to meet my father in Arandelft."

Instead of becoming angry, Gilbert threw back his head and laughed with real amusement. "I wondered why a scrap of a girl was the leader over grown men, but now I see you carry the sharpest weapon in your wicked tongue."

"Why have you brought us here?" I demanded.

Gilbert smiled. "I am the one asking the questions. Tell me, where have you come from, if you insist you are going to Arandelft?"

I hesitated. "We have been in the high mountain country."

I heard a smothered gasp from Kella, but fortunately Gilbert was too intent on my answer to register it.

"Then . . . you must have seen Obernewtyn?" he said.

I shrugged carelessly. "Of course." From the corner of my eye, I could see Matthew looking at me as if I had gone mad.

"Why did you go up there?" Gilbert asked guardedly.

"Why does a gypsy travel anywhere? For silver. My father said there would be winter lodgings there and work to trade for it. He wanted to try trapping a snow bear. One sold in Sutrium last moon fair for a Councilman's ransom." I smiled as if the thought of such wealth excited me, then I let my face fall.

"But everything went wrong. There was a curse on that place, and we laid another in leaving. A firestorm had all but laid it to waste. There was nothing left but a few rough huts made of the ruins. The people remaining had no room or food to spare. Then my cousin fell sick, and I had to wait for him while the rest went on without us. And now this," I snorted petulantly.

"So, there *was* a firestorm," Gilbert murmured.

"We were supposed to meet the troupe at Arandelft in time for the harvest of eben berries," Matthew said.

Gilbert looked at him and grinned. "So, you *can* speak. I thought you were all mute, having this grubby wench speak for you."

I held my breath, hoping Matthew would have the sense to see he was being deliberately needled. He only shrugged sullenly and fell silent.

The robed man returned, and Gilbert spoke to him in a low voice. His pale eyes rested thoughtfully on me.

"Take the men to the compound, the boy to the other children, and the girl to Rilla," the robed man told Gilbert. "You will come with me," he instructed me coldly.

He led me down the hall to another door.

". . . but how can we have missed it . . ." A deep voice floated out as we entered. I blinked, dazzled by the sunlight streaming from a huge window. The room was an

79

enclosed fern garden. There was a long table covered in books and papers and surrounded by chairs. A number of robed men and several dressed like Gilbert clustered around the head of the table.

"Forgive me, lord," said the man who had brought me there.

Those bending over the table drew back to reveal a white-bearded man seated in their midst. He wore a plain cream-colored robe like the others, yet there was an aura of authority about him. He had the thin face and body of an ascetic, but his features were curiously mismatched—a beaky nose, a jutting chin, and beetling silver brows. His eyes were his sole visible beauty, dark and strangely compelling. Such eyes might easily see into a person's mind. I met his penetrating gaze uneasily.

"Who is this?" he asked in a low, sweet voice.

"This is the gypsy girl I mentioned a moment ago. But I had not realized then that she and her family have been in the high mountains," he added pointedly.

The old man's eyes glittered. "You have been to Obernewtyn?"

I nodded, wondering if I had made a mistake in mentioning Obernewtyn. I told them what I had told Gilbert. "Why have you brought us here?" I asked at last. I wanted to impress on them that I was a gypsy, interested in nothing but my own skin.

"Tell me what you saw at Obernewtyn," the old man invited.

"I've told you everything. They wouldn't let us stay because there was no room. Some of them were sick." I let distaste show in my eyes.

"My acolyte told me you were looking for a Beforetime pass."

I nodded.

"There is no pass," the old man said. "Now, what is the truth for your avoiding the main road? I suspect you were trying to leave the highlands without being seen. Gypsies are known for being light-fingered." I hung my head to hide my relief. He thought we were thieves trying to reach the lowlands without being arrested!

"What are you going to do with us?" I asked, hoping to encourage his assumptions.

"What was the name of the Master of Obernewtyn?" the old man asked.

A chill ran down my spine. "There was a youth in charge, if you would call him master. He seemed half out of his wits if you ask me. Kept raving about Obernewtyn belonging to him and wanting to restore it. Who would want to bother with such a ruin?" I chewed my lip as if trying to recall. "Rafe . . . Rushton, I think his name was."

An unreadable look flickered over the old man's face.

For a long moment, there was silence in the room, and I heard the muted sounds of children at play. The old man rose slowly and came round to stand in front of me.

"Do you know who I am?" he asked.

My heart sank. If he would tell that openly, he had no intention of letting us go. "Are you . . . the Druid from the old stories?" I asked shyly.

The old man gave me a quick, rather beautiful smile. "I am," he said. "It pleases me to know my name has not been forgotten. And what do gypsies know of Henry Druid?"

"My father told me the Council and the Herder Faction forced you into exile. He said you were not dead no matter what was said and that you would one day return."

A fanatic gleam flashed in the old man's eyes. "Your father is wise, for I do mean to return."

The door opened suddenly, and a pretty blond girl entered. She scanned the room lazily, her eyes stopping on the Druid. "Father, you promised to come to mid-meal. We are all waiting." She pouted.

The Druid smiled indulgently. "I will be there very soon, Erin. In the meantime, take this girl to Rilla for me."

"Another gypsy?" she inquired disparagingly. Without waiting for an answer, she gestured languidly for me to follow.

The Druid's voice followed us into the hall. "And, Erin, tell Rilla the two girls will attend nightmeal with us tonight. See that they have some suitable clothes."

Erin nodded and closed the door behind us. She led me wordlessly out of the building, across the green, and down a number of streets to a square building near the edge of the settlement. A delicious smell of cooking food flowed out the door. My mouth watered, but we by-passed the door, going round a narrow path to another building at the rear. The less appetizing smell of soap-suds met my nostrils. I cast a regretful look over my shoulder.

Erin glanced at me with as much interest as if I were a piece of cheese. Her eyes were hard and bright like pieces of blue glass.

A woman came out to meet us. Plump and pretty, she introduced herself as Rilla.

Erin looked bored at this exchange. "This one needs a good scrubbing. I don't wonder Relward mistook it for a boy. Still, do what you can. Both these gypsies are to come to nightmeal at the Druid's table tonight."

"Your friend is already bathing," Rilla said when Erin had gone. My stomach growled loudly as if defining its own priorities, and Rilla laughed. "Ye'd nowt be let into th' kitchen lookin' like that. But bathe quick and ye can have yer fill before yer tum gives up growlin' an' takes to bitin' ."

The bathhouse was filled with billowing steam. I squinted, making out a number of tin barrels all round the walls with fires burning beneath. In the center of the room were two vats. Kella's head popped above the rim of one, and Rilla pointed me to the other.

"There now," she said kindly, handing me a drying towel.

I turned to set the towel down and caught sight of myself in the mirror. I gaped. My face was barely visible for filth—I scarcely looked human. My clothes were stiff with dirt, and my long hair was one lank rat tail. I had not bathed since Gahltha's riding lessons. With a grimace, I stripped off my clothes and slid into the soapy water. I scrubbed thoroughly, massaging gritty dirt from my hair and ears. Kella handed me a thick calico robe like the one she wore as I clambered out.

"Was it the Druid?" she asked worriedly.

I nodded. "Did you notice anything else since we came here?"

Kella sighed. "You too? I hoped your powers would be strong enough not to be affected. What do you think it is?"

"Some sort of machine, but no one mentioned it. Maybe this is how they test people to find out if they are Misfits. Yet I'm almost certain they believe we're real gypsies."

"Rilla won't be long. I think she's been told to keep an

eye on us. What are we going to do?" Kella asked urgently.

"I'm going to try breaking through the barrier as soon as I have a moment alone. If that doesn't work, I'll have to get to the machine and damage it or switch it off somehow. If only Pavo were here. I wonder why we've been separated?"

"Didn't they say anything to you about this night-meal?" Kella asked.

Puzzled at her tone, I said, "We're to eat with the Druid. What else should I be told?"

"We are to eat with the Druid and all unbonded men," Kella said pointedly. "Have you noticed how few women there are around here? Rilla let it slip. Tonight we are going to be looked over like batches of scones. For bonding."

Rilla returned carrying a green dress in one arm and a blue one in the other. "These will match your eyes," she said. Her own eyes widened. "Well, ye do clean up nice an' proper."

I had never seen such fine clothes before, let alone dreamed of wearing them. But where had such finery come from, if not Sutrium? And how would an exiled Herder priest obtain such luxuries?

"These will make ye pretty fer tonight," Rilla said, holding out the dresses.

"Pretty as lambs to the slaughter," I murmured sarcastically. I held mine up as if it were a shroud cloth. And well it might be, for I had no intention of being bonded to anyone.

✦ 9 ✦

It was an odd, strained occasion.

The Druid and his guests were formally attired, and the courses of food were lavishly presented. It was hard to believe we were in the middle of the White Valley.

The Druid's armsmen, as those of Gilbert's type called themselves, drank heavily, both red and white fements as well as a spicy warmed cordial. The latter could be made anywhere, but the highlands were no place to grow the delicate fement grapes. Like the dresses Kella and I wore, the fements could only have come from the lowlands, probably Arandelft.

The Druid had the head of the table, and his daughter, Erin, sat by his side, clad in a dazzling blood-red dress. Her long hair was elaborately plaited and beaded around her head.

Beside her, Gilbert smiled in welcome. "So, gypsy girl, how are you finding our rough-and-ready camp?"

Laughter met his words. All the Druid's captives were probably equally astounded at the lavish way the Druids lived. Gilbert was hardly recognizable in a fine white shirt and black velvet jacket, though he was less extravagantly clad than many of the other armsmen. None of the white-robed Druid acolytes were present.

"What? No words for us, gypsy girl? Have we disarmed you at last? Perhaps the fire was quenched when the dirt was washed off," Gilbert teased.

Erin laid a dainty hand on his arm. "Dirt will wash away, Gilbert, but that particular hue of skin will remain the same grubby gypsy color, no matter how hard she scrubs."

The table fell silent, but before I could draw breath to respond, Gilbert laughed, smoothly drawing his arm from beneath hers. "I find that dusky tone more pleasing than the fashionable pallor of a fish underbelly," he said, smiling into my eyes.

I found myself seated some way down the table and apart from Kella. On either side, the men spoke only a few polite words to me. Their eyes said they shared Erin's attitude. It was funny, in a way. If they had known I was a Misfit, I would be far more despised.

A while later, Erin's voice rose above the buzz of talk. "Father, I am only saying that this desire to bond the armsmen is going too far. Surely you want to maintain some sort of standard. Yet you permit grubby gypsies to dine with us." I had no doubt she had raised her voice deliberately.

I stood abruptly. "Lord, my father told me enough to make me admire Henry Druid, but I will not be insulted by a painted doll!" There was a gasp from some of the men, and Erin's pouting mouth fell open in astonishment.

There was a long silence. I did not take my eyes from the Druid's, but I was not to hear his reply since someone had begun to clap.

"Well done, Lady Erin. I salute you for your wit," Gilbert said. He raised his mug to Erin. "I feared our gypsy girl had lost her tongue." He drank deeply, and a few hardy souls around him laughed.

Erin's face filled with rage, but the Druid laid a restraining hand on her arm. I wondered at Gilbert's recklessness. It was clear he had some rank in the camp, but now I wondered exactly what his position was.

He grinned at me down the length of the table, but I did not smile back. Beside him, Erin's eyes glittered with malice. Perhaps Gahltha's cynical comment that poisoned trees bore poisoned fruit was right, for I suspected the Druid shared his daughter's prejudice.

I finished my meal, ignored by my companions. I had a fierce longing to be back at Obernewtyn, where people were judged by their actions rather than their ancestry. Rushton would laugh to know how much I hungered to be home. With a painful lurch of my heart, I realized I missed him.

A young boy and an old man played a merry dance tune on a drum and a small flute. I was not surprised to see people rise to dance. I had never learned how. Orphan homes did not organize such frivolous pursuits. On both sides of me, the seats were empty, my dinner companions having deserted me for less controversial partners. My outburst had made me doubly an outcast despite my finery.

I looked up to find Gilbert standing beside my seat. "Come, let me see if you dance as well as you talk."

I lifted my chin. "I wonder you dare ask a gypsy to dance."

Gilbert frowned. "Hatred of gypsies is a foolish, unfounded prejudice that I do not share."

"It seems you are alone in that. Who are you, that you can safely voice such unpopular opinions?"

"I lead the armsmen. The Druid values my expertise. But I am known for my outspoken nature. It has not got me killed so far."

I smiled a little despite myself. Another place and time, I would have liked the bold armsman as a friend. But the knowledge that he was the leader of the Druid's fighting force made me nervous. His kindness might be no more than a strategy to put me off guard.

Gilbert slid into the seat beside me. "I am my own fellow. Dance with me," he invited softly.

I found I did not want to hurt his feelings with a plain refusal. I lifted the hem of my skirt and showed him my scarred legs and feet. His face tightened at the sight of the scars. "And I made you walk back to camp. Why didn't you say something?"

I smiled and shrugged wryly. "You didn't seem the sort to worry about a prisoner's feet."

"Then we will talk," he said firmly. "You may direct the course of our words."

The opportunity was too good to miss. "Tell me how you came to be here."

Gilbert smiled and obliged. It proved an unexpected tale.

He had been born to a seafaring family in Aborium, but his father had been taken by slavers and his boat sunk. As a child, Gilbert had worked as a harbor laborer to support his mother and sister, until they died of a plague that swept the coast one year. Weary of the sea and lonely, he had gone inland to seek his fortune as a hunter. He had been on his own in the White Valley when the Druid had recruited him. He smiled wryly at the euphemism.

"At first I was determined to escape, but where

would I escape to? I had no home, and I loathe the Council. And, as you see, this is a pleasant enough life for one so skilled and useful as I."

"The Druid has a good supply of luxuries," I said.

He grinned. "He has a friend in Sutrium." He stopped abruptly.

I continued on, pretending not to have noticed his slip. "Are there really such things as slavers?" I asked.

He nodded. "There are at that, black-hearted souls. They prey on small fishing vessels like those belonging to my father, shanghai the crew, and sell them. I have also heard it said the Council sells seditioners they do not want brought to open trial. Those taken are never heard of again. Who knows where they end up? It is a wide, strange world."

"But . . . what do you mean? There is only this Land and the two islands," I said. "The rest is Blacklands."

Gilbert shook his head. "A myth spawned by the Council, who have a vested interest in ignorance. There are other places on the earth where the white death never reached or where the poisons have faded. My father always said so, and he had seen more of the world than most."

I stared. "But how is it no one talks of this?"

Gilbert smiled, not unpleasantly. "Any seafarer stupid enough to talk of such things disappears, no doubt himself sold to the slavers. After all, the Council do not want their subjects sailing off in search of greener pastures and freer lands."

I was fascinated. I had never dreamed of questioning Council teachings on the extent of the holocaust.

"Why not take to the sea yourself and go where there is no Council?" I wondered.

Gilbert sighed. "I could have done that, but a harsh lore is better than none. It is said that incredible mutations of plant and beast run riot beyond our horizons. And even lands untouched by the Great White must have suffered in the Age of Chaos that followed. No, better to work here with the Druid to overcome the Council. Besides, unlike my father, I get seasick," he added.

I laughed, then sobered quickly. "You think the Druid and his acolytes are any better than the Council?" I hardly expected an answer to such a question, but he had certainly been forthcoming to this point.

"I don't know. I hope so. He is hard, but there is always hope of change. At least he has standards and rules to live by. He values order and normalcy."

I looked at him sharply. "You said the world is full of mutation. Who has the right to decide what is normal?"

Gilbert looked taken aback at the change in my tone. "I do not mind mutants; in my experience, those deemed Misfit are harmless. But the Druid was a Herder, after all. He is fanatical on the subject. And most of the others think as he does. Perhaps I'm not fine enough to distinguish between the smells of people as if they were so much spoiled meat."

I frowned, deciding whatever the Druid knew or guessed about Talents, Gilbert knew nothing. Perhaps only the Druid's acolytes knew about the machine blocking my abilities.

"And what about freedom? He would not let you leave here."

The armsman smiled. "No one keeps me where I do not want to be. But freedom is not a matter of that. You are a gypsy, so you think it is only the ability to move from place to place at will. Real freedom is a thing no one can take from you because it is of the spirit. I keep it here." He tapped his head, then rose. "I have promised a dance, but we will talk again."

I watched him go, surprised to find myself wishing we could have gone on talking, grateful that he had allowed me to question him without asking me questions in return.

I shook my head. He was an enemy, yet I liked him. And I was as certain he liked me. It had never occurred to me that I might be found desirable. Yet clothed in the fine dress, I had only been able to gape at my reflection as I'd caught sight of myself in a long mirror on my way to the dining hall. The girl who had looked back at me, with her cloud of dark silky hair and mysterious green eyes, had seemed a dazzling stranger. In that moment, I'd had the curious wish that Rushton might see me so transformed.

To my relief, the meal ended without talk of bonding. Like all farseekers, I knew bonding for me would mean more than a physical communion. A mindmeld would be far more intimate than any bodily merging. It would be an ultimate kind of nakedness with one of my own kind; to bond with an unTalent would be like bonding to a statue.

I prepared for bed in a private chamber; Kella had been housed in a separate room. Dismissing all thoughts of the nightmeal from my mind, I concentrated my senses for a final, unrestrained attempt on the barrier of static.

The block lay like a wet blanket over my senses. I felt suffocated as I tried to farseek. I used more power, but the static seemed to respond, strengthening in direct proportion to the force I used.

Finally I lay back with a defeated sigh. It was no use. I would have to find the machine.

◆ 10 ◆

"WHAT ARE YE up to, Emmon?" Rilla demanded suspiciously of a slight boy with a lopsided grin who had entered the kitchen.

He looked exaggeratedly hurt. "Th' Druid sent me to bring the gypsy called Elspeth," he said in a wounded voice.

I had spent the morning with Kella helping to do the encampment chores. I had tried questioning Rilla, but she appeared to know no more than Gilbert about the existence of Talents, much less the blocking static. She also didn't seem to know where the rest of our friends were. I'd begun to worry.

Kella had learned that Rilla's dead bondmate had been one of the Druids slain in the last Teknoguild expedition, and the older girl's general ignorance of the incident confirmed that the Druid only told his people what he felt they needed to know. "Rilla knows that others were involved but has no idea that they were from Obernewtyn," Kella had said. "She did say the Druid believes the explosion had been caused deliberately with a Beforetime weapon. That and his interest in Obernewtyn must mean he suspects Rushton of treachery."

I wondered now what the Druid wanted of me.

As we left, Emmon stole a slice of meat and got a

hard smack for his troubles. Outside, he rubbed his ear and grinned broadly. "T'was worth it. Come on." We had not gone far when I realized we were going in the wrong direction.

"Well, that's true . . . ," Emmon admitted. "As a matter of fact, I were nowt told to bring ye at once, so we've time to spare. I'd rather walk about than wash dishes or work at spellin' an' th' like. Wouldn't you?"

"Won't we get into trouble?" I asked warily.

He shook his head. "Ye won't. If we gan caught, I'll say ye knew nowt of it."

"Will you show me around, then? I haven't had much chance to see the camp," I said.

Emmon nodded enthusiastically. He marched off, at once setting out to describe the variety and uses of the buildings we passed. I tried in vain to lead him to talk of the Druid, in the hope of getting a clue about the location of any machine. Eventually, I concentrated instead on committing the camp to memory.

We passed a long series of windowless buildings, which Emmon identified as storehouses.

"Where do all the Druid's supplies come from?" I asked.

Emmon grinned. "From th' Council's own stores. Th' Council dinna know that one of their own trusted agents is oath kin to th' Druid."

Oath kin? That meant someone as close as blood without being related. The Druid was as canny a strategist as I'd ever encountered.

Emmon pointed out another building. "That's th' library." It seemed his dislike of spelling did not extend to reading. The Druid had obviously instilled his followers with his own love of books.

"I hear Erin dinna take to ye much," Emmon said.

"Who told you that?" I asked sharply.

Emmon smiled. "I'll take ye to visit a friend of mine."

Before I could question him, he ran off, and I was forced to follow. I found him knocking on the door to a small cottage.

"Who lives here?" I asked. I heard footsteps inside.

"Erin's twin sister lives here," he whispered. I gave him a furious look, but it was too late. The door opened, and a delicious odor wafted out.

"Gilaine, it's me. I've brought a visitor," Emmon announced. He sniffed and sighed, identifying the smell. "Honeyballs."

I stared at the girl who had answered the door.

There was no question whose sister she was. But they were as much alike as the sun and the moon. Where Erin's hair was spun gold and elaborately dressed, Gilaine wore her long, ashen tresses loose about her shoulders. Erin's eyes were bright blue, but Gilaine's were as gray as clouds lit from behind by the sun. The greatest difference, though, lay in their expressions. Erin's face was ever haughty and querulous, but Gilaine's was gentle, the smile on her mouth echoing in her eyes. I was immediately drawn to her.

"This is Elspeth. She's one of them gypsy folk," Emmon said, slipping behind her into the house.

I wondered why she did not speak. As if in answer to my thought, she raised a finger to her lips. At first I thought she was trying to tell me to be quiet. Then I realized she was mute.

"The honeyballs are burnin'!" Emmon wailed.

Gilaine smiled anew, gesturing for me to follow her. The cottage was tiny, consisting of three sections: a closet of a room with a bed in it, a front hall, and a cozy and relatively large kitchen.

The honeyballs turned out to be tiny, crisp sweets. My mouth full, I asked Emmon why I had not seen Gilaine at the nightmeal. He managed to look wrathful over bulging cheeks. "She is nowt asked," he said.

I could figure out the rest. The old Druid was a perfectionist. His hatred of Misfits extended to anything he considered flawed. And Gilaine was mute. Seeing my look, she smiled sadly and shrugged.

We stayed with Gilaine until it was time to go. I was surprised to hear Emmon confess his deception in retrieving me early, but she only shook her head helplessly and ruffled his hair with an expression of mingled concern and exasperation.

Crossing the green to the meeting house, I spotted Jik playing ball with some children and asked Emmon if I could talk to him.

"Well, yer nowt supposed to, an' ye know what a stickler I am for rules. But if I was to gan over an' wash my hands at th' spring, I'd nowt see what ye were up to. I'm a gullible fellow," he said with a smirk.

I called Jik away from his game. "Do you know where the others are being kept?" I asked him immediately. There was no time for greetings.

He shook his head. "I think they're someplace outside the walls."

"What about the block, can you feel it?"

He nodded, saying he had heard no talk of machines but that the Druid's acolytes worked in a shed forbidden to all others.

I nodded impatiently, frustrated that Emmon's tour had included neither this shed nor the compound I'd heard mentioned before. "Keep an ear out but don't ask any questions that will make anyone wonder about you. Remember, you're a gypsy. Where's Darga?"

"He's disappeared," Jik said miserably.

"Darga's a smart dog," I said. "He's probably gone to look for the others, or even to find Domick."

Jik's face brightened. "Do you think so?"

"Come on, Elspeth," Emmon called.

I patted Jik on the shoulder and ran to join Emmon.

I was taken in to the Druid by one of the acolytes. Struck again by his building's similarity to the Councilcourt, I wondered curiously if the Druid was indeed trying to start up his own opposing order. I had the feeling his order would be as bad as the Council's, whatever Gilbert believed. Entering the Druid's meeting chamber, I heard a tantalizing snatch of conversation.

A voice said, "If she is telling the truth, I don't see any need to waste more time on the mountains. I said all along it was your old friends in the Herder Faction that we bumped into."

"That may be, but it is likely too late to stop the soldierguards from investigating Obernewtyn. And better to have them in the mountains than here." That was the Druid. I hesitated at the door, hoping to hear more, but the Druid looked up.

"Come in, Elspeth. I want you to tell me again all you saw at Obernewtyn. . . ."

I was there for the rest of the afternoon. Fortunately, my story was simple, and I resisted the temptation to embellish in case he asked me to repeat it again. I quickly realized what he really wanted to know was if Rushton were continuing Alexi's researches.

I was unsure how much he knew of the truth. It was

common knowledge Alexi and Madam Vega had been involved in illegal research into the Beforetime and that Rushton had stopped that research when he had claimed Obernewtyn, as was his legal right. At one time, Henry Druid had befriended Rushton and had even supported him in his work to undermine the usurpers. But the Druid's motivations were less than admirable—he had sought for himself the same Beforetime weapon-machines that were the object of Alexi and Madam Vega's researches, and so far as I knew, he had hoped to eliminate his competition without getting the Council involved.

Rushton had severed ties without revealing his true plans for Obernewtyn, recognizing that the Druid's obsessive hatred of mutations was a danger to us. Ironically, this must have made the Druid wonder whether Rushton was continuing Alexi's search for Beforetime weapons, and our occasional exploration of the Blackland fringes would have only supported his suspicions.

The snatch of conversation I had overheard told me the Druid no longer saw Rushton as an enemy. Just the same, while taking care to present myself as an ignorant, self-centered gypsy, I made sure Rushton sounded as if he were verging on mania, committing all his resources to rebuilding the shattered Obernewtyn.

Dismissed at last, I went back to the kitchens. "What did he want?" Kella asked. "You've been ages!"

I told her of Emmon's antics, then recounted what I had heard.

"But it sounds like they now believe the Tekno-guilders they clashed with at the ruins were Herders. How odd that they should jump to that conclusion, when Herders discourage any interest in the Before-time," Kella said.

I nodded. "I think there is much about the Herders' activities that is secret. The important thing, though, is that the Druid now seems to believe Obernewtyn is a ruin. Even so, he seems to have set something in motion—there are soldierguards coming to the mountains. That means the rumors about renewed interest in Obernewtyn are true, and I'm almost sure this friend of theirs who works with the Council organized the investigation. It wouldn't be hard. The Council is so suspicious anyway."

Kella wiped her hands slowly on her apron. "We have to warn Rushton."

I nodded. "But first, I have to do something about this machine. Let Rilla think I'm still with the Druid. I think I can home in on the source of the static if I put my mind to it."

"Don't get caught," Kella said.

I climbed out the window at the back of the kitchen. Walking slowly, I let my mind explore the oddly pliant nature of the blocking static. Again I was reminded of a blanket and brushed my mind against it instead of using force. I had the eerie feeling it liked this, as if it were rubbing up against my mind like a kitten. I thought I could sense a core and moved in that direction.

Before long, I found myself in a part of the camp I had not seen before. I walked purposefully, trying to look as if I were running an errand, and avoided the eyes of the few people I passed.

Two men coming out of a doorway looked at me but made no move to stop me. As soon as I rounded a corner, I ran, keeping to the walls. I was determined nothing would keep me from at least locating the machine. A young girl looked out of a window curiously. I slowed abruptly to a walk, but her eyes followed me up the street.

I noticed a bank of ominous black clouds roiled along the horizon. An omen, though for good or ill I couldn't decide.

Suddenly I found myself on the very perimeter of the settlement. There was no one in sight. This part of the camp looked deserted. Uneasily, I wondered if the whole thing was some sort of trap.

I was about to turn back when, suddenly, I sensed the source of the block was very near. I couldn't resist. It came, I was certain, from a long, low-slung building with a flat roof. There was only one door to the building, and no guard stood by it. My trapped powers prevented me from knowing if there were guards inside.

Pressing one ear against the door, I heard faint voices. Dry-mouthed, I made my decision. The door swung open soundlessly.

I gaped at the complete unexpectedness of what lay inside. The building was composed of a single, long, almost bare room filled with babies and very young children. On the far side of the room, a thin dark-haired girl wiped the face of a bawling tot.

In the middle of the room, playing with a group of happy children, was Gilaine.

She looked up idly, and her face registered my own shock.

I could not think of a single thing to say. The room was obviously a kind of communal nursery, but I was convinced it was also the source of the block. The machine had to be concealed somewhere in the room.

The dark-haired girl came over. "Yes?" she said pleasantly.

Gilaine touched her arm and made a few intricate hand motions. "Gilaine says you're a friend. Come in."

Gilaine made another agitated hand movement and the girl nodded. "I'll do it. You talk to your friend," she said kindly.

"What is this place?" I asked Gilaine when we were alone.

She frowned and pointed to the children. One of the toddlers waddled after her and lurched at my knees. Reaching out to catch him, my hand brushed against Gilaine's.

The baby gurgled in delight, oblivious to our stunned looks. The moment our hands touched, I had immediate access to her mind—and she to mine! Gilaine was a Talent. She had the same unusual combination of empath and farseeking abilities as Jik.

She pulled away almost immediately. I leaned forward slowly, not wanting to alarm her, and touched her forearm. Again contact was established. It seemed the block did not work if I was actually touching the person I wanted to communicate with.

"Gilaine?" I sent gently. She recoiled. I stood waiting, and she reached out, touching my shoulder with a tentative finger.

"Elspeth?" her mind responded. It was a weak signal despite the strength I had found in her mind.

I nodded. Gilaine sat on a chair as if her legs would not hold her and pulled the toddler onto her lap. I reached forward, pretending to look at the baby, and touched her. "We must not make ourselves obvious," I sent, at the same time wondering if Gilaine was the trap.

"You . . . are like us, but different," Gilaine sent timidly.

"Us? There are other Misfits here?" I asked, astounded.

She nodded almost imperceptibly. I sensed that she did not want to talk about them.

"Does your father know?" I asked.

She shook her head vehemently. "Must not know." The baby began to struggle to be put down. Gilaine jiggled her knees up and down, and he gurgled contentedly. "Fatherdruid thinks Misfits only feebleminds or dreamers. He does not know about us/you. He thinks Misfit/mutant evil," she stressed.

"And you? Do you think this is evil?" I asked.

She shook her head but without much conviction.

"It's dangerous for you and your friends here. Why do you stay?" I asked.

She shrugged, but I was startled to see a familiar face in her mind. It was the boy I had met in the Councilcourt in Sutrium years earlier, when I had been waiting to be sentenced to Obernewtyn. In her vision, he was older, but it was unmistakeably the same person. He had spoken to me of running away to take refuge in the mountains. He had even mentioned Henry Druid, saying the rumor of his death was a lie. Clearly, he must serve the Druid. I fumbled in my memory for the name he had told me. "Daffyd," I murmured aloud triumphantly.

Gilaine almost dropped the baby in fright. The startled child hitched in a breath and began to scream. When it was quieted, Gilaine touched my hand. "How do you know that name? Did you read my behind-thoughts?" she asked suspiciously.

I shook my head without bothering to explain that I could have if I'd chosen to. People always thought I wanted to eavesdrop on their private thoughts, whereas the notion actually embarrassed me. "I saw his face in your mind. I met him once, in Sutrium. Is he a Misfit, too?"

She nodded, still wary.

"Where is he?" I asked, for surely I would have seen him if he were in the camp.

"Druid sent him to Sutrium/lowlands. Druid-business."

I noticed the dark-haired girl watching us curiously. We had been silent too long. In another moment, she would begin to wonder who I was and why she had not recognized me. I was putting Gilaine in danger and said as much to her in a low voice.

Rising, I sent a final, vital question. "Where is the blocking machine?"

She frowned. "Machine?"

"The block on our minds. Surely you can feel it?"

"Feel what?" Gilaine sent.

Confused, I sent a brief impression of the block.

"Oh, that," her mind sent, amused. "No machine. Lidgebaby." She pointed to a cot near one of the walls. "Lidgebabymind."

My mouth fell open. The incredible numbing effect blanketing the camp that had resisted all my strength was the uncontrollable mental static of a Misfit baby!

◆ 11 ◆

SOMETHING WOKE ME.

It was a dark night, with no moon showing beyond the window glass. Rain was falling softly on the roof of the washhouse and its adjoining sleeping chambers.

Then I heard a voice, calling softly. "Elspeth?"

I sat bolt upright in bed, afraid to answer in case it was a trap. Trying to think how a real gypsy would react, I climbed out of bed and went across to the window.

"Who's out there?" My voice came out low and anxious, not quite a whisper.

"Shh!" the voice hissed urgently.

Apprehension prickled along my spine. "What do want? Who are you?"

There was a pause, as if the caller was wary, too.

"I come from a friend," the voice whispered at last, reluctantly.

I frowned. "I have no friends here."

Again there was a pause. "Gilaine," the voice grated, with a hint of irritation.

I bit my lip and peered into the rain-streaked night, wishing there was a moon. Whoever was out there had the perfect cover. I could see nothing.

"I have a key to unlock your door," the voice said.

I made up my mind. If it was a trap, I would blame gypsy curiosity.

A moment later, there was a faint click, and the door opened to reveal a man wearing a dark hooded cloak pulled low across his face. Pulling my own cape hastily over my nightdress, I padded out barefoot, closing the door behind me.

"Who are you?" I demanded.

"My name is Saul. And you don't need to know any more than that," he added brusquely.

We hurried along, keeping close to the walls, cloaks flapping in gusts of wind that blew along the dark, empty streets. Coming to a cobbled square, Saul stopped, intently scanning the square and the streets leading into it. Trees growing up through the cobbles flung bare branches about, sighing mournfully. After a long moment, he flicked his hand curtly and strode directly across the square.

On the other side, I stopped. "Wait a minute. This isn't the way to Gilaine's house."

"It is the way to mine," Saul answered.

His house proved to be as small as Gilaine's but looked dark and deserted. He opened the door, and light spilled out onto the wet ground. Dark heavy curtains had hidden the light from prying eyes. Reassured, I followed him inside.

Removing his cloak, Saul shook it and hung it on a peg in the wall. Studying him covertly in the light, I decided he was handsome in a cold sort of way. He was tall but too thin, and his skin was pale. His hands were as long and slender as a woman's, his facial features sharply defined beneath a fringe of straight light brown hair. He looked at me fleetingly with eyes the color of mud-stained ice. I smiled tentatively, but he did not respond. I pretended to stumble as I followed him along the hallway, clutching at his arm to steady myself.

I had a brief impression of an intelligence bordering on brilliance, resting on a frighteningly unstable personality.

"Get out!" commanded an icy mental voice. He pushed me away with a look of revulsion.

I followed him wordlessly into the kitchen, knowing I had seen such stress before in people unable to tolerate the realization that they were Misfits. I guessed Saul had been ruthlessly orthodox before discovering his true nature. His very personality was disintegrating under the stress of being what he loathed. I wondered if the others knew how poorly he was coping.

The kitchen was almost the exact replica of Gilaine's but without cooking smells or flowers. It reminded me of an orphan-home kitchen before Council inspection.

Seated at a scrubbed timber table were Gilaine, the two musicians I had seen at the Druid's nightmeal, and an older heavyset man I had not seen before.

For a moment, they looked up at me with collective appraisal. Then Gilaine rose. Smiling welcome, she touched my arm. "I am glad you came. See? I am getting better at this strange way of communicating. But Lidegbaby does not like it. You know Saul. I think you have seen Peter and Michael." She gestured at the musicians. "And last is Jow, the brother of Daffyd."

"This is dangerous," I said aloud.

Gilaine nodded gravely. "You told me this afternoon that you meant to escape. We want to help, but you must answer questions first," she sent.

From the expressions on the faces of the others, I

guessed they had been less eager to help than Gilaine. I wondered what she had said to convince them—especially to Saul, who made no pretense of liking my presence and was prowling back and forth like a caged animal.

"The others with you—Misfit also?" Gilaine asked.

I nodded, aware we would not get out of the camp without help. I had to take the risk. And I did trust Gilaine. I guessed she was reporting my answers to the others but could find no trace of their communication, though her hand rested on my arm. She seemed not to need physical contact to farseek with the others.

She looked back at me. "Have you really been to Obernewtyn?"

I nodded, and again told the story I had told the Druid, with one difference. I told her we had welcomed Pavo's illness as an excuse to split off from the rest of the troupe. "It was getting too dangerous for us to stay. Most gypsies hate Misfits."

"Then you never meant to rejoin your father?" Saul asked accusingly when Gilaine had relayed my answer. "You say Obernewtyn is a ruin. How can we believe you?"

I shrugged. "Believe what you want. Why would I bother to lie?"

It was odd how everyone seemed to know that the firestorm story was a lie, though no one but our own people had been up to the mountains since Rushton had staked his claim to Obernewtyn. I decided to ask my own questions.

"How did you discover your powers?"

Gilaine smiled. "It happened the night Lidgebaby was born," she sent.

The baby coercer had woken the entire group to operancy. Gilaine sent a graphic impression of the night the baby was born. She had been in bed asleep when the sound of a baby screaming woke her. She was in the street in her nightgown before she realized the cry she was hearing was inside her mind. She had gone back inside and dressed quickly, her mind reeling at the effort of fighting the summons. Only when she reached the street outside the birthing house did she begin to understand what had happened, for she was not alone. They had all answered the call: Saul, acolyte apprentice; Jow, an animal handler; his younger brother, Daffyd; and the two musicians.

Daffyd had sobered first to the peril of such a gathering, and they had dispersed at his urging, planning to meet again in less dangerous circumstances. It would prove the first of many such meetings. They all understood two things at once, though. They would never again be alone in their own minds, for Lidgebaby was with them constantly, linking them irrevocably to one another. And they were in terrible danger.

In that dramatic birthbonding, Lidgebaby had forged an indelible emotional link between himself and the group. None could ever consciously harm the baby. All were coerced to love and protect.

Little monster, I thought, keeping my mind shielded. No wonder I could not hear their communication. They talked through the baby, using their own powers only to maintain contact with Lidge. It was the combined network of minds, and the child's mental overflow, that was blocking me.

This incredible situation gave me a clear idea of Lidgebaby's mental prowess. A baby, his coercive demands were selfish but basically innocent. But what would happen when he grew up and became conscious of the power he wielded? I shuddered, seeing them smile in the collective memory of that first enslavement/wakening of their Misfit minds.

Seeing my eyes on him, Saul frowned and turned away.

"Where will you go, if we help you?" Gilaine asked.

"We hadn't thought that far ahead. We meant to use an Olden pass we'd heard about to reach the lowlands without going along the main roads."

Saul snorted. "No one can get through that pass alive."

I stared. "You mean there *is* a pass?"

Gilaine nodded. "But Saul is right. No way to go there. Dangerous."

Jow shifted in his seat and the others fell silent. For the first time, I glimpsed a hint of Daffyd's features in his face. "Where are you headed?" he asked aloud.

I shrugged. "To the west coast. We thought of getting a boat. I've heard there are places . . ." I hesitated.

"Over the sea," said the boy musician wistfully.

"I have heard there are places over the edge of the world, where there is no Council or Herder Faction," Jow said pensively.

"Why do you stay here?" I asked. "It's terribly dangerous."

Jow shook his head. "Better to wait until winter is over. And we must wait until Lidgebaby is weaned."

"Couldn't you get the mother to go with you?"

"The mother is bonded to an acolyte and has already had one babe burned. She denounced it," Jow said.

I stared at him in horror. "Why are you offering to help us?" I finally asked.

Jow frowned. "You are a danger to us as long as you stay. You are a danger to Lidgebaby. We'll help you, but you must understand we can't let you talk if you are caught. The acolytes are very persuasive."

I nodded, understanding what he left unsaid. "How can you help?"

"There are two things," Jow said. "First, we can absorb Lidgebaby's emanations so that you can communicate with your friends in the compound. Second, we will organize a diversion to give you all time to get away. The timing is good because soldierguards from the training camps below Gelfort Range will leave in a few days to witness the ordination of new Herders in Sutrium. That will mean the main road will be safe for a week or so, and you can cut right through their camp and make for the coast between the lower mountains and Glenelg Mor."

I bit my lip. It would take several days to go that way, but it seemed there was no choice.

At a word from Jow, Saul seated himself at the table, and the group linked hands. "Be quick," Jow said. "I'm not sure how long we can hold it."

They closed their eyes. For a long moment, there was silence. A log cracked noisily in the fire, spitting out an orange flame. Beads of perspiration stood out on Jow's face.

Then the block was gone.

I gasped in delight, realizing how greatly the restriction had oppressed me. I sent a specific probe tuned to Matthew's mind. There was too little time to locate him physically. He was asleep when I found him, and I woke him with an ungentle mental jab.

"Wha?" his mind inquired stupidly. "Elspethelf?" he sent.

"I don't have much time, so listen carefully," I sent. "Some Misfits here are going to help us escape. They'll create a joint diversion to give us the chance to get away."

"We canna use th' Olden way," Matthew warned.

I told Matthew about Jow's alternate route. "They still believe us gypsies—I can't let them know the truth about Obernewtyn if they intend on staying here. So I told them nothing about Domick. I'm going to try to reach him now."

Matthew interrupted eagerly. "I was able to farseek with him." I was astonished. It was impossible to communicate over significant distance with anyone but another farseeker unless communicator and communicant each possessed some deep-probing ability. It seemed Ceirwan was right about Matthew's developing powers. But there was no time to think about that now.

"Are the horses with Domick?"

"An' Darga," Matthew sent. "Wait a minute! If ye haven't escaped, how can ye be contactin' me? We're in a compound, outside the settlement, but you—"

"The Misfits here helped me stop the block temporarily. It's not a machine. The static is caused by a baby with coercive powers."

"A baby!" Matthew echoed.

"Where is this compound? Show me," I demanded.

Matthew made his mind passive so that I could use his eyes. At once a ghostly vision unfolded in my mind. He was looking down a long, narrow rift between two mountains. There was a fence dividing a barren foreground from a heavily vegetated background. I thought I could see patches of glowing gas in the faint moonlight beyond the barrier. It took a moment for me to realize what I was seeing.

"The Olden pass . . ."

Matthew confirmed it. "It's there, but so is tainted ground, poisoned air, an' gigantic growling beasts."

"Why build a compound there?" I wondered.

In answer, Matthew turned again. Dirt, rocks, and dispossessed trees lay in mounds on either side of a broad hole in the ground. A row of rough huts sat amidst the debris. "Th' ground here is safe enough. We're here to pander to th' Druid's favorite obsession: Oldtime ruins. He thinks th' Great White was made by one of their machines and that th' machine is here somewhere. Mad as a snake is our Druid, to think it would still be workin' after all this time."

Not so mad, I thought with a feeling of cold dread.

"How is Pavo?" I asked.

"He says he refuses to die in a dirty, damp Druid hole," Matthew sent. "He's convinced you'll be along any minute to rescue us. 'Elspeth is a survivor,' he keeps sayin'."

"I wish I shared his faith. There's no hope now of getting to the lowlands and back before wintertime."

"If only we could farseek Ceirwan at Obernewtyn," Matthew sent.

I shrugged. He knew as well as I that it was impossible. But he was right—we needed to contact Obernewtyn. "I want you and Louis to take Mira and Lo and go back home as soon as you're free. Make sure you don't leave tracks or get caught. Someone has to warn Rushton about what the Druid is up to here." I made Matthew repeat the message back to me before bidding him goodbye.

Next I sought Domick. This was harder, and he instinctively responded by trying to repel me.

"You!" I saw him assimilate my ease in demolishing his defenses. "Have you escaped?"

I told him all I had told Matthew. "Then we are still going?" Domick asked when I had finished. "You know we can't make Maryon's deadline if we go that way. We are already cutting it too close because of the delay here."

"We dare not head back to Obernewtyn anyway, since the Druid would follow," I said flatly. "I'm sending Matthew and Louis to warn Rushton. The rest of us will continue, if only to draw the Druid's attention away from the high mountains. I'll contact you as soon as we get outside the baby's static. In the meantime, stay out of sight. A group of armsmen went out this morning to hunt. Where are you now?"

Domick was unable to let me use his eyes, but he projected a picture with painful force into my mind. Cross-guild farseeking had its drawbacks. The coercer was right at the foot of the mountains. "Tor," he sent in explanation. "I've been hiding in the cave where the Suggredoon goes into the mountain. There's a good wide ledge. Pity it doesn't go right through alongside the river, or we could simply walk to the other side."

Severing the contact, I found myself back inside the room. The group was still hand-linked. Gathering my exhausted senses, I reached out to Jik. He was overjoyed to hear Darga was safe. I was in the middle of explaining the escape plans when the contact was severed neatly, and Lidgebaby's static filled the air.

I opened my eyes in time to see Gilaine pitch forward. Jow picked her up gently and laid her on the floor, using his coat as a pillow. She moaned, and her eyes fluttered open. I went to her side, stricken with guilt.

"She was the focus. Lidge likes her best," Saul said petulantly.

"Did you get through?" Jow asked.

I nodded. Gilaine reached out for my arm and projected a message to us all. "It will be difficult. Perhaps they should stay through the winter and leave when we go."

"They can't stay!" Saul broke in angrily. "They endanger the baby. They endanger us all. It was bad enough to reveal ourselves. . . ."

The older musician shook his head reproachfully. "Saul, we have already gone over this. Once Gilaine was revealed, it was the same as if we were all exposed. If the Druid forced her name from Elspeth, she in turn would be forced to betray us. I'm sorry, Gilaine, but it would be better for them to go."

She hung her head.

A queer expression flitted across Saul's intense features, and I felt certain he was thinking Gilaine's death would solve everything.

"We won't be staying," I said firmly. I looked at Jow. "You'll never have cause to regret this," I promised. "And someday you might be glad."

I vowed to myself that I would return to bring Gilaine and her friends up to Obernewtyn as soon as I had completed my quest to the west coast. By then, Lidgebaby would be old enough to travel.

❖ ❖ ❖

I woke the next day to Rilla shaking me impatiently. "Elspeth. Ye sleep like th' dead," she scolded.

Outside, rain was falling steadily, and thunder rumbled in the distance. Hurrying across the gap that separated the washhouse from the kitchen, I glanced up at the drear gray sky with faint apprehension.

To my surprise, Emmon was sitting at the kitchen table with Kella. Seeing me, they both stood abruptly.

"What's the matter?" I asked.

"Gilaine sent me to tell ye," Emmon said. "Only ye mun nowt let on ye know, or she'll be in for it."

"I promise. Now what?"

"Yer to be bonded tomorrow," Emmon said, refusing to meet my eyes.

"To whom?" I asked in a strangely distant voice.

He made a warding-off gesture with his hand. "To . . . Relward. The gatewarden. This is Erin's doin'," he added in a rush.

"But why?" I asked faintly.

"She's jealous. She thinks Gilbert means to request ye in bonding. He's gone off to hunt, an' by th' time he gans back, it will be too late for him to protest," Emmon explained.

I blinked rapidly, fighting off an unexpected rush of tears. I had always used Rushton's stern, dark face as a talisman against despair, but this time the thought of him only evoked a fierce pain in my chest and a bittersweet longing to be home.

Then the irony of it struck me, helping me gain a measure of calmness. Here was Erin, violently jealous of the fleeting and surely lighthearted interest Gilbert had taken in me, willing to go to incredible lengths to stop something I had no more desire for than she.

"I can't let it happen," I said, and in that moment, a daring idea came to me. With Emmon's help, I managed to speak privately with Gilaine. She agreed the bonding must be avoided and said she would talk to the others about an immediate escape. I also told her I had heard Pavo was getting sicker and that I wanted to make sure he would be able to walk unaided. But that night, when Gilaine and her friends damped Lidgebaby's emanations, I contacted Domick instead.

"Has something gone wrong?" he asked, responding to the agitation in my thoughts.

I told him of the intended bonding and that Kella would likely be next. I was surprised at the vehemence with which he said it must not be allowed to happen. "If I can help it, it won't," I sent. "Our friends here have set their plans for tomorrow night. But after we get away from here, I have an alternative to going round the mountains. It's dangerous. Rushton would never approve. But if it succeeds, we will be on the other side of the mountains in less than two days."

"Impossible. Unless your undisclosed Talents include teaching giant birds to carry us across the sky."

I ignored his sarcasm. "I want you to build a raft. A strong raft."

"A raft. But . . . you can't mean . . . ?"

"We're going to raft through the mountains on the Suggredoon," I sent determinedly.

◆ 12 ◆

ERIN SMILED.

"Wait in here," she said. She opened a door off the hallway, and I entered a small, musty-smelling antechamber.

Inside the Druid's house, it was unexpectedly quiet. The room was dark, though it was not yet evening. The day had been dreary, overshadowed by banks of foreboding storm clouds. A single candle burned in a sconce on the wall, offering meager light.

As soon as Erin's footsteps faded, I crossed to the window facing the street and pulled aside a gauzy pleat of curtain. I peeped into the windswept street. A brilliant flash of lightning gave the fleeting impression of a blighted daytime. Then it was dark again.

I hoped nothing had happened to delay the others.

There was another flash of lightning, and I wondered uneasily at the building storm. I did not mind the rain but thought warily of firestorms and of a theory of Pavo's that they were increasing in frequency in the lowlands. He had explained that they were not real storms, despite the lightning and thunder, but were an electrical imbalance in the complex forces holding the earth together—another legacy of the cataclysmic disturbance of the Great White. He could not explain why firestorm rain burned the skin, nor why that rain alone could extinguish the destructive flames that always preceded it. He was certain, though, that there had been no firestorms in the Beforetime.

The Herders also believed firestorms followed the holocaust but claimed they were sent by Lud and would continue ravaging the earth until the world was again pure. Naturally, the only way to achieve such a state of grace was to adhere to Herder doctrine. If there *was* a firestorm brewing, we could not think of escape. Firestorm flames burned even stone, but there would be more protection in the Druid encampment than in the open, at the mercy of the lethal flames.

Outside, the wind muttered sullenly, echoing my inner disquiet. Erin and her traditional lecture about the duties of a bondmate were the least of my worries. Though not yet told I was to be bonded that very night, I did not doubt it.

Scanning the length of the street visible from the window, I wondered anxiously if Kella had managed to get a message to Gilaine. She should have contacted her as soon as I was sent to the Druid's house. Jow had decided that was the best time to make our move. But if they did not come . . .

More lightning flashed, followed by a sharp crack of thunder. The time lapse between the flashes and the thunder was growing shorter. Rain fell in light flurries, but the heaviness of the clouds illuminated in the intermittent light indicated a deluge was coming.

Hearing a movement at the door, I dropped the curtain and moved quickly away from the window. Erin came in cautiously, as if she had thought I would be waiting to attack her. Her hand rested lightly on the hilt of a short knife she wore in a jeweled waist scabbard.

"You have been sent here so that I can tell you some wonderful news," Erin said, her eyes glittering vindictively. I was taken aback at the force of her dislike.

"Yes?" I asked calmly.

Her lips stretched across her teeth in a smile that looked more like a snarl. "You are to be bonded—to Relward."

Knowing took the force out of my reaction, and I was glad to see her look disappointed. "This is your news?" I asked sourly.

For a moment, Erin looked nonplussed; then her cheeks mottled with anger. "You are to be bonded tonight," she added viciously.

I shrugged. "I don't bother with such things," I said lethargically.

"You . . . w-what?" she stammered.

"What does it matter to be bonded or not? It is all the same in the dark," I added crudely.

Her face reddened, and she stepped away from me as if she thought I would contaminate her. "You dare speak of such things to me?"

I shrugged. "If you don't like such talk, why are you the one to tell me of this bonding?" Taking advantage of her loss of balance, I stepped toward her.

Her hand groped for the knife in her belt, and she held it up between us. "Stay back." There was a loud noise in the street, and we both jumped. "What was that?"

"The wind?" I said quickly, stepping forward again in my haste to distract her.

She lifted the knife. "What's going on?" she asked, suspicion flaring in her eyes. She backed to the door, holding the knife out menacingly.

Unable to think of a way to stop her, I stood still, heart banging against my ribs. If she caught the others and gave the alarm, we would all be lost. Erin groped behind her back, opening the door without taking her eyes off me.

My knees felt weak with relief. Blocking the hall behind her were Kella and Jik. I smiled at them in greeting.

"That is an old trick," Erin sneered. "Trying to make me think there's someone . . ." She stopped abruptly as Kella's knife pressed into her neck.

Jik reached round and took the knife carefully out of her fingers.

"Get inside the room," Kella ordered, her face pale but determined. I was momentarily astonished to see a healer waving a knife in such a businesslike way. Erin obeyed, shock turned to fury.

"You will all die for this. My father will burn you," she snarled.

"Did you bring the rope?" I asked Jik, ignoring her. He nodded. "Tie her up."

Erin stood rigidly erect as Jik bound her hands and feet. "What do you think this will get you?" she grated. "There are men in all the watchtowers and guards at the gate. And even if you *did* get out, my father will come after you. You will be caught, and then you will wish bonding was the only fate awaiting you."

I touched Jik's arm, sending a swift thought. The next time she opened her mouth to speak, he thrust a ball of cloth into it, then tied another round her head to stop her spitting it out. It was a relief to have her quiet. I checked the ropes. They were tight, and I guessed Erin's hissing threats had made Jik more efficient than he might otherwise have been.

I forced myself to face her. "Daughter of Henry Druid, we are gypsy folk and not meant for staying in one place. My father waits for me in Arandelft, and I mean to meet him. I bear no ill will to the Druid, but I cannot stay. That is why you have to be tied up. To stop you raising the alarm too soon."

"Perhaps we should kill her," Jik said, obeying my covert prompting.

I pretended to consider it, gratified to see the first sign of real fear in Erin's eyes. Slowly, as if reluctant, I shook my head. "I would be just as happy to kill her, but that might make her father annoyed. Besides, we will be long gone down the main road before they find her." I had no doubt Erin would faithfully relay all I had said, sending her father off in the wrong direction.

I nodded to Jik, and he opened a large chest under the window.

Erin's eyes widened with real horror. I did not like the idea of locking anyone in a trunk, even someone so detestable, but we had to make sure she was not found too quickly. If the Druid came home early, he was un- likely to think to look for his daughter inside a box in a spare room. With Kella's help, we lifted her into the trunk, leaving the lid slightly askew so she wouldn't suffocate. Then we went into the kitchen, where she would not be able to hear us.

"Phew," Jik said. "If eyes were knives, we'd all be dead."

Jik went to fetch Jow from outside. We gave the all-clear signal, and Jow came in the back door. "Where is she?" he asked in a low voice. I told him and, unexpectedly, he grinned.

"Do her good," he murmured. Then his face became serious. "Now, you know what you have to do?"

I recited the route he expected us to take, and he nodded.

"You'll be a bit ahead of schedule now. You might have to wait in the wilds until the soldierguards leave their camps. I wish we could give you more help."

"We'll be all right. Gypsies know a few things about hiding," I said, sorry to be deceiving him.

He opened a bundle and handed me boots, stout trousers, and a jumper and coat. I threw aside the silky red dress Rilla had made me wear, without regret. Fine clothes were no substitute for freedom.

Outside, thunder cracked loudly.

"This is an ordinary storm?" I asked Jow.

He nodded. "An ordinary storm, but bad all the same. Worse for the armsmen who will have to track you."

I pointed to the dress. "You could use that to lead them astray."

Jow shook his head. "You can't go in two directions at once. If he eventually found your tracks, the Druid would know for certain you had help."

"What are we waiting for?" Kella asked, looking round uneasily.

"A signal from Peter," Jow said. "He should have been here by now; I'll go and look."

A cold blast of wind swept through the back door as he left. I shivered, less from the cold than at what lay ahead. I prayed Domick could do his part in freeing Matthew and the others.

When the door swung open again, Jow had brought the older musician, Peter. With them, to my surprise, was Gilaine.

She took my hands in hers. "The others did not want me to come, because I am known to have associated with you. But I wanted to say goodbye. I wish you did not have to go," she sent wistfully.

I squeezed her fingers. "We'll meet again someday. I'm sure of it." I leaned forward and kissed a cheek that smelled faintly of honey.

"Come," Jow said impatiently. "There's no time to waste."

Gilaine gave me a gentle push and waved as we followed Jow and Peter into the stormy night. Looking over my shoulder, I saw her disappear round the corner of the house.

It began to rain in earnest then, as if it had been waiting for us. To my consternation, the flashes of lightning lit up the streets. Anyone glancing through a window might see us.

I trotted to keep up, trying to ignore the pain in my feet. We stopped to rest in one of the alleys running between the dark storehouses alongside the gate. Peter left at once with a terse farewell.

"I live near, so it's safest for me to be seen here," Jow explained. "I've left two horses in the front yard nearest the gate. They've agreed to run the minute they're let out." Jow was a beastspeaker.

"Your job is to break the latch on the yard gate," he told Jik. "Wait until a crack of thunder and smash it with a rock. Then get out of sight. I'll come out and call the gatewarden to help me catch the horses. They're to run down to the other end of the camp. There'll be enough noise to attract the attention of the posted guards in the corner lookouts. Even so, you'll have to be quick. And don't leave any tracks showing which way you've gone. There must be no doubt you're making for the main road around the head of the river. Elspeth, you're sure you'll be able to relock the gate from the outside?"

I nodded. "My powers aren't blocked when there's physical contact. If I'm touching the door, I'll be able to lock it mentally."

Jow looked up as a flash of lightning lit the alley. "Count five and thirty once you're in position, to give me time to get back to my hut. Then bash away," he told Jik. Then he was gone.

We stared at one another, frightened and excited. "Go on," I prompted Jik after the time had passed. He darted off into the shadows, and Kella and I edged closer to the main gate. The whole aim of Jow's plan was to give us a head start. Jow hoped no one would even realize we had gone until we were discovered missing at nightmeal. And even then, the locked gates would make them think we were hiding somewhere inside the camp.

But everything depended on our getting away unnoticed.

I jumped as a loud crash of thunder mingled faintly with the sound of splintering wood. Two horses thundered past us into the street, their hooves making a great clattering noise on the stones. We watched as Jow burst out of a door, shouting for help. Two other doors were flung open and men came out, wondering what was happening. A man poked his head out of the gate-warden's hut, and Jow called him to help catch the horses before someone was killed. He pulled on a coat and ran after the shouting group without looking back.

As soon as they were all out of sight, we hurried across to the gate, Jik running up behind us. My heart beat loud enough to drown the thunder. We were completely exposed, and my hand trembled as I reached for the lock.

But even as my fingers closed around the bolt, a hand shot out of the gatewarden's hut and fastened on my arm. Kella screamed and jumped back, knocking Jik to the ground.

Still holding my arm, the black-bearded man who had caught us in the first place came out into the rain, an unpleasant smile on his mouth. "What have we here?" His eyes ran over our bundles and dress. "Not running away, are we? And Relward so eager to have a maid in his bed." He laughed, and rain shook from the wiry beard hairs under his chin. "What a pity, since runaways here end up as bonfire fodder."

Kella moaned in terror, snapping me out of my own trance. Anger flowed through me in a molten tide. If I did nothing, we would all burn. I gritted my teeth.

There was nothing subtle in what I did next. The armsman's bruising grip on me made him vulnerable, since the contact negated Lidgebaby's static net. I simply lashed out with all the frustrated power in my mind. Even so, it was less effective than it should have been. He recoiled in shock and, instinctively, tried to let go of my arm. My other hand snaked out and caught his wrist, keeping the connection. He fought me in earnest then, and when I clung like a limpet, he struck me across the face. It was too awkward a blow to have full force, but my ears rang and I suddenly felt a long way from my hands. I could feel my grip weaken.

Terrified of what would happen to us if I failed to get us away, I reached inside my darkest mind for the power I had once used to kill Madam Vega. I had not accessed it since the night we had taken Obernewtyn. I had tried to pretend to myself that it was gone. But it rose at my call like a great black snake, and only fear of that dreadful secret power gave me the strength to temper it. Even muted, the power of my attack on the armsman's mind was terrible. His mouth gaped wide in a soundless shriek, and he slumped half-dead at my feet. I slid to my knees behind him, retching and coughing.

Kella looked down at me, stunned. "What did you do to him?" Then her face changed. "Elspeth, you're bleeding."

I shook my head and climbed to my feet. "No . . . time. We have to get . . . away before they find him." I could taste blood and spat, but the taste persisted. Dazed, I wondered if it was my imagination that it was raining more heavily.

Kella visibly gathered herself, unlocking the gate and pulling us through after her. I put my hands on the door and relocked it. With luck, the locked gate would still throw off the search, and the Druids would assume the unconscious armsman had been struck by lightning.

We picked our way with careful haste across the spine of rocks Jow had said would hide our tracks. When we had gone some distance, I decided speed was more important. "Run!" I yelled over the noise of the rain. All around us, trees creaked under the weight of the downpour. It was like standing under a waterfall. I staggered after them, my head spinning and my feet hurting badly. I was too disoriented to know which way we should go and plodded after Kella, hoping she knew.

Then, abruptly, we were outside Lidgebaby's range. I sent a probe to Domick. Fortunately, he was waiting for me, because I had no strength left to fight his defenses or the interference of the rain. To my relief, Pavo was there already.

I stumbled over an exposed tree root and fell to my knees hard. Kella and Jik helped me up. The healer's hair was plastered to her head, and her face dripped with water. I struggled to stay conscious as they half dragged, half carried me between them. Crashing through the trees moments later, Domick ordered the other two to run and hefted me effortlessly over one shoulder. My teeth felt as if they were rattling round behind my eyes.

We reached the clearing where Pavo waited with Gahltha and Avra. Like Domick, Pavo was still clad in the ragged remnants of the clothes we had worn from Obernewtyn that first day.

"What's happened?" the teknoguilder asked. "Kella says you killed a man with your mind."

Domick gave me a startled look.

"Not killed . . . stunned," I said groggily.

"He hit her in the face. There was blood all over, but the rain's washed it off. Wait . . ." Before I could stop her, Kella reached out and touched me, drawing my pain off into herself. At once the dizziness faded.

"Hurts . . . ," moaned Kella, white-faced.

I took her hands away. "That's enough. I can think now. You've stopped the faintness."

Kella smiled wanly.

We were all huddled under an eben tree, the only real shelter. Rain drummed down heavily on all sides.

"Matthew and Louis are on their way back to Obernewtyn, and no one at the compound pursued them. Did anyone follow you?" Domick shouted over the noise.

I shook my head. "No one will come after us until this storm is over. And even if they do, we'll be long gone on the raft."

Something in Domick's expression struck me.

"You *did* make the raft?"

Wordlessly, he pulled me to my feet and pointed through the trees to the water.

My heart sank.

Swollen by the phenomenal rains, the Suggredoon was a roaring torrent overflowing its banks, carrying whole trees and chunks of rock. Domick's raft was fastened to the bank by a thick, twisted rope and bobbed like a creature mad to be set free. Only a lunatic would set off on such a river.

Domick hauled the raft in and looked at me, panting. "What do we do?"

I took a deep breath. "We'll wait until daylight. Maybe the river will have calmed down by then?"

Before he could respond, I heard a bark and turned to see Darga pelting into the clearing. "Many funaga coming," he sent.

I translated. Domick's face hardened. "Then we've no choice. We'll have to go now." He pointed to the raft. "There are ropes. Tie yourselves down."

"Quickly," I shouted when no one moved.

I helped Kella tie herself, and Jik tied Darga and

127

himself down. Avra stepped into the large space in the middle obviously reserved for the two horses, and Domick bound her gently. I sat next to Pavo, trying not to look frightened.

My mind was reeling. How could anyone have followed so quickly?

Domick's cry broke into my thoughts. He was standing on the bank with Gahltha.

"What is it?" I shouted.

Domick waved his hand helplessly at the black horse. "He won't move."

I tried to reach Gahltha's mind, but it was as smooth and unassailable as a mountain of glass. I looked at Avra and sent an urgent query. Through the noise of the rain, I could hear men's voices and shouts.

"They come," Darga sent.

Domick threw his hands up and began to push the raft off the bank.

"Gahltha," I sent, forcing through his shield. He whinnied, a high quavering note, the whites of his eyes showing. But he made no move toward the raft.

"He's afraid!" Jik cried.

Domick jumped into the raft just as the water dragged it from the bank. There was a hard jerk as it reached the end of the tether rope. Still Gahltha stood on the bank unmoving, staring out at us.

"Gahltha!" I sent. "Go back to Obernewtyn."

He made no response. I saw figures running. "They're coming. Cut the rope!" I cried.

Domick lifted his small ax.

"Gahltha. Go now, or the funaga will trap you!" I sent forcefully.

He reared violently and plunged into the night. At

the same time, Domick let the ax fall. It landed badly, and the rope was not severed. Several armsmen had reached the bank and were attempting to reel the raft in. Domick raised the ax again, and this time it fell true.

At once, the roaring water carried us swiftly away from the bank. Lightning flashed, and in that moment, I saw Gilbert among those who stood watching us. I knew he had been out hunting and realized our poor luck—we had not been followed from the encampment but had been found out all the same.

His eyes falling on me, Gilbert cried out something in evident dismay, but the sound of rain and rushing water made his words impossible to hear.

Then the raft carried us from his sight, and within seconds, we were speeding toward the dark bulk of the mountains. For a moment, it seemed we would be smashed to pieces against the side of the mountain. Then the black gape of a cave opened up before us.

I looked back and caught sight of Gahltha pawing at the raging water as if it were tongues of fire.

"Here we go," Domick said grimly, and we plunged into the heart of the mountain.

· 13 ·

THE SUGGREDOON BORE us along its ancient course at the speed of a bolting horse.

Domick stood up on the raft, slipping his feet into rope loops, and took hold of the paddle, which gave him rudimentary steering. I was surprised to find a dim light in the cavern instead of dense blackness. The walls glowed gently and eerily, and only when a cloud of insects stirred and rose did I see that the light came from their tiny bodies. A stiff, cold draft blew in my face from somewhere ahead, but I knew we had far to go before we would see the sky again.

It was not long before the way narrowed and twisted, creating the first turbulent stretch of rapids. The water boiled savagely, sending the raft shuddering and careening through foaming torrents, barely missing jagged rocks. Luck as much as steering kept us from being overturned or having a rock smash the raft to splinters.

And there were many such stretches. Each time we began to breathe easy, thinking ourselves lucky to have reached calmer waters, we would hear the familiar hollow roar ahead and would tighten our grips on the raft.

At one point, the entire surface of the river seemed to tilt, and we were as much sliding as being swept by the current. The wind whistled past me, whipping strands of hair wildly in my face.

We knew the Suggredoon flowed down to the lowlands, but I had been secretly afraid that the tunnel it had carved through the stone roots of the mountain might become too narrow for the raft to pass. My heart sank when the walls began to close in around us, and for a moment, the mountain seemed to throb with brooding malevolence.

I tried to ignore the roof drawing steadily nearer and more dim, as if the glowing insects disliked the closeness as much as we did. Gradually, it became so low that Domick could not stand. I needed no empathy to sense Avra's fear. If the cavern became much more cramped, she would not fit. And we all knew there was no turning back.

But the way began to widen again, and I shivered with reaction. In my wildest fancies, I had never imagined the trip to the coast would be such a road of trials. I had worried only about soldierguards, yet in all that had befallen us, we had not even laid eyes on one.

Hearing a roar ahead, I prepared myself for another battering, but instead the raft flowed round a bend and through a natural stone arch into a vast, dark cavern. If not for the stalactites and stalagmites and the rock columns rising from the water to the roof where some had met and fused, I would have thought we had somehow got out onto the sea at night. The cave was lit by millions of the tiny insects.

The raft slowed but was still drawn along by a deeper current.

Our wonder at this great lake under the mountain dissolved into greater amazement as we drew near to what at first appeared to be strangely symmetrical rows of rocky mounds rising from the water.

Pavo realized first what we were seeing and gasped. I was struck by the wonder in his gaunt face. "This is a Beforetime city," he whispered reverently.

Squinting, I saw that he was right. The shapes were too square to be natural, but the height of them astounded me. These, then, were the skyscrapers of the legends.

I stared about me as the current carried us between two of the monstrous constructions, along what must once have been a street. There was no way of telling how far below the surface of the water lay the floor of the dead city. Out of the distant past, I seemed to hear Louis Larkin telling me there were certain to be rare niches in the world where bits of the Beforetime were preserved.

And what wonders lay inside these buildings with their thousands of dark windows?

Up close, the surfaces were badly eroded, especially at the water line. One day the currents' ebb and flow would eat the foundations, and the remnants of the ancient city would topple. Gaps in the rows of buildings suggested this had happened already in some cases.

Many of the smooth façades were crumbled, revealing the great black steel frames inside them, like the bones of some moldering animal. Much of the remaining walls were covered in a livid yellow fungus. The glowing insects either lived or fed on it, for wherever the fungus grew, they were clustered thickly, and their collective light was brighter.

I wondered if the city had somehow sunk into the mountain during the Great White or if the earth had spat the mountains on top of it like a gravestone.

I found myself wishing Matthew could see it. He had long worshipped the Oldtimers with a glib surety that had always troubled me, but the city told a story of people who were certainly great—but people just the same, with flaws that all their brilliance had not helped.

It was a somber and sobering experience. It was not hard to think of the people who had built such cities as capable of any wonder—or terror. Looking around me, I had no doubt that such a people could create a weapon that would live far beyond their span. The stark reality of the brilliance and insanity of the Oldtimers struck me then as never before.

"This is a bad place," Avra sent uneasily.

As much to distract myself as the mare, I asked her about Gahltha's strange behavior.

She whinnied forlornly. "The funaga who owned him almost drowned him when he was first brought to them. It is a funaga way of breaking the spirit of an equine, to use water and fear. They did not break him, for he took refuge in a savage hidden hatred, but since that time he has a dread of water that goes beyond reason."

"I'm sure he's safely on his way back to Obernewtyn," I sent reassuringly.

"He is proud," she sent. "Too proud to bear such shame easily."

I stared at her, puzzled. "There is no shame in what happened. No one will blame him."

Avra sighed in a very human way. "He will blame himself. I do not think he will return to Obernewtyn."

Hours later, we were still gliding through the ancient city. The immediate wonder having worn off, we lapsed into silence for a time. I watched from the corner of my eye as Kella helped Domick to steer, thinking that the stresses and perils that had beset us since leaving Obernewtyn had eroded the old enmity between co-ercer and healer. I was imagining what effect their un-expected friendship would have on their guilds, when we suddenly passed out of the big cavern into a tunnel. Immediately, the raft picked up speed, and in seconds we were in rapids again.

Another hour passed with little respite from the fe-rocious white water, which seemed more frequent on this side of the underground sea. Domick was swaying on his feet with exhaustion.

Then we heard a noise. At first we checked our binding ropes, thinking there was another bout of rapids ahead, but as we came nearer to the source, the roaring became louder, taking on a curious vibrating quality.

I noticed that Pavo was listening intently. There was no fear on his face, only fierce concentration.

"What is it?" I shouted. "More rapids?"

"Let's hope that is all it is," Pavo answered.

I opened my mouth to ask what he meant when the raft tilted abruptly sideways. Being tied on was all that kept us together. I heard Kella scream, and then we were falling as the Suggredoon became a giant water-fall, plummeting us into a black void.

My face felt hot and damp at the memory of that fall.

I tried to open my eyes but saw nothing. I lifted my hand to feel if my eyes were open, wondering if I had gone blind.

"Shh, lie still," Kella said softly.

"My eyes," I croaked. My throat felt as dry as old paper.

"Your eyes are fine. They're stuck shut by blood from a cut on your forehead. Wait . . ."

I heard footsteps on a stone floor and the murmur of voices. It was strange to hear and not see; that was how it was for Dameon. Two sets of footsteps approached, and there was the sound of curtains being drawn. I felt a warm cloth on my face and gasped at the unexpected sting.

"There are lots of small cuts from the rocks," Kella explained gently. "Some of them reopened in the night. There now."

I opened my eyes. I was in bed in a small white-washed bedroom with sun streaming through a window and birds chirping outside. Kella was sitting beside me on a stool, a bowl of bloodied water on her knees. Her cheek was badly bruised and her arm was bandaged. Behind her was a plump matronly woman I had never seen before.

"I am Katlyn," she said with a warm smile.

I did not know what to say and looked helplessly at Kella. "Katlyn and her bondmate, Grufyyd, found us washed up on the banks of the Suggredoon. They know we escaped from a Councilfarm," she said pointedly.

"Dinna worry about that now. Ye need to rest," Katlyn said, her highland accent strong. "That is the best healer of all, but first I will bring ye some food."

She went out, taking the stained water with her, and returned in a moment with a bowl of soup.

"That smells wonderful," I rasped.

She smiled. "It is an old recipe, a special healing mixture. Eat an' then sleep. Ye can talk later."

"Where are the others?" I asked Kella as soon as the woman had gone.

"Everyone is fine," Kella said, and pointed firmly to the soup. "Now eat. If Katlyn says it will heal, it will. She knows so much about healing and medicines. I've never seen such an herb garden."

"Herb?" I asked sharply.

"Katlyn is an herb lorist. She learned it from her grandmother. Apparently people came to the woman's village from all over the Land, and they used to come see Katlyn before herb lore was banned. Many still come. I wish Roland could meet her."

"Does she not fear the Herders?"

Kella smiled. "She talks about the Council and the Herders as if they were a collection of naughty boys. She knows what she does is dangerous, but she says it's her job."

"How long have we been here?" I asked, anxious that we had stayed too long in the house of a woman who cared so little for her safety.

"Only a day, but without her help, we would have taken much longer to heal," Kella said sternly, seeing my disapproval.

"I'm grateful for her help," I said. "But it's my job to keep us safe and finish this expedition without getting caught by the Council or the Faction—who are a lot more dangerous than bad boys. Now, tell me, where are we?"

Kella shrugged. "We're not far from Rangorn and the Ford. It's only the two of them here. There's a son, but he's a seaman. They seemed to think we might have heard of him when I'd told them we were runaways. I thought it best not to pry."

"Good. How did you come to tell them we had escaped from a Councilfarm?"

"We had to tell them something. There was no way of hiding that we had been in a boating accident, but no one would have crossed the Suggredoon this far north unless they were trying to avoid being seen. Gypsies would hardly travel by water, and besides, our coloring has all but faded now. The Councilfarm runaway story seemed most plausible."

"It's risky," I said. "You are certain they didn't send word to the Council? There is a reward for information leading to the capture of runaways."

Kella shook her head emphatically. "I don't think it occurred to them."

I frowned. "I suppose if Katlyn is an herb lorist, she wouldn't want soldierguards here. So we're probably safe enough for now."

A flicker of anger crossed Kella's face. "You're too cynical, Elspeth. It makes you blind to things right under your nose," she added obliquely.

"What about the others?"

"Everyone's fine except for a few bruises and bumps. Pavo is not too good, but that has nothing to do with the accident."

"Jik?" I asked.

She smiled. "A cracked rib. He's milking the goats with Grufyyd. Domick has gone off to scout the area. Once a coercer . . ." I was astounded to see her eyes soften and wondered if friendship was all that had developed between them.

Kella stood, taking the empty bowl from my fingers. I could not even remember drinking the soup.

"Sleep and get better. The world will wait," the healer said.

Weary as I was, I could not rest easy. The expedition

seemed to be in tatters, without disguise or papers, two all but unfit to travel. I wondered if we would ever get home again.

Domick returned late that night.

"Elspeth?" he whispered outside the window.

"I'm awake," I answered softly, sitting up. "Come in."

He climbed through the window. "I am sleeping in the stables with Jik and Darga, but I wanted to talk to you while it was quiet. Katlyn and Grufyyd are good people," Domick said. "Kella believes it, and so do I. I don't like lying to them."

I hid my amazement at these uncoercer-like sentiments. Domick went on. "They seem . . . accustomed to people like us—people on the run, scared, and without anything but a flimsy cover story. The medicines, the food, the lack of questions . . . it makes me think they have done this before—sheltered runaways."

"Are you sure? How do you know?"

He shrugged. "Instinct as much as anything. But Jik can sense their sincerity. If we were forced to leave him or Pavo behind, I think it would be safe for them here."

I did not respond to the question in his voice, knowing that Jik must accompany us however dangerous the expedition had become. "You're right to think of leaving soon, or we'll waste the time we gained coming through the mountain. You scouted ahead?"

Domick's face was impassive. "Yes. We're above Rangorn, but we can easily get to the ford without passing through the town. The ford is unguarded, though Grufyyd says there are guards at the ferry terminal. You will need papers to cross."

"We'll have to manage without them until we reach Sutrium. We need to try to get hold of another cart.

That way we should be able to leave together—all of us." I touched his hand. "Go to bed now."

He slipped out as soundlessly as he had entered.

The next morning, Katlyn came in to change the bandages on my feet. "Poor ill-treated feet," she said gently, unwrapping them. "I put on a salve to numb them so you could sleep. The scars are deep and have not healed well, though they are old."

"I have to be able to walk," I said.

Katlyn nodded. "If you must, these will carry you. But walking will increase the hurt. If they are ever to heal properly, you must rest them completely for many months, perhaps even longer."

Katlyn looked up at me, her expression serious. "Child, there is something I want to say to you. Kella told me you are making for the west coast, in search of sanctuary. But I dinna think you will find any safe place on the coast. I want ye to think of staying here with us."

"Here?" I echoed, astounded by the offer.

Katlyn reached out and touched my hand. "This is a safe house, a refuge for runaways . . . and for others. You could help us in our work. Help others like yourself . . ."

I stared at Katlyn, my heart beating fast, for her eyes told me clearly that she knew we had not told her the truth about ourselves.

"Think on it," she said softly. "Talk with the others. Let us know tonight what you decide."

✦ 14 ✦

"WHAT WILL YOU tell her? Won't she find it odd that runaways refuse refuge?" Pavo asked when I told the others of Katlyn's offer.

"I will tell them the truth," I said. "As much of it as we can. I think we owe them that."

Grufyyd turned out to be a big, silent man with a brown beard and somber, smoke-gray eyes. After we had eaten nightmeal, my first out of bed, I asked the couple if I could retell our story.

"We have so often had to lie that it's hard to see where the truth can be told," I began. "It is true we are escapees, in one sense, but that was a long time ago. Now we, and others, have a secret . . . place in the highlands. There are a lot of us there now, mostly no more than children and many runaways. Some came to us, more we helped get away.

"Until recently, we thought our existence a secret. Then we started to hear rumors that the Council meant to investigate the highlands, so our leader decided to send down a delegation to see what we could find out. And at the same time, we came to find a . . . a friend who is hiding somewhere near Murmroth and Aborium."

Katlyn and Grufyyd exchanged an odd, tense look.

"How did you come to be half-drowned on the banks of the Suggredoon?" Grufyyd asked in his rumbling voice.

"We were in the White Valley looking for an Oldtime pass through the mountains. We didn't want to use the main roads. But we stumbled on a secret camp run by Henry Druid. He takes prisoner anyone who gets too near. He uses the men for labor or else makes them join his armsmen."

Katlyn cast an appalled glance at Grufyyd. "Armsmen. Then he still means to get revenge?"

Grufyyd shook his head sorrowfully.

"We managed to escape, but the Olden way proved impassable. We were desperate with the Druid's armsmen close behind us, so we rafted the Suggredoon through the mountain."

Katlyn gasped. "But is it possible?" No one answered, since we were the living proof of our story.

"Looked overmuch damage for an overturned boat," Grufyyd observed dispassionately.

I continued. "Now . . . all I have told you is true, but I have not told everything, mostly to protect the ones we left behind. But I would not have said this much unless I trusted you and because we want you to understand why we can't stay here."

"We are no strangers to necessary secrets," Katlyn said gently. "But since you will not stay, then we would like to offer you further help, in return for a favor."

"What favor?" Domick asked.

Grufyyd rose suddenly and decisively. "Our son, Brydda, does not live strictly according to Council lore. In short, he is a seditioner. He helps people who are to be burned—helps them to get away an' start afresh.

141

Our problem is that we have lost contact with him. Brydda has neither visited us nor sent people to be hidden for two moons. We are afraid something has happened to him. We are too old for intrigue, and we ask that you will go into Aborium to give Brydda a message from us."

"Aborium," Jik said and paled.

Domick looked at me. "No," he said decisively. I was startled at his brusqueness after his words the previous night. "If I was coming with you, it might be different, but . . ."

"We mean to part before Morganna, you see," I explained. "Domick will remain in Sutrium. The rest of us will cross the Suggredoon, and on the other side we meant to stay away from the towns. Especially Aborium, for it does not have a good reputation, even in the highlands."

Grufyyd nodded. "It is a bad place. Yet all west coast cities are the same. Ye will have to enter one for food and fodder. And it may be that we can help."

"I do not see how asking us to deliver a message to your son can help us," Domick said belligerently. He stole a glance at Kella, and suddenly I understood his agitation.

Grufyyd nodded with a grave courtesy that made Domick seem rude and brash. "I meant to offer you the use of a cart. Ye will travel more swiftly and safely that way. And I can provide you with some false Normalcy Certificates."

"We will be happy to deliver a message to your son," I said. "It is the least we can do."

Grufyyd's face broke into a beguiling smile. He

crossed abruptly to the door, gathering up his coat. On the threshold, he turned. "It will be best for you to go soon. I will ready the cart for tomorrow morning." Without waiting for a response, he went out, leaving a startled silence behind him.

I looked around to see Katlyn giving Domick an apologetic look. "He has been frightened for Brydda; we both have. But dinna fear for your friends, Domick. No one checks papers, save at the main entrance to Aborium. And it is even possible Brydda can help you find th' refuge ye seek."

Katlyn looked at me and smiled. "Now . . . food and drink to travel." She turned to her store cupboards.

"How are we to find your son?" Jik asked timidly.

Katlyn smiled over her shoulder at him. "Ye mun go to the Inn of the Cuttlefish and ask for Brydda Llewellyn—that is the name he calls himself. Wait then, and he will come to you."

"And if he doesn't?" Domick asked.

Katlyn's back faced us, but it seemed to shrink. "Then that will mean he cannot come. The journey takes two days. If you leave very early tomorrow morning and travel steadily, you will arrive at Aborium at daybreak. That is the best and safest time to enter the city. Tradesmen from outlying regions come then, when the gates are opened."

"It is a walled city?" Domick asked sharply.

"The gates are open freely and unguarded in the daylight hours," Katlyn assured him.

She turned to us suddenly, her face serious. "I dinna think ye will come to harm seekin' Brydda out, but take care just th' same, for there are other dangers on the west coast besides the Herders and the Council soldier-guards. Those Brydda helps to run away do not account for all the disappearances from the city."

"Slavers . . . ," I murmured.

Katlyn's expression altered subtly. "You have heard of such things?"

"I heard a story while we were in the Druid camp. A man whose father had been to sea. I didn't know if it was the truth or not."

"Many things that seem impossible are true of Aborium. In its own way, it is worse than Sutrium. There the Council rules, but Aborium belongs to the Herder Faction, for that is where ships from Herder Isle and Norseland dock." Katlyn was silent for a time, her eyes anxious. She shook her head and said, "Dinna linger there, is all I'm saying."

✦ 15 ✦

We arrived at Aborium two days later.

Bypassing Morganna on Grufyyd's advice, we traveled on a lesser road. Only when we were near Aborium did we venture near to the coast.

From a distance, the city was curiously ugly. Sprawled along the shore, it seemed to be made up of smaller versions of the square skyscrapers we had seen under Tor. Above the rooftops hung a dense, bleary mire of smoke.

"I don't like the look of this place," Kella murmured.

"All such places where the funaga live like rats in a nest stink," Avra observed with a disparagement that would have pleased Gahltha.

The mare was more interested in the sea, which truly provided a dazzling setting for such a grimy jewel. Being mountain bred, she had never seen so much water and was fascinated by it.

We had meant to arrive outside Aborium at dawn, but the loss and slow repair of a wheel delayed us. By the time Kella, Jik, and I had repaired it, the day was drawing to an end. I did not want to enter the city by night, so we made camp on the shore. We would enter

Aborium as Katlyn had suggested—at dawn with the tradefolk.

We used the last of the wood Grufyyd had provided to build a small fire in the dunes above the high-water line in the sand so it would not be seen by soldier-guards in watch-huts along the top of the city walls. Kella began cooking pancakes from the coarse flour Katlyn had given us while Pavo reorganized the cart, concealing the all-important maps that were to lead us to the Beforetime library in a concealed pocket in Avra's halter. I had brushed down the mare and was putting out grain and a bowl of water for her when the sun fell into the sea in a blaze of colored glory.

Avra went down to the water's edge, and on impulse I followed her and took off my boots. Stepping into the water, I sighed with relief as the cold soothed my scarred feet.

"There is a story among the equines that there is a land beyond the sea where there are no funaga, and beasts rule themselves," Avra sent. We stood for a time in silence, half-mesmerized by the murmurous sighing of the waves on the shore.

Returning to the fire, I found the others seated, staring into the flames with the dreamy expressions a fire always seems to evoke.

We ate the pancakes slowly and fell to talking of Katlyn and Grufyyd.

"I wonder what their son will be like," Kella said.

"Like Grufyyd. Big and soft-spoken. A man of few words," I guessed.

"Perhaps he will be like Katlyn, short and plumpish and always smiling and singing," she suggested.

Pavo smiled. "More like a bit of both. And what will

he make of us? I doubt he'll be as free and easy as his parents. He can't afford to be." We all looked at the city behind its wall.

I felt my own smile fade. "I trust them, but we know nothing of this son. I'll keep my judgment until we meet."

Kella bridled angrily. "If he is Katlyn's son, how can he be other than honest?"

Pavo gave her a reproving look. "The guildmistress is wise to be cautious," he said with a faint emphasis on my title. I caught his behindthought that the trip had made Kella too outspoken.

Jik shifted uncomfortably beside me, disturbing Darga, whose head rested on his knee.

"I wonder if Domick has found lodgings yet?" Kella asked.

I was tempted to tell her what I had seen in Domick's mind when he had bid us farewell, despite his coolness with her. Then I realized the knowledge would only intensify her regret at his loss. Better not to meddle.

"Much better," Darga sent laconically.

I stared at the dog in amazement. He had passed through my shield with an ease that astounded me.

"My mind grows stronger," Darga sent.

I was about to answer this when a blinding realization struck me. In my excitement, I shouted, "What if the Talent is not human?"

"What?" Kella asked, looking at me as if I had gone mad.

"I meant, what if the Talent that registered on the Zebkrahn isn't human? What if it's a dog or an equine?" I said.

"Does it matter?" Avra inquired coolly.

I was taken aback. *Did* it matter? If we were to accept animals as equals and allies, this must lead eventually to animal rescues. Sobered, I shook my head.

"I'm an idiot. Of course it doesn't matter," I sent.

"Gahltha hoped it would be a beast, to break the funaga prejudice," Avra sent, mollified.

"Prejudice?" I said.

"The worst prejudice is that which goes unrecognized," Darga explained. "You think you treat us as equals, but in your deepest heart, you regard the funaga as superior. In part, this is because you yourself are powerful. But that does not make the race of the funaga better than that of dog or equine." Darga's gentle criticism cut like a knife. I was not certain I believed the funaga admirable as a race, but there was some truth in his accusation. And how could one fight such an insidious prejudice?

"You are less prejudiced than most of your race," Darga sent. "But Gahltha hoped we would find a beast mind to rival yours. He believes that is the only way to alter the funaga's deepest attitudes, even at Obernewtyn. Perhaps he was right."

"It might be a girlfriend for Darga," Jik sent with a shy grin. The others had not been part of our silent beastspeaking.

"We'll know soon enough," said Pavo.

"How many hours do you calculate from here to the hidden library?" I asked.

Pavo considered. "Half a day, if the distances shown on the map are consistent. I hope we will not be delayed too long in Aborium."

❖   ❖   ❖

Coming to the side gate of the city just after sunrise, I was startled and unnerved to see how many soldier-guards were posted. There was no mistaking the yellow cloaks they wore as a badge of office. But though they looked searchingly at our faces, they neither spoke nor sought our papers. Just as unexpected as the guards were the huge crowd of people and carts clamoring to be let in the gate. Many of those waiting were laughing and singing, and one girl did a cheeky jig to the calls and encouragement of her friends. I was puzzled by the crowd's high spirits but reassured, too. Surely a city that had so many eager visitors could not be such a bad place.

The sun was well risen by the time our cart was allowed to enter, and we made directly for the seafront and the Inn of the Cuttlefish. Grufyyd had given us directions, but it was harder than we had expected to follow them, for we were swept along by the crowd past the turns we had wanted to take. The city was of a tortuous design, so there was no working our way back. Streets ran off in all directions, bisecting, curving, and turning back on themselves.

"If we can find the water, we can work our way along," Pavo suggested. We were loath to mark ourselves strangers by asking the way, but morning passed into afternoon and still we were lost. I did not even remember how to get back to the gate. "No wonder people come in and never come out," I said wearily. "They probably can't find their way."

"We'll have to ask," Kella said.

I asked a woman, then a boy and another woman. All claimed not to know the inn. That struck me oddly. Aborium was large, but Grufydd had said the inn was

149

big and well known. Still trying to decide what to do, we continued to be carried along within the milling crowd. Jik warned us that Avra was on the verge of panicking at the way people were pressing all around her.

"Let's get out of this," I said, and directed Avra to force her way to the edge of the crowd and take the next turn away from the throng.

"I didn't know there were so many people in the Land," Kella said in a shaken voice, when we had reached a quiet side lane.

I looked at Jik, who wore a puzzled air. "There were not so many when I was here."

We came to the end of the lane and stopped in dismay, for it ended at an enormous central square. Here people swirled and butted one another like goats in a pen. I could hear laughter and strains of music, and the smells of food and warmed drinks wafted to our noses.

"It's a moon fair!" Pavo said, slapping his forehead. I laughed aloud in relief. That was the reason for the number of people waiting to come into the city. And the people of whom we had asked directions were strangers, too.

Avra managed to take a turn just inside the square, and we halted the cart in a quiet byway. A foul stench filled the air.

"What is that?" Kella asked in a disgusted voice.

"Seaweed," Jik said with a grin. "We must be near the wharves."

"Fancy having an inn near such a smell," Kella muttered. Then she noticed me climbing down. "Where are you going?"

"I'll have a look for the inn on foot. It will be easier than trying to maneuver the cart."

"I will go with you," Darga offered, and jumped down.

"Darga will come back alone if anything goes wrong. If he does come back without me, go back out of the city and wait for me where we camped last night," I said.

Kella and Jik looked aghast, and I laughed. "Nothing will happen, but we must have a plan just in case." They looked only slightly reassured.

I set off, ignoring the slight pain in my feet. The gypsy caravan, the raft, and the cart meant I had done little walking, and they were much better, though still tender. I hoped I would not have to walk too far on them. I was glad of Darga's company, though once or twice I noticed people looking at him so oddly that I wondered if I was breaking some city law, letting him walk unchained.

I looked around, trying to see someone who appeared to belong in Aborium. Spoting an old woman struggling with a load of washing down an alley, I hurried to catch up, hoping kindness would beget kindness.

"Mother, let me help you," I offered.

She gave me a long measuring look before letting me take one of the handles. " 'Tis good of ye, sure enough," she said. "I dinna mean to be so slow at takin' yer offer, but a moon fair dinna improve manners, an' a helpin' hand is rare at any time. What be yer name, lass?" she asked, squinting at me.

"Elspeth," I said.

"Well, I'm Luma," she said cheerfully. "I live just round th' next corner. I went out to gan th' wash an' were near swept away wi' moonies. It gans worse every year," she added despondently. She prattled on as we walked, complaining bitterly about the damage done to the city during the fairs. At a narrow door, she set down the basket to find her key.

"No doubt it's been picked from me," she said, searching all her pockets and folds in a haphazard way. "I'm from th' highlands. There ye dinna have to lock yer door, but in a city, leavin' it open is a right invitation to any robber." At last she found the key. Bidding me help her a little further, she told me to call Darga in.

"Things have a way of disappearin' in Aborium," she said confidingly.

Stone steps led down directly from the front door. We carried the basket awkwardly between us, down the stairs and into a large, rustic kitchen.

"What an effort," gasped Luma, panting and fanning her red face. "Ye'll have a glass of cordial to wet yer whistle?" Taking a squat jug from the cooling cabinet, she poured two mugs. " 'Tis me own brew I'm givin' ye, though I'll thank ye nowt to speak of it after. We are bound by lore to buy th' Herders' bitter cordials, an' makin' it is an offense." She drained her glass with relish and watched me drink mine.

"Ye be a moonie? I'm sorry for all that I were sayin' of them, but it gans on a body's nerve to have so many at once."

"I'm a traveler on my way to Murmroth. I only called into Aborium to deliver a message," I said.

Luma beamed. "An' I might ha' guessed it. Ye look to have too much sense to be part of that nonsense.

Who do ye carry a message to? 'Tis nowt of my affair or care, but I know most folk hereabout, an' might save ye some trouble."

I took a deep breath. "He's staying at the Inn of the Cuttlefish."

She nodded thoughtfully, her eyes on Darga. "A fine creature that, for all he puts me in mind of th' Herder breed."

"I've heard they use dogs to protect the Isle," I said.

"An' th' cloister here in Aborium. But who in their right mind would want to break into one?" She looked at Darga again with faint unease. "Yet he's a match, though small an' th' wrong shape. Well, th' inn ye seek is just a step from here. Ye dinna say who ye were lookin' for."

"A seaman," I stalled.

She cackled. "A seaman? Ha! Well, what else would ye find a man doin' in a seaport? I myself ha' two strappin' sons, an' my bondmate were a seaman, too, Lud rest his head."

"The man I'm looking for is called Brydda Llewellyn," I said.

The color drained from the washerwoman's face.

"What is it?" I asked quickly.

She smiled, a horrible false twist of her lips. " 'Tis naught. I were thinkin' somethin' else for a minute. I hardly heard ye. I dinna know th' name."

"She is afraid," Darga sent as the old woman took me onto the street and pointed the way to the inn. I felt her eyes boring into my back until I was out of sight.

"What happened?" Darga asked when we had gone out of her sight.

"I don't know. One minute we are talking like two sisters, and the next she looks as if I murdered her best friend. And all after I mentioned the name of Katlyn's son."

"He is well known?" Darga suggested.

"I don't know what it means, but I don't like it."

The inn was not far from Luma's house, and rather than being the grand place I had half imagined, it was a modest establishment with a faintly dingy air and peeling paint. Along the front was a stone veranda where men sat in the fading twilight talking in low voices. Wishing I had reached the inn before dark, I told Darga to wait in the street. "If I don't come out within an hour, go back to the others."

"Better not to go in," he sent.

I glanced down at him, wondering what he sensed. "I don't want to, but I promised."

The men on the porch fell silent as I approached. I asked for the manager of the inn in what I hoped was a confident voice. One of the men jerked his head toward the door.

"Thank you," I said.

The reception room was dim and cool. For a moment, I could see nothing and blinked, trying to accustom my eyes to the lack of light.

"What do you want?" asked a sharp voice. I jumped and heard a snicker of laughter. A woman and two men were sitting near the window, silhouetted against the fading pink sunset.

I swallowed dryly. "I'm . . . looking for a man. I have a message to deliver."

"What is his name?" the woman asked coldly.

I made myself speak, though I was regretting not listening to Darga. "Brydda Llewellyn."

A match flared and a lamp was lit on the table, illuminating the narrow, ratty face of the manageress and the hard, wary faces of the men.

The woman smiled, a folding rather than a curve of thin lips. "Brydda lives at the inn, but he has been on his boat this last moon. He will be here tomorrow morning. I can let you have a room for tonight."

Again the sour smile, and as she rose, dark satin skirts rustled around her feet like a nest of snakes. "Come with me," she commanded, and I dared not refuse. The inn was larger than it looked, and I was filled with unease as she took me downstairs where there were a number of bedrooms. The room she gave me was halfway down a hall and had a narrow window, level with the street. It was sparsely furnished.

"This is the only room we have free. Best if you keep to it until morning. The men who stay here are not used to having women around. I'll send water for you to wash and some supper."

Forcing a smile, I went across and tested the springs of the bed. "It's been a while since I've slept in a bed," I said casually. "I don't mind a bit of rest."

"I'll lock the door so you're not disturbed. Ring the bell if you want anything." She nodded smugly and departed.

My false smile fell away the minute the door closed, for I had no doubt I was a prisoner. The moment I tried to leave, the thinly veiled pretense would end. I pushed a bench to the narrow window and climbed up to peer out. There was no possibility of getting out that way.

I could fiddle locks, but I could not magic myself through the ground. I sent a call to Darga.

"Can you get out?" he asked as soon as he appeared at the window.

"I can open the lock, but I will have to wait until everyone goes to sleep. I want you to go back to the cart and get the others out of the city."

"Why have they locked you up?" Darga asked.

"I don't know, but I think it was because I asked for Brydda Llewellyn." I wondered what Rushton would do in such a situation.

"He would not risk you," Darga sent.

I stared. "What do you mean?" I shook my head. "Look, there's no time for this. You have to get the others out of the city before the gates are closed for the night."

An hour later, I could wait no longer. The door lock was a simple device, and I tampered with the mechanism so it would seem to be broken. Then I wrapped a towel round my hair and stuck my head out into the hall. The man outside started in astonishment at the sight of me. "How—?"

I interrupted him. "I've rung the bell three times, and no one comes. I was promised some water for a wash," I complained. Amazement gave way to confusion and then indecision. He had obviously been told to guard the door, but I was not acting like a prisoner. My querulous demand for water and the towel on my hair had confused him, and I sensed him wondering if he had somehow got his instructions muddled.

"Go on, then, tell her," I snapped, and shut the door.

I listened to his footsteps receding. Then I threw off the towel and slipped out into the hallway. I had barely taken two steps before I heard voices coming. I dared not go back to the room. Turning, I hurried in the other direction, trying every door I passed. A locked door had to mean the room was occupied.

My heart leaped as I recognized the manageress's voice. "What do you mean the door was unlocked? I locked it."

The last door was also locked, but I had no choice. If there was someone in the room, I would have to coerce them. I bent my mind to the lock, but before I could do anything, the door opened and a young, bearded man looked out. We stared at one another in surprise; then the voice of the manageress came clearly down the hall.

"Find her! She can't have gone far. She has a limp. Search all the rooms on this level."

Without saying a word, the man reached out and pulled me through the door, shutting it quickly. He made a sign for me to be quiet, and we listened intently. I heard the manageress shriek in rage at finding me gone.

The young man turned to look at me. He was not much older than Rushton, and his skin was the clear smooth brown of a seaman. He wore trousers, but his wet face and bare chest told me I had caught him in the middle of a wash.

"You are the girl who asked after Brydda Llewellyn?" he asked in a low voice.

I nodded, dazed that he should know.

There was a loud knock on the next door, and I looked at him in a panic.

In two strides he crossed the floor and flung open the lid of a big trunk. "Get in."

There was a knock at his door. I climbed in the trunk and heard him turning the key slowly.

"Why did you take so long to answer?" It was the manageress. I held my breath in terror.

"I was washing. What's going on?" he asked crossly.

"Ah . . . well, we have had a girl staying, as a favor to her father, who is a seaman. She is subject to manias and brainstorms. For her own safety, she was locked in, but she has got away."

"Is she dangerous?" asked my rescuer seriously. Despite my fear, I grinned at his convincingly anxious tone.

She grunted.

"Well, I heard this was a respectable place, but with all the noise and murdering madwomen running around, I am glad I am heading out to sea this night. Send someone to bring up my trunk."

My heart thumped in fear that she would demand to see what was in it.

"Carry your own trunk!" she snapped rudely, slamming the door. There was silence and some movement, then I felt myself lifted. I slid to the bottom of the trunk, half-suffocated by clothes.

"Don't make a sound," he hissed in a strained voice that told me he had hoisted the trunk—and me—onto his back.

In the hall, I heard enough to chill my blood. "The Council won't like this," said one voice.

" 'Tis nowt th' Council troubles me but th' priests. They're th' ones he's plagued," said another voice. The two voices faded, and I realized we were climbing the stairs.

Suddenly there was another voice. "Ho, Reuvan. Where are ye goin' at this hour?"

"I'm for the sea tonight," said my rescuer.

"Tonight?" There was an edge of surprise in the other's voice.

"The Herders have given permission to my master," Reuvan said. "But I don't know why he can't wait till a civil hour to set sail."

I wished he would get moving. The air in the trunk was beginning to foul. I felt sweat trickle down my spine.

At last the other laughed. "Better you than me. I'll see you."

"Not here you won't," Reuvan said easily. "It's a damn sight too noisy, and that sharp-tongued manageress is no enticement."

The other man laughed, and we moved on. At long last, I felt myself being set down, and the distinctive sound of hooves scraping over cobbles told me we were in the street.

The chest jerked, and I realized I was in a cart. It set off, and after an eternity, the latch was undone. "Stay down. It's not safe yet," the seaman whispered softly.

"Why are you helping me?" I asked in a low voice.

There was a pause. "You wanted to talk to Brydda Llewellyn, didn't you? Well, I'm taking you to him."

◆ 16 ◆

BRYDDA LLEWELLYN WAS a giant of a man, towering head and shoulders above the men around him. His face, illuminated fitfully in the guttering candlelight, was as stern and craggy as weathered rock.

Reuvan gave me a slight push. "Brydda, here is the girl who asked for you at the inn. I caught her trying to escape the old crow's clutches."

The buzz of talk from the men in the room ceased. My heart thumped unevenly under their hostile scrutiny.

"You have taken your time in coming," said Brydda, for all the world as if he had expected me.

"If you were where you were supposed to be, I would have been quicker," I said.

An astounded silence followed my words, then the giant roared with laughter. "Well, well, so they have sent a kitten that snarls and spits. I could crush you with one hand, little sad eyes, but I don't. Let that be a sign of my good faith. Now, what do you have to tell me?"

I was less intimidated by his threats than reassured by his laughter, for I had seen Katlyn in it. "I come from Rangorn. I bring a message from your—"

To my surprise, Brydda's smile disappeared and he

held up an imperious hand. "Speak no more of that for a moment." He glanced around, and silently the men filed out, giving me curious looks. Then we were alone except for Reuvan, who went to stand by the door.

"Don't be afraid," Brydda said in a softer voice. "I thought you were a messenger from Sutrium. I did not think . . . You come from my parents? Are they well?"

I nodded. "They are worried because you haven't sent word to them in so long. I think they feared something had happened to you."

Brydda ran a massive hand through the dark, springing curls on his forehead. "So it has. I suppose they told you about me?"

"They said you help seditioners."

He smiled faintly. "Well, that is as good a way as any of putting it. How did you come to meet my parents? You are not from Rangorn."

"We had an accident, and your parents helped us. We offered to bring a message to repay their kindness."

"You are with friends?" Brydda said sharply.

I nodded, hoping Darga had got the others away. "When I left them, they were in an alley not far from the inn. I'm not sure whether they made it out of the city before nightfall."

Brydda started, a look of concern on his face. "Quickly, Reuvan, go and take some of the others. Bring them back." He turned to me. "What do they look like?"

"A girl and a boy not much younger than I am, and a much younger boy," I said. "A wheat-colored mare is pulling the cart."

He nodded, and Reuvan hurried away. "It is dangerous to be out in the streets at night, though less than usual because of the moon fair. Is there no one full grown among your companions?"

Slightly indignant, I told him we were perfectly able to look after ourselves. Changing the subject, I asked why I had been locked up at the inn. "Your parents told us to mention your name. I didn't reckon on such an unfriendly reception," I said resentfully. Brydda only laughed and gave me a slap on the back that winded me.

"Much has happened since I last spoke to my parents. I was betrayed by one of my men. Once I could go to and from the inn openly, an ordinary seaman, but now I am known to be the notorious seditioner they call the Black Dog. You are lucky I had friends keeping an eye out at the inn for the messenger I mistook you for. Once she comes, I will leave Aborium. I dared not send word to my parents while I am here, because I was afraid of having their connection with me exposed. But I am glad to hear they are safe."

"Those soldierguards at the gate," I said in sudden realization. "It was you they were looking for."

He nodded. "The Council would like to catch me, and so would the Herder Faction. But I will slip through their fingers like snow during the moon fair."

"Where will you go?" I said unthinkingly.

Brydda looked at me for a long moment. "Few would expect an honest answer to such a question. But I believe I can trust you. Does it seem strange to you that a wanted man trusts his instinct over caution?" He smiled when I did not answer. "I have a kind of infallible knack for judging people."

"Yet you say you were betrayed . . ."

He nodded grimly. "By a man I loved like a brother.

But I did not misjudge him. He was tortured and made to speak, and there will be a payment for that. Come, tell me the truth. Are you not a seditioner or a runaway yourself, that my mother should tell you my secrets?"

I stared at him in fright.

"I told you. I have a knack at guessing. But don't look so unnerved. It makes us allies, not enemies," he said.

I nodded, shaken, entertaining an odd notion about this uncanny "knack" of his. "My parents were burned by the Council as seditioners, and my brother was killed by soldierguards," I said.

Brydda nodded triumphantly. "I thought as much, though I think there is more to your story than that. But it is enough to know we fight the same fight. It is my aim to rid this land of the Herder Faction and its tyranny. I have many allies who think as I do, and for now we oppose the Herders in a thousand small ways. But the time is not too distant when we will challenge them openly."

I was filled with excitement, for his words were almost identical to Rushton's, except Brydda seemed to think the Herder Faction worse than the Council.

He continued. "The message I wait for is to ensure there are no Herders waiting for me in Sutrium. It is too dangerous for me here now, so I will go elsewhere and harass them anew. Sutrium. They will not expect me to be so bold."

Reuvan came in, grim-faced. He bent and spoke into Brydda's ear.

"What is it?" I asked.

"Your friends are gone," Reuvan said.

I sighed in relief. "They will have gone outside the

city when I didn't come back. That was what we planned."

Brydda said, "Reuvan means they have been taken prisoner. I have allies who let me know who has been taken by the Herders and the soldierguards. It seems your friends were among today's intake."

I shook my head in disbelief.

"Rumor says the boy was a runaway Herder novice," Brydda went on.

"No!" I whispered in horror. "Where have they been taken? Who has them?"

"The Herders," Reuvan said. "They'll have been taken to the cloister for interrogation."

"I have to help them," I cried.

Reuvan shook his head. "No one escapes the cloister cells. There are priests everywhere and killer dogs. And the place is built like a labyrinth."

Brydda scratched his head. "Only a madman would attempt such an impossible rescue."

There was a commotion at the door, and a girl entered. Weary and travel stained, she half staggered into a chair. "You are the messenger?" Brydda asked.

The girl nodded. "Sutrium and all the other branches are safe. It seems he died before they could make him tell any more. . . ."

Brydda's shoulders slumped. "I should be glad. . . ."

I did not wait to hear any more. Taking the chance offered by the momentary confusion, I slipped into the street.

It was dark and very cold, the moon obscured by clouds. I shivered and wished I had not left my coat on the cart. I had delivered my message, I thought bitterly, but at what cost?

When I had gone a safe distance from Brydda's hovel, I stepped into a darkened doorway and closed my eyes, sending my mind to the other side of town. My mind played back and forth, seeking Jik's familiar pattern. It seemed ages before I spotted a dull glimmer at the farthest edge of my reduced lowland range. I sent a farseeking probe gratefully.

"Elspeth?" Jik's thoughts were faint.

"Jik, are you in the Herder cloister?" Lightning lashed overhead, making it a strain to communicate at such a distance.

"Yes," he sent.

"What about the others?"

"I'm on my own in a cell. Kella and Pavo are here somewhere. Avra is in the stable," Jik sent. I was filled with loneliness and apprehension but realized Jik was empathising his own emotions to me.

"What happened?" I asked.

"One of the priests recognized me from Darthnor. I tried to tell them Kella and Pavo didn't know about me, but I don't think they believed me. They want to know how I got here and how I made it look like I died. They want to know where I've been and if I had help. I'm scared. I think they mean to take me out to Herder Isle." Jik's terror spilled over into my own mind, and for a moment, I saw his nightmarish vision of the interrogation methods awaiting him.

"I won't let that happen. I'm coming," I sent, but the contact had begun to fade.

I found myself slumped in the doorway, gritty water seeping through the knees of my trousers. Sweat was freezing on my cheeks, and my teeth were chattering violently.

I had meant to try farseeking Darga as well, but that would have to wait. I needed to reach the cloisters as fast as I could and get Jik away from there. Get him away, or erase his mind, a darker voice reminded me. I shuddered and walked faster.

I was limping badly by the time I reached the area of the city nearest the cloister, certain that all Kella's good work on the scars had been undone. It was not hard to tell which building was the cloister. Set apart from the other buildings, it had its own high wall. Branches of trees and leaves visible at the top told me there was a garden inside. I made my way carefully around the perimeter, looking for a weak point. There were two small gates, barred and guarded, and one larger gate, open but heavily guarded. The contact with Jik had left me too depleted to coerce a guard, let alone more than one. Somehow I had to get in without being seen. I decided I would have to climb over the wall.

Leaning against it to gather my energy for the climb, I realized a dog was pacing on the other side. He had sensed me and was about to bark. I sent a quick greeting, and his urge to bark diffused into curiosity.

"Who/what are you?" It was a dog named Kadarf.

"I am a funaga. I mean no harm. I want to come over the fence and visit a friend," I sent. Fighting a wave of nausea, I gave his mind a coercive push. I climbed the fence with the help of a spindly tree growing by the wall. Sitting on the top, I could see the Herder cloister through the trees, a dark, squarish building with few windows and no visible doors.

At the foot of the wall, a muscular, brindled dog watched me slither awkwardly to the ground. He bore a strong resemblance to Darga, and I remembered how the townspeople had eyed him warily.

I closed my eyes and reached out with my mind for Jik. When I farsought him, he almost overwhelmed me with a wave of emphathised terror.

"Elspeth!" Jik sent. "They're taking me to the Herder Isle tonight!"

"I'm right outside. Now, how long before they come?"

Jik made a concentrated effort to control his panic. "In . . . in an hour, they said. But that was a while ago. Is Darga with you?"

I sent a gentle negative. "I was delayed at the inn and sent him back to the cart, but you must have already been taken. He's a smart dog. Remember when he disappeared in the Druid camp? He'll turn up."

I left Jik for a moment to locate the others. Kella and Pavo were in a cell together, and I let Kella know I was coming. Avra was in a stable near the perimeter of the grounds.

She responded with relief to my probe, and I realized she had been afraid we would abandon her. Quickly, she outlined the arrangement of the stables. I told her Kella and Pavo would come to get her shortly.

Returning to Jik, I was glad to find him calmer. "I've found Kella and Pavo. I'm going to free them first, because they're on the top level, and they can free Avra," I sent.

"If the Herders come for me . . . ," Jik sent fearfully.

"I'll get back in time," I sent.

"Promise you won't let them take me to the Isle," Jik urged.

"I promise," I sent.

I looked down at Kadarf and probed him to locate a lesser house door. Following me, Kadarf stretched himself outside the door to wait.

Inside was a short hall branching in two directions. I took the left way, leading to Kella and Pavo, noting the other way would bring me to stairs leading down to Jik's level. Passing numerous closed doors, a slight farsense probe was all I needed to warn me if anyone was coming.

My limp had grown worse, but there was no time to rest. Turning warily into another hall, I jumped at the sound of voices, but no one was visible.

I could hardly believe I was creeping through a dread Herder cloister. I would not have imagined I would have the courage, but Jik's fear of being taken to the Isle and my own fear of having to erase his mind spurred me on. I stopped abruptly, realizing I had found them. A brief straining, and the lock clicked. Kella and Pavo looked up, relief flooding their faces.

"There's no time to talk," I said, forestalling their questions. "I'll take you to an outer door. There is a dog there who will lead you to the stables where Avra is kept. Avra said you can get out of the stable to an exercise yard, and from there to the street. Leave at once, and get straight out of the city. You might have to bribe the gatekeeper. Head for Murmroth until the lights of Aborium dim. Camp on the beach. I'll find you. Now let's hurry."

"I will slow you down," Pavo said faintly. I was shocked by his ravaged face. He seemed to have aged years in a few hours.

"Help him," I said to Kella brusquely. She looked

hurt at my tone, but some of the dazed horror had faded from her eyes.

Moving back down the hall, I was puzzled to note how awkwardly Pavo moved. Had the disease begun to affect his limbs? Then I saw a bloody streak on one ankle and understood. He had been interrogated.

For a second, I was overwhelmed by a black tide of hate. This dissolved into fear as my senses warned that a priest was approaching. There was no door near enough to offer refuge, and the hall was long and straight with no turnings. Neither Pavo nor I was capable of running fast enough to get back inside the cell before he came round the corner.

Desperation gave me an idea.

"Get close to the wall and face it. Don't move, no matter what happens," I whispered. I blew out the candles on either side of us, throwing our hall into shadow. Flattened to the wall in the dimness, I mustered my strength and sent out a fine coercive probe. I let it mesh with the priest's mind. The alignment was perfect, and for a time, I simply mirrored his thoughts about the power-hungry manipulations of an ambitious senior priest. Then, gently, I began to exert my own force beneath the conscious level and into the semiconscious region of the mind.

My brother, Jes, and I had played hide-and-seek as children, and I had always won when he searched, no matter how bare the boundary we set, because I could make his mind look everywhere but directly at me. Our only hope was that this child's trick would work on the priest.

He came around the corner, and Kella quivered with fright. I willed her to be still as he came nearer. It would only work if we were completely motionless. Pushing the priest's mind fractionally, I made him turn his head absentmindedly to the opposite wall where the candles were extinguished. He passed us looking steadfastly the wrong way, entirely unaware of us or my subtle coercion. I did not dare release him until he had turned the corner, then I slumped back, exhausted.

"He didn't see us," Kella whispered incredulously. "How could he not?"

"Quickly," I snapped.

Outside, I bade Kadarf take them to the stables and prevent their harassment by any other dogs. I did not stay to see them go. Time was running out for Jik. Nearly hobbling now, I sent my mind ahead to let the boy know I was coming.

To my dismay, he was not alone. There were two priests in the room with him. I was too late!

Agitation made me careless and Jik perceived me. "Elspeth?" His mind groped for mine. I was filled with remorse at the terrible duty that lay before me. I dared not let them take him without erasing all of his knowledge about Obernewtyn. No matter how brave he was, in the end they would make him talk, just as Brydda's friend had been made to talk. But I knew I had neither the heart nor the strength for such an operation.

I had another idea.

Hobbling back into the garden, I called to Kadarf. He followed me back to the fence and watched me struggle to climb it. "I'm sorry you are going," he sent.

I waved a brief salute, then dropped to the path on the other side of the wall. Kella and Pavo were nowhere in sight. I hurried around to the ornate double gate Kadarf said was used for most coming and going among the priests, praying they would bring Jik out that way.

I waited, sitting cross legged in the shadows beneath a bush to give my feet a rest. It was some minutes before I saw any sign of life. One of the guards brought a large cart out and harnessed up a white horse. Then a group of priests came out, carrying boxes and parcels. Peering from my hiding place, I saw Jik between them, looking small and frightened. My heart ached for him, but I turned my mind resolutely to the horse. My only hope was to create some sort of diversion to give Jik the chance to run.

Suddenly a hand touched my arm. Whirling, I stifled a scream of fright as I looked into Brydda Llewellyn's face.

"How . . . ," I began, only to be interrupted by the sound of horses and a carriage.

Frantically, I tried to collect my thoughts, but I was too slow. With a cry of despair, I saw the carriage draw away and knew I had failed. I had a brief glimpse of Jik sitting upright among the grim-faced priest masters.

Then he was gone.

✦ 17 ✦

I STARED DOWN the empty street, knowing I had failed Jik—and all of Obernewtyn.

"Quickly," Brydda said. "We will have to move fast if we are to catch them."

He half dragged me across the street and around a corner where a grinning Reuvan sat behind the reins of a carriage embossed boldly with the gleaming Herder seal.

"Courtesy of the Herder Faction," he said with a mock bow.

Dazed, I let myself be lifted in. The cart lurched as Brydda climbed in behind me. Reuvan shook the reins, urging the horse on to a wild pace.

"You are hurt?" Brydda shouted over the clatter of hooves on the cobbles. He nodded at my feet.

"Old wounds," I shouted back. "You followed me?"

Brydda shook his head. "You were gone before I realized, before we could talk of ways and means to rescue your friends. But I knew where you had gone."

"You said helping them was impossible," I protested.

Brydda shook his head. "I said only a madman would attempt such a rescue. I forgot you did not know me well enough to realize that I am just such a man."

I was struck dumb at his words.

"Besides," Brydda said, "you had not meant to come to Aborium, except to deliver my parents' message. Therefore, I am the direct cause of your troubles and honor-bound to help you. And if the Herders are so keen to have your friend, I am just as eager to stop them." He grinned. "We were waiting to see you arrive, never dreaming you had already magicked yourself inside. . . ." He hesitated, obviously curious, but I said nothing. "A lad and a girl came out stealthily leading a horse. They fit the description you gave, so we stopped them. It took us a minute to convince them we were trying to help, and then they told us you were inside. I sent one of my people to show them a safe way out of the city. I wanted them to take the cart, but I have never seen a pair more attached to a horse." •

"I don't know how to thank you . . . ," I began, but Brydda held up a hand.

"No need for thanks among allies. Now, the Herders will be going to the wharf. The girl said they want to question the boy. . . ." For a moment, his face really did look like stone, and I understood that Brydda Llewellyn would be a savage enemy. "There's no time for subtle planning. I meant to leave town tonight anyway, so it does not matter if the Herders think I freed the boy. It will madden them trying to understand the connection. Was he really a Herder novice?"

I nodded. "What can we do? There are five priests in that cart," I said as Reuvan suddenly reined the horse to a slow walk. I could smell the sea and the sour odor of old seaweed.

"We're nearly to the wharf," Reuvan said over his shoulder.

"Go softly, then," Brydda said. "We can handle five between us, six counting the shipmaster."

I nodded, praying they would succeed, for I knew I couldn't wipe Jik's mind clean of his dangerous knowledge.

The clatter of stones ceased as the wheels ran onto board. We had reached the wharf.

The waning moon broke through the clouds but shed a wan light, and all was darkness. The smells of oil and spices mingled with that of sea and fish scales. Moored vessels bobbed in the dark, gurgling water, bumping occasionally into their mooring posts with a dull thud.

"The Herders cast off from there," Brydda whispered, pointing to the very end of the wharf. Lanterns swung from either end of a long, slim boat moored there. Illuminated fitfully in the gritty, shifting light was the carriage that had brought Jik. It was empty, and there was no sign of him. Priests were moving between the ship and the carriage, transferring boxes to the vessel.

"Why do they travel at night?" I whispered as Brydda signaled for Reuvan to draw the carriage into a shadowed corner.

"They are a secretive lot, and night suits their fell purposes. Most ships go out at dawn or just before. Folk know the Herders come here at night, and that is enough to discourage anyone else. People who seem too interested in Herder business have a way of disappearing. There's the boy."

Jik was standing between two priests, half obscured by their flapping gray cloaks. His hands were bound behind him, and his shoulders slumped hopelessly.

"Jik," I sent.

His head jerked in surprise, but he subsided when one of the priests gave him a hard look.

"Careful," I warned, and sensed him make an effort to maintain his dejected pose.

"Elspeth," he sent in a powerful wave of gladness that twisted my heart.

"We are at the other end of the wharf, in the shadows. We're going to help you."

I broke contact, feeling Brydda's hand on my arm. "It's no good. There are at least seven priests down there. And there is the shipmaster. Two of us might barely overcome the lot, and I'd take the risk but for the dogs. They are trained by the priests to tear a man's throat out on command," Brydda said.

I blinked at him, trying to reconcile the savage picture his words evoked with Kadarf's simple kindness. "But you said . . . we've got to get him away from them. I . . . I . . ." I stopped, gulping back tears.

"It's not possible, lass. You see that, don't you?" Brydda asked.

"You don't understand. He . . . he can tell them about us, and about you and your parents."

Brydda shook his head. "That's bad, but there is no way to help the boy or silence him. Getting ourselves killed trying won't help anyone."

I threw caution to the wind. I felt I had no choice.

"Brydda, I am a Misfit," I said. "I can stop those dogs from attacking. You think—everybody does—that Misfits are only true dreamers and defectives. Useless. But there are other kinds, too. Misfits like me and my friends. I can make those dogs do what I want, and I can talk to Jik from here, inside his head. If you can handle the men, I can deal with the dogs."

I could hardly believe myself revealing so much. Reuvan was staring at me as if I had gone mad.

"I'll prove it," I said desperately. "Watch Jik. I'll make him look toward us and nod." I sent a message to Jik, asking him to respond as obviously as he could without alerting his guardians. He turned his head slowly and nodded with a subtle wink. Reuvan hissed in astonishment.

"You can hold the dogs?" Brydda asked.

I nodded, hoping they would be as easy to convince as Kadarf. "Help me save Jik. Please."

After a long tense moment, Brydda grinned. "Well, I'm probably finally going mad, but we'll have a go at it. Seven men—we can handle that many between us, eh, Reuvan?"

"Seven men, yes. But those dogs . . . ," he said doubtfully.

Brydda clapped him on the back. "Come, man, you heard the girl. Those dogs will be all bark and no bite."

Reuvan looked at me warily, as if I myself might bite, but such was the strength of Brydda's personality that he nodded.

"Good lad. Now, Elspeth, tell the boy to run for it as soon as he gets the chance. Don't wait for us. As soon as you have him, get out of the city as fast as you can. There is a gate back near the cloister. Go out that gate and no other. Wait with your friends, and I'll find you."

"What about you?"

"I'll worry about me. Make sure you do as I said."

I reached out and touched his arm. "It was a glad day when I first heard the name of Brydda Llewellyn," I said.

He smiled. "Life is an adventure, is it not?"

They melted into the shadows and began making their way toward the Herder vessel.

I groped about until I found the mind of the shipmaster. He was in the hold, organizing the loading of the cargo. I pinched a nerve experimentally and he groaned and doubled over. I grinned, catching his thought that he must have eaten a bad fish stew.

I tweaked the nerve again, more firmly, and this time he groaned loudly enough to be heard by the priests on the wharf. They looked at one another. One stepped onto the deck and climbed down into the hold.

Taking advantage of their preoccupation, Brydda and Reuvan attacked with wild cries, brandishing knives. One of the priests standing on the edge of the vessel fell overboard in fright. Another Herder, with stronger nerves, reached down to unloose the dogs he had on leash. Quickly, I beastspoke to the dogs, asking for help. I had no strength left to coerce more than very slightly, but they agreed to help. I saw that the dogs had no love for their masters, for all their savage training. As soon as they were loose, they began to bark wildly and snarl, jumping and running in circles. The look on the Herders' faces would have been funny if there had not been so much at stake.

Then Reuvan jumped onto the deck, delivering a stout blow to the emerging priest and slamming the hold shut. That left five. One of the priests held on to Jik while the others divided into pairs to attack Brydda and Reuvan. Brydda was more than a match for two men. A blow from his fist and the first priest crumpled at his feet like a wet cloth. The other had drawn a knife and tried to sink it in Brydda's belly, but the big man was agile for his size and whirled on his toes like a dancer before dealing a blow with the haft of his sword. He stepped over the unconscious priests and turned around.

Reuvan had dispatched one of his attackers and was busy with the other. Brydda turned menacingly to the priest holding Jik. Calmer than his brothers, he drew a long knife from the folds of his cloak and let go of Jik's arm.

"Run!" I sent.

He lurched forward, stumbling, hampered by his bound hands. Panting, he fell as he reached the cart.

"Quick, get in," I whispered. His nose was bleeding and his breath came in sobs, but he clambered awkwardly into the cart and fell across my feet. I gathered up the reins. I hated to leave Brydda, but he had struck me as a man used to having his orders obeyed.

I beastspoke the surprised horse, and we rode away from the wharf.

I was afraid someone would spot us crossing the dark city in the Herder cart and slung a bag over the side to obscure the insignia. As we drew up to the gate, my heart was thundering. But the gatekeeper barely looked at me before letting us through. There was not a soldierguard in sight.

Incredulous, we found ourselves outside the city.

Sheer relief made us both hoot and laugh like madmen the moment we were out of hearing. I laughed till my stomach hurt and tears rolled down my face.

"Who were those men?" Jik asked when the laughter had died away.

"The big one was Brydda Llewellyn," I said, and tried to untie his wrists, but they were too tight. They would have to be cut off.

I beastspoke the horse again, telling her where we wanted to go and promising freedom once we got there. She was a beautiful creature. I was interested to learn that she thought of her masters as jahrahn, the cold ones. She appeared unconcerned at the strange events of the night and even at leaving the walled city.

It seemed the Herders often rode out at night beyond the city limits to meet with funaga on the seashore. Sometimes they brought men and women and children, bound as Jik was. These were always left behind. *Slavers*, I thought bleakly.

I thought I saw a faint flicker of fire in the distance. Closer, we could see it was a shore camp, but we were almost on it before a figure jumped up and Kella's voice rang out gladly.

After the first excited greetings, Kella introduced me to a tall blond youth called Idris, who cut Jik's bonds and left us to unharness the horse. Jik and I warmed our hands and explained Brydda's role in our escape.

Pavo looked pale and fraught. His feet were freshly bandaged, but he refused to talk about what had been done to him, save that his tormentors had made no real attempt at questioning him—they'd only meant to assert their dominance.

Our talk reminded Kella of my feet, and she insisted on examining them.

My shoes and stockings had to be soaked and cut away from the wounds. I was dizzy with pain before a grim-faced Kella had finished her ministrations. Then she looked up, not with the reproof I had expected but with tears in her eyes.

"I don't know how you walked so far on them,

yet . . . if you had not . . ." She stopped abruptly and hurried down to the sea to wash her instruments.

I looked at the others with faint embarrassment. "Anyone would have done the same."

Pavo smiled wanly. " 'Would do' and 'have done' are two different things."

I felt my face redden and was glad of the darkness. To turn attention from myself, I asked Idris how he had come to know Brydda.

The boy said his father and two sisters had been taken by the Herders. One night, he and his mother had returned from a visit to find their house a charred ruin. Neighbors said the Herders had come and taken the husband and daughters away, but the priests claimed Idris's mother was mad with grief and that her husband and children must have burned to death in the fires.

Idris had never seen his father or sisters again. He met Brydda after his mother had gone to the rebel for help. She had died shortly after learning her husband and daughters had been sold to slavers. Brydda had taken the shattered boy in, and though Idris did not say it out loud, it was clear he worshipped the big rebel.

It was near midnight before Brydda and Reuvan found us. They had dealt with the Herders quickly, binding and locking them into their own hold before setting the ship adrift. Brydda said in casting off he had offered up a fervent prayer that the ship would be seized by slavers. They had gone back to Brydda's hovel for supplies since they would not be returning to Aborium.

Hearing my amazement at the ease of leaving the

city, Brydda grinned and said the real gatekeeper and three soldierguards had been tied up securely and uncomfortably in the watch hut to ease Brydda's departure. All we had to do now was wait for a message from the city to tell us how the Herders had reacted and if it was safe to move.

We were all weary, but Brydda's suggestion that hot food would do us more good than sleep was met with enthusiasm. We deferred serious talk until after we had eaten. "It is bad for the stomach," Brydda said with a comic roll of his eyes. Kella and Idris unpacked and prepared a meal, and Brydda regaled us with stories of his travels on the sea and his adventures as a seditioner. He made it sound like a game. I suspected he was telling only the brighter side of the tales, but even Pavo laughed at some of his more absurd stories, and we sat to eat at last in good spirits.

With shining eyes for his rescuer, Jik asked shyly how Brydda had come to spend his time fighting Herders. Brydda said it was a long tale and refused at first, but finally, when we all pleaded, he agreed to tell his story.

"I traveled to Aborium as a lad to get a trade as a seaman. Like many a boy, the sea called me. While I sought work, I heard rumors of slavers. I thought them no more than another salty tale at the time, but as I grew and worked on different ships, I learned that there were indeed slave boats that called at our shores. No one said openly how the slavers got their cargo, but it was whispered that the Herders filled their moneybags by selling prisoners and innocent folk they brought in for questioning.

"I pitied those taken, but I thought it was none of my affair and meant to mind my business," Brydda said.

"Then a lad who was the son of my landlord, and very dear to me, was taken. He had simply been in the wrong place at the wrong time. I had no hope of doing anything, for I did not learn of it till days after when I came back from a fishing trip.

"I swore then that I would never again stand aside and let some injustice happen simply because it was none of my business. From that, it was not far to the next step, finding others who thought as I did and were prepared to fight back.

"And so we have done these long years past, stealing their cargo and silver when we could, disrupting their festivals and plans, rescuing prisoners and spiriting them away. And we have bided our time, longing for the day we might be strong enough to revolt openly."

He looked at me speculatively. "If I had a hundred like you, I would dare to try it."

"Don't you fear and despise me for my deformed mind?" I asked so coolly that Kella gasped.

Brydda spat into the flames. "If the Herders are normal, then let me also be called Misfit. As to fearing you, I fear no man—or girl. Even if she can talk to dogs."

Pavo and Kella exchanged a quick look, and Idris regarded Brydda in confusion. I took a deep breath. "Then maybe one day you'll have your wish."

Brydda's eyes flashed. "What do you mean? Your people would fight with me?"

I shook my head. "You go too fast. I'm not the one to decide."

Brydda looked angry, then he laughed aloud. "That's me all over. My mother always said I was like a wild bull at a fence. Yet I think we will one day be allies." His eyes had a familiar faraway look.

I was more convinced than ever that Brydda had some sort of Misfit ability, a combination of empathy and futuretelling—just enough to make him an infallible judge of character and a lucky guesser. But if he wanted to think of it as a "knack," past experience told me to say nothing of my theories.

"I have always thought of Misfits as unlucky mutants, but maybe I was wrong," Brydda mused. "Life is too short for all there is in it. A man with his eyes open learns something new every day," he added so ironically we all laughed.

Gradually, the others dozed, but Brydda and I stayed up talking far into the night.

The rebel organization was very large, extending throughout the Land. By comparison, Obernewtyn was a very small operation. But Brydda was far from dismissive, saying more like me might shift the tide of a battle. He was taken aback to discover how young most of us were but still believed we could help one another. I agreed to advocate a meeting between him and Rushton, but I was not sure the extent to which our aims coincided.

"At the bottom of everything, we are Misfits, and few men would have reacted as you did. Can you say for certain all your people would think as you do? Not be disgusted by us or frightened?"

Brydda looked thoughtful at this. "I don't know. Maybe the thought of someone who can talk inside your head or make animals do anything they want *would* seem frightening. Yet if people are frightened, it is because of their ignorance and the Herders' lies about mutations. They could learn," Brydda said at last.

"Maybe, but we have to be sure," I said. "There is no good in our exchanging one kind of tyranny for another."

The others rose, too anxious to sleep for long, and we discussed our plans. Brydda asked Pavo where he thought we would find the Beforetime library. He frowned at the teknoguilder's mention of ruins.

"I don't know about a library, but there are ruins of an old city near here."

Pavo looked excited. "That must be it," he said, then his face fell. "But if it is near and common knowledge, the library is sure to have been found and ransacked."

Brydda shook his head. "No one goes there."

"Why?" Pavo asked in a puzzled tone. "It's not in Blacklands territory. It is not even tainted badlands."

"It is haunted by ghosts of the Beforetime," Reuvan said.

Pavo gaped at him, then burst out laughing. "But there are no such things."

Brydda looked at him without smiling. "So I once thought, but these are real enough. I have seen them."

"And I," Reuvan said with a shudder. "Terrible, monstrous faces twisted in mortal agony."

"Ghosts?" Pavo echoed, confounded by their joint testimony. I stared from one to the other, just as astounded.

"Ghosts," Brydda said decisively.

◆ 18 ◆

WELL BEFORE DAWN, a man rode out from the city with news for Brydda. The Black Dog's attack on the Herder ship and the escape of three dangerous seditioners were the talk of the town. Huge rewards were being offered for information leading to their recapture. There was also a reward for a girl, escaped from custody at the Inn of the Cuttlefish, believed to have been an associate of the Black Dog.

The Herder ship had been found floating aimlessly, and those on board had described Brydda's attack as ruthless and bloody, claiming thirty cutthroats had descended without warning.

"Now you see where I came by my terrible reputation," Brydda said.

He was delighted with the way the Herders had linked the events. "How they will sweat wondering what a Herder novice has to do with the Black Dog," he crowed.

More disturbing was the messenger's report that a search party of soldierguards was combing the town. "It will only be a matter of time before they come upon the unguarded north gate and realize you have got out. There are enough of them in Aborium that they would attempt to pursue you into the plains," the messenger said grimly.

After he had ridden away, Brydda turned to us. "There are four watchtowers with a clear view together of the plains. They will be scanning for any movement away from the main roads, and all roads will be guarded. We must go at once, while it is dark. I have no desire to visit your ruins, but right now it is probably the safest place for us."

We packed up the camp and left immediately. Reuvan and Brydda rode the two horses they had stolen to leave the city, I rode Avra, and the rest went in the cart with Idris at the rein. We could not gallop or trot because although most of the west coast was plains, they were stony and pocked with holes that a horse might stumble into in the darkness.

To while away the time, Brydda asked me to help him devise a method of signaling that would let him communicate directly with the horses. He was intrigued by their intelligence. "I always liked animals better than people," he confided.

Later, he asked Jik to demonstrate his empathy. He was amazed to find his emotions swayed by the boy. "Imagine such an ability in battle. He could shatter the nerve of a dozen good men without firing an arrow."

"It wouldn't be very fair to make brave men act like cowards," Jik said.

Brydda gave him an incredulous look.

Pavo spotted the ruins first.

He had always seemed ageless to me, but now he looked ancient, shrunken with pain; Kella told me the illness raging freely through his body had progressed more quickly than she had anticipated. Yet he seemed untouched by his physical transformation, in better spirits than anyone, apart from his perplexity over Brydda's ghosts.

We had been riding in silence, each busy with his own thoughts, when Pavo stiffened and pointed.

At first we could see nothing. Then I saw the square shapes of buildings barely distinguishable from the dark night. Up close, they were in far worse condition than the ruinous buildings we had seen under Tor. Here the walls rose only slightly above our heads, the stone cracked and grown over with a weedy beard of green scrub and moss. The faint moonlight gave the buildings an intangible look, as if they were a mirage that might dissolve any second.

We were within two lengths of the first building when Brydda called a halt. "We'd better stop here. The ghosts will rise if we go nearer. I think it will be safe enough. No one would dream of us taking refuge here."

I looked at Pavo's determined face. "Pavo and I will be going in to look for the library. The rest of you may wait here with Brydda or come, as you please," I said.

Idris said he would wait with Brydda, but the rest, even Reuvan, said they would come. We left all the horses except Avra, who would draw the cart to bring back the books we found. Pavo and I rode while the others walked. The teknoguilder held his precious drawings and maps tightly but did not even look at them; he had pored over them so often that he knew them by heart. Occasionally, he led us to a road that rubble had made impassable, then he would frown and take us another way.

I did not believe in ghosts, but the deeper we went into the dark maze of stone and crumbled walls, the more uneasy I became.

It was clear some disaster had befallen the ruins, for there was far more damage here than to other ruins I had seen on the Blacklands fringes. In one place, pale moonlight glimmered on a charred wall that showed the burned, black shape of a man running. I did not know what it could mean, but I felt a deep chill in looking at it.

I began to think of all the stories I had heard of the Beforetime ghosts, how vengeful they supposedly were when their territory was invaded. The cold crept into my bones, and I wished we had waited until dawn to begin searching. My apprehension increased with each step, though there was no overt reason for it other than the strangely compelling atmosphere of the city.

The others were showing signs of disquiet, too. Kella's breath was coming fast despite our slow pace, and Jik stayed very close to the side of the carriage. Even Pavo's enthusiasm gave way to a distracted frown.

Then there was a faint moaning noise, and we all froze, looking around nervously.

"What was that?" Kella whispered.

"The ghosts," Jik said in a high, frightened tone.

"The wind," I said, but my voice sounded uncertain. I looked at Pavo.

"I don't understand it," he said. "I am afraid, too, but what have I to fear?" He reached out and took up a brush torch and set a flint to it. The flame flickered and blazed, throwing light onto his bony face. "We are not far from the library now. Just down here."

Yet the lane ended in a mass of twisted metal and rubble.

"We'll have to clear this," Pavo said.

I looked at him in dismay. "It will take weeks."

He frowned, then climbed out of the cart with an energy that belied his illness. Taking the torch, he clambered over the rubble.

"It doesn't matter about the light," Reuvan said gloomily, mistaking my look of concern. "We often see ghost lights moving around the city. No one will come to investigate."

Watching Pavo peering about, then scrambling higher, I found myself unable to believe anything could have survived the devastation that had overtaken the city. Nothing was left but enduring stone, and even that was greatly weathered with time. Paper was a thousand times more vulnerable. But Pavo seemed undaunted by the look of the city.

My neck prickled, and I had the queer feeling we were being watched. With shaking hands, I lit another torch.

"Here!" Pavo shouted, disappearing over the crown of the rubble mound. "The entrance is over here."

I had no desire to go into the dark alley, which waited like a toothless mouth. But Pavo was alone and calling for me. I climbed after him, the pain in my feet a welcome distraction from the fear. The mound did not extend very far into the alley, and Pavo was kneeling on the ground beyond it, scrabbling in the dirt and muttering to himself.

He looked up excitedly. "This is the entrance according to my maps, but the lock is strange. It seems to be locked from the inside. Do you think you can open it? It will be complicated." He described the mechanism, which was indeed complex. I wondered why such a lock would be wanted to protect books when they had been so plentiful in the Beforetime.

I looked around, not liking the way the dark seemed to crouch just outside the wavering circle of torchlight. Pavo had marked out the squarish shape of a door. There was a great deal of earth layered over it, but he assured me it would make no difference. I let my mind feel out the lock until I understood how it worked. It was as much a seal as anything, more secure than any door I'd encountered—all the more so because the mechanism had malfunctioned, jamming so that it could not be opened from either side.

After a long moment, I had it. There was a distinct whirring sound, and the door swung inward. The mounded earth near our feet seemed to drop, sliding away into the revealed space, showering dirt onto the metal steps that ran down from the opening. I had expected the air to smell bad, but it was odorless, dry, and cool.

I knelt and peered in, instinctively raising my hands in defense, certain something was about to leap out at me.

"I'll go first," Pavo said impassively.

"Wait for me," I said.

Climbing back to the top of the rubble, I told Reuvan to stay with Avra. Kella and Jik came to help, carrying their own torches.

"Warn us if there is any danger," I sent to Avra.

We descended into the dark with as much joy as if it were our own grave. Except for Pavo—he went first, fearless. I came next, and behind me, Kella and Jik holding hands. As soon as my head was below ground level, I realized the ground was slightly tainted—enough to prevent me from staying in contact with Avra.

The steps took us down to a long, dark corridor.

I was struck by the smooth sameness of all the surfaces. There was no hint of the owner's personality, no feeling that human beings had ever been there. Now that we were inside, my attack of nerves had faded, and I found myself curious about the library. Why would a library be built like a secret fortress?

"What is this place?" Jik whispered.

"Why are you whispering?" Kella whispered. They stared at one another, then exploded in a fit of nervous giggles.

"It was more than just a library," Pavo said in a normal voice. "The Oldtimers eventually used machines to store their knowledge, and books became less important, even old-fashioned. Luckily for us they never fell completely from favor. This place was an historical storehouse. Among other things."

I did not like his tone, but before I could ask what he meant, we rounded a bend in the corridor.

Pavo stopped dead ahead of us with a hiss of indrawn breath. I looked over his shoulder and gagged. Kella screamed, and Jik looked close to fainting.

Before us, leaning against the side of the hall, were a number of human skeletons. One was small, the size of a young child. Almost certainly the skeletons of Beforetimers.

"They're dead. They can't hurt you," Pavo said, but he sounded shaken, too.

"What . . . what happened to them?" Kella whispered.

Pavo sighed. "There was evidence that this storehouse . . . was meant to store more than just books. The Oldtimers actually wrote about the possibility of the Great White, which they called 'First Strike.' This place was supposed to be a possible shelter, because it could be completely sealed off. They must have survived the holocaust only to be trapped here. And there was no one alive on the outside to help them escape."

"They . . . they were trapped?" Kella said, aghast.

Pavo patted her arm, and we passed single file and ashen-faced.

There were no other unpleasant surprises, although we walked down the corridors leading to the main storage area with as much trepidation as if skeletons might wait around every turn. Eventually, we came to a series of solid and immovable doors. Pavo explained the locking mechanism. I rested my hands on the cool metal and went to work on the locks. Each time a door opened, there was a hiss.

Opening the last door, we found ourselves in a gigantic storage room filled with endless rows of books on shelves, reaching high above our heads and running away into the shadows.

For a long time, we simply stood there and stared. Even Pavo, who must have anticipated such a find, was struck dumb by the scale of the storehouse. Surely all the knowledge of all the ages of man before the holocaust must be contained in the thousands of books we saw before us.

Then Pavo stepped forward and laid his hand reverently on one of the books. "Just think of it," he said in a voice that trembled with excitement. "We are the first in hundreds of years to come here. The first since the Oldtimers." He gathered himself visibly.

"The books are old and frail. Only the dry air has preserved them. Handle them lightly and as little as you can. Look for books on Oldtime machines like the Zebkrahn and books on healing. Also any showing maps of the old world. The Beforetimers were very orderly. If you find one map book, you will have found all such books," he said. "We will each take a different section. Bring anything worth looking at to me, but mark your place so you don't forget where it came from."

I padded to the far end of the vault, amazed at the scale of it. Despite the orderly arrangement of the books, the sheer volume made it hard to find what we wanted. And though I understood the words, many of the books made no sense to me, being filled with references to things I did not understand. Some of those I *could* piece together offered up bizarre notions and ideas.

One book claimed there had once been midget races of various kinds—squat, wizened men with huge axes and tiny people with wings. Another book talked of a land where there were men and women taller than skyscrapers. Kella came hurrying down to show me a book she had found showing drawings of people with fish tails instead of legs.

I began to feel bewildered. If there had been so many different kinds of races, what had happened to them all?

Jik gave a shout. He had found a book showing wonderfully clear pictures of a Beforetime city. Pavo stopped his sorting to explain that the remarkably lifelike pictures had not been drawn by artists but were actual images of reality, somehow preserved by a process designed by the Oldtimers.

Jik's book seemed to be composed entirely of such images showing a number of Beforetime cities in all their glory. Here were the dark towers we had seen in the city under the mountain but lit by bright lamps, thousands of them. "Cities of light," Kella whispered, awed. It was hard to reconcile the dark, decaying city under Tor, or the rubble above us, with the sheer beauty of those images.

Jik was the first to find a map, though whether it was real I couldn't say. It's fringes showed beasts unlike any I'd seen, lizard-like and menacing. "Here be dragons," it read.

"And that was before the mutations of the Great White," mused Pavo.

Soon after, I came across a section containing books on machines. They meant nothing to me, but Pavo went through them carefully, rejecting this, keeping that.

He waved away the books of half-fish people, saying the creatures must have been of a race that had become extinct before humans came. However fascinating, we did not have room for such things, he said.

There were hundreds of books on very trivial subjects—books that told how to dress your hair or make a garment, books on how to set flowers in a jar, and even a book showing how to fold paper into the shapes of animals. It struck me that the wondrous Oldtimers had possessed a silly, trivial side.

There were books on every conceivable—and inconceivable—subject. Books on machines that carried men and women over land, over sea, and even up to the stars. The more I read, the more I understood that the old world really had passed away forever. So much had changed; so much knowledge lost that could never be regained. The teknoguilders' fascination with the past suddenly struck me anew as pointless. The future was what really mattered. And perhaps the past was better lost, if it had led the Beforetimers to the Great White.

"It is such a waste," Pavo lamented, wrapping books in waxed cloth to be carried by Jik to the foot of the stairs. "Now that we have broken the seal, the books will decay quickly. You must tell Garth to send another expedition soon, before they are lost to us." I felt a chill at Pavo's calm acceptance that he would not be there to do the telling.

I was about to turn into another aisle when my gaze fell upon a particular title.

Powers of the Mind.

I stared at the book as if it had eyes and might stare back. Breathing fast, I took it down. I let it fall open where it wanted, then struggled to read the tiny script.

> *Every mind possesses innate abilities beyond the five known senses. For most people, these abilities remain hidden and untapped. Sometimes, they are used accidentally or imperfectly and called* hunches, insight, *or* inspired guesswork.
>
> *Even those who have demonstrated these mental abilities, or extrasensory perceptions, are barely touching the edge of their true potential. It would take some immense catalyst to break through the mind's barriers and allow men and women to use and develop that hidden portion of their minds . . .*

I felt hot and faint, for what could it mean but that the Oldtimers had speculated about Talents? I trembled at the revolutionary idea that the powers we had always imagined to be caused by the Great White might have existed before the holocaust—that they were not mutations but some natural development of the mind.

I flicked a few more pages and read.

For time eternal, some men and women have exhibited flashes of future knowledge and been called fey. But who is to say they are not simply the forerunners of some evolutionary movement, destined to be scapegoats and ridiculed, tormented and even killed for their strangeness, until the rest of the human race catches up. . . .

My eyes flew down the page. Flicking back and forth feverishly, I found the book mentioned many of the abilities I knew to be real and even some I had not encountered.

My head ached with the tremendous feeling of having made a discovery that might well change our future. If the Council saw such a book, they would have to admit Misfits were not mutations. But the Council called such books evil and burned them.

And the discovery might only make things worse for us; if our kind was the future and not some freakish sideline, what were ordinary people but a dying breed?

I shivered and read on more soberly.

The Reichler Clinic has conducted a progressive and serious examination of mental powers and has produced infallible proofs that telepathy and precognitive powers are the future for mankind. Reichler's experiments have taken mind powers out of the realms of fantasy and set them firmly in the probable future.

I shivered again, knowing in my deepest heart that the truths contained in the book would not make us more accepted.

"Elspeth?" Jik asked. I started, instinctively closing the book. "Are you all right?" he asked curiously.

I nodded. "What is it?"

"It's Reuvan. I was taking books to the stairs, and I heard him call out," Jik said.

I bit my lip, slipping the book into my pocket and cursing the unyielding tainted earth that would not let me reach Avra mentally. Then I told myself to be glad the taint was not lethally strong, as in the Blacklands. I left Pavo to his books and returned to the stairs, climbing up to poke my head aboveground. It was nearly dawn, and pink light showed faintly in the east. I sent a query to Avra.

"He has gone," the mare sent perplexedly. "I could not find your mind. The funaga ran away."

"Why did he leave?" I asked.

"I saw nothing. There was nothing," she sent.

Bewildered, I lifted my torch and climbed out, wondering what could have frightened Reuvan badly enough that he would desert us.

I opened my mouth to call down the steps, but the words died in my throat.

Fear had seized me.

My heart pounded and the night was suddenly ice-cold as I watched the air before me shimmer and smoke in a way that could not be natural. The smoke coalesced into a spectral face so grotesque and malevolent that only some Herder hell could have spawned it. Almost reptilian, it watched me from the end of the alley, a shadowed creature of roiling smoke and razor-sharp teeth.

Terror flooded my mind; the lantern slid from my nerveless fingers. I screamed then, barely registering the footsteps coming up the metal steps behind me. I heard Kella cry out before I saw her, falling at my feet in a dead faint. That shook me enough to break my trance. I dashed the books from Pavo's arms and half dragged him and Jik out of the doorway. They stared at the specter in astonished wonder.

"Ghosts . . ." Pavo moaned.

I grasped his shoulders and shook him to make him help me lift Kella, all the while keeping an eye on the creature. It did not advance but opened its mouth menacingly. Then there was a savage growling, but not from the monster—it came from the far side of the mound of rubble and was followed by a high-pitched scream.

Then, just as abruptly as it had appeared, the smoky demon vanished.

"What just happened?" Pavo asked.

Jik looked at me, his face transformed. "That growling. It was Darga!"

I thought fear had deranged him, but there was barking nearby, and this time I recognized it. I sent out a probe and immediately encountered Darga.

"There you are," he sent imperturbably. "Come to me."

Startled, I told the others to wait inside and picked my way over the rubble, tracing his probe to what remained of a building fronting the alley. It was little more than four walls, and in one corner a growling Darga held a thin, ragged figure at bay.

I was beside him before I realized it was a girl cowed against the wall, her skin as black as if she had rolled in the mud. To my bewilderment, she hissed and bared her teeth at the sight of me.

All at once, fear assaulted me.

Darga growled again, and the fear vanished.

I stared at the girl in wonder. "*She's* doing it!"

"I learned from a dog that you had left the city. I followed your scent," Darga sent. "Then I saw the child-funaga's mind making you see things. I frightened her enough to break her grip on your mind. She does not know how to speak to my mind, so she cannot make me afraid."

The urchin snarled at me, pressing herself deeper into the corner.

"She is like a wild wolf pup," Darga sent.

I looked at the girl. "Well," I said aloud in a gentle voice, "if you are wild, then I will have to tame you." I backed away, telling Darga to follow. The girl suspiciously watched us withdraw, then ran forward and slithered through a hole in the wall, swift as a snake.

I reached out but could find no trace of her mind.

There was a joyous reunion between Jik and Darga. The others were astonished and relieved that the demon we had seen was no more than a vision. Pavo suggested returning to the library, but I decided we had better find Reuvan, Brydda, and Idris.

"It's been a long night. And we have plenty of time to go through the books. We'll have to stay until I can tame our wild girl."

We found Reuvan unconscious, having run into a jutting piece of stone in the darkness, then returned to Brydda. He was fascinated to hear the truth about his ghosts and, though still wary, agreed to cross into the city. But he was skeptical about my intention to tame the girl.

I shook my head wearily. "I can't give up. I have to win her trust."

"Why?" Brydda asked. "What does it matter?"

I looked at him. "Don't you understand? *She* is the one I came all this way to find. She's one of us. And I have a feeling she needs us as much as we need her."

✦ 19 ✦

WE CALLED HER Dragon, after the picture I had seen in the library.

We had set up a comfortable camp inside the roofless shell of a building with a clear view of Aborium and the surrounding plains. Each night, I set food out, hoping to make her understand that I meant no harm. But though the food had been gone each morning, we did not catch sight of her. Sometimes I sensed her watching us but could not reach her. After a few initial attempts to instill her particular brand of fear into one or another of us, and being fended off by me, she had given up trying to frighten us away.

The third night fell, and I was silent and preoccupied with thoughts of the ragged urchin girl. Kella was trying to force Pavo to set his notes aside and eat. Finally, losing her temper, she shouted at him.

"If you don't eat, you'll be dead before you have the chance to get your precious books out of their hole in the ground!"

She broke off, looking horrified at herself. But Pavo burst out laughing. "Kella, what would I do without you? All right; you win."

We all laughed at the martyred expression he gave the flushed healer.

"No luck with the girl?" Pavo asked me over night-meal. "Have you given thought to what sort of powers she has?" Pavo said.

I frowned. "Empathy and coercing, though I have never encountered that combination."

Kella gave me a quick look. "It's more than coercing. Domick can't make things appear in the air."

I shook my head. "The creature she conjured looks so like the ones on the map. I think she took the image from my unconscious and somehow projected it into all our minds."

Brydda yawned. "Whatever she does, it's kept the soldierguards from looking for us here. And I saw no patrols out on the plains today. I think they have moved the search to Half Moon Bay or Morganna. I doubt they will bother with Murmroth or Port Oran, given the distances involved. As soon as you've finished with the books, we can leave."

Pavo nodded absently. "I feel as if I could never be finished, but I'll have as much as we can safely carry by tomorrow."

No one looked at me, but I knew they were thinking of Dragon.

Time was running out, yet I seemed no closer to reaching the girl than when I had begun. I went out with a pot of stew and sat down to wait, determined to make some sort of contact. Hours passed, and I was beginning to drift off to sleep when I heard a faint sound.

Snapping wide awake, I sensed her trying to drive me off. Frustrated and baffled, she paced outside the light like a hungry, wild cat.

"Hello?" I called softly. The wind hissed in scorn,

but there was no answer. I took up the pot of stew and held it out.

Still no answer, but instinct told me she was watching. I sighed, feeling suddenly defeated.

Then I heard a movement, and she was there, the half-moon shedding a wan light on her grubby face. I was careful not to make any sudden movements as she crept forward, never taking her eyes from me. She reached out abruptly and snatched the pot from my hands, turned, and ran into the night.

I sighed heavily and went back to the campfire. Reuvan sought to comfort me, saying he thought sheer curiosity would make Dragon follow us when we left. That and our food offerings. I was not so certain, but we had no more time to spare.

That night, we left the city after concealing the entrance to the library under rubble. If Dragon did follow, the city would have lost its guardian, and we did not want the books and all their secrets to fall into the hands of the Herder Faction.

There was no sign of Dragon as we left, but I sensed her eyes watching us from some dark corner of her lonely city.

I sent out a broadspan beckoning call, but there was no response.

Brydda had said that we ought to reach the sparse, distorted trees of the fringes before the moon rose, if we did not stop, for once again we were not able to move at more than a plodding walk. I asked what he would do if we could safely cross the Suggredoon.

"To begin with, I will ride to Rangorn to see my

parents. Then I will return to Sutrium and join the group of rebels working against the Council there. I have already been in contact with their leader," Brydda said.

Pavo, Jik, Kella, and I traveled in the cart with the books, and the others rode. Brydda had become adept at communicating with the horses through gestures and spent more time conversing with them than with his human companions. Pavo looked pale and ill, the energy of the last days having deserted him as soon as we left the city. He lay back against his precious books and slept.

Huge flies plagued us by day, and the unseasonable heat made me long for the cool of the mountains. I consoled myself by thinking the weather was good for my feet, which had begun to heal again.

I felt weary when we stopped at dusk the second day. The others talked and sparred while setting up the camp and nightmeal, but I could not help thinking of Dragon and wondering if she would go on as she had before our departure. I had given up hope of her following us and wondered if Maryon's prediction meant that all aims of the expedition had to be achieved to avoid whatever disaster she foresaw. If so, then everything we had done was for nothing, because I had failed to bring the Talent back to Obernewtyn.

Remembering how Dragon had cowered back against the wall, I was filled with self-reproach for my failure to reach her. I ought to have tried harder. Under all the dirt and savagery, she was little more than a child. Depressed, I went to bathe in a stream after summoning Darga to assure me that it had not flowed from

Blacklands. The air had a misty mauve tone, and in the west, streaks of dusky sunset ran across the horizon.

Darga's mind broke abruptly into my thoughts. "She follows."

My heart leapt, understanding instantly whom he meant. "Where?"

"Behind the trees," he sent.

I forced myself to walk naturally to the stream. Darga sniffed the water and pronounced it clean. Stretching himself out on the bank, he pretended to sleep. I stripped off my clothes and slid into the icy water with a gasp of delight. Rubbing sand against my grubby skin, I reveled in the coolness, but only half of me was enjoying the bath. The other half was searching for the slightest evidence of Dragon's presence. I was forced to concede that without Darga, I would never have known she was there.

I took up a handful of sand and rubbed it against my scalp until the tangled mass of my hair felt clean, then I ducked under to wash it out. Floating beneath the surface and holding my breath, I opened my eyes and looked up.

To my astonishment, Dragon was leaning over the stream, staring with openmouthed terror into the water. Gasping and spluttering, I bobbed to the surface. She sprang back, and gently I fended off the waves of fright she was generating. I reached for her mind but again was unable to penetrate her shield.

"It's all right," I said softly, realizing she thought I had been drowning. "I'm Elspeth," I said slowly, extending a dripping hand.

She cringed away.

"She fears water," Darga sent.

Dragon looked at him uneasily, though he had not stirred. I gathered up my towel and dried slowly.

I looked up to find her looking at my naked limbs with a hint of bafflement. I stood very still as she reached out one blackened finger and touched my pale belly. Her finger left a dirty smear, and she stared at it, frowning.

Very slowly, I reached out a wet finger and touched her bare stomach. A rag twisted around her body exposed most of her skin, but rag and skin were indistinguishable, merged together in uniform grime. She suffered my touch, then looked amazed at the clean streak my finger had made. She gazed from the dirty mark on my stomach to the white mark on her own flesh, as if our skins had rubbed off on one another.

"Elspeth," I said, pointing to myself. I bent down to put my clothes on. My trousers were worn to shreds, but Kella had given me an old skirt and underskirt to put on.

I saw Dragon's eyes flicker toward the blue underskirt, and impulsively, I held it out to her. Eyes shining, she reached out, then froze, mistrust clouding her expression. I did not move, and finally, she reached out and grasped the underskirt, folding it into her arms and stroking it as if it were an animal. I went on dressing, pulling on Kella's knitted stockings, my shoes, and a cloak.

"Esspess?" she said suddenly in a rusty whisper.

I gaped, for I had begun to suspect she was mute. I had even thought this might be why she had been abandoned.

I pointed to myself. "Elspeth," I said distinctly. "Elspeth."

Then I pointed to her.

"Elspess," she said obligingly. I grinned, wondering if my name was the only word she would say. I pointed to myself again. "Els-peth." I pointed to her. "Dragon . . . Dra-gon." Later, when she could talk, she could choose a more suitable name.

She frowned. "Drang-om."

I nodded. She pointed to me. "Elspess." She pointed to herself. "Drangon."

"Close enough," I said. "Food?" I asked, rising slowly. Alarm flared in her eyes. I mimicked eating, and hunger replaced her fright.

Summoning Darga and warning him to move slowly, we made our way back to the camp. Whenever Dragon stopped, I would mimic eating. I sent a probe to Jik, telling him to warn the others not to do anything to frighten her.

Approaching the light of the fire that glimmered through the trees, Dragon hesitated. I had to coax her the last few steps with exaggerated mimicry of how delicious the food would be. When we were close enough to smell Kella's stew, she sniffed at the savory odor like a hungry animal. The others were sitting very still around the fire, fascinated, for this was the first time they had seen her. To my surprise, she barely looked at them. Her eyes darted about hungrily. Kella had set a pot to the side, and I took this up and held it out to Dragon.

The firelight showed her as an emaciated scarecrow with a mop of filthy hair, clutching the blue underskirt to her chest.

Taking the pot, she squatted unceremoniously and plunged her filthy fingers directly into it, scooping the stew to her mouth with ravenous dexterity.

Kella grimaced and softly wondered aloud whether she had not already poisoned herself with dirt. I was filled with compassion rather than revulsion. I had never imagined that the Talent I had come so far to find would be a half-wild savage who could barely speak. I had imagined a calm discussion ending in an offer of a refuge.

No one spoke while she ate with much lip smacking and slurping, and when she was finished, she licked out the pot, sighed gustily, and sat back on her haunches.

"Well," Kella said faintly. Dragon's lambent eyes turned to her.

"Meet Dragon, our newest recruit," I said with a broad smile.

For the rest of the night, Dragon sat close by my feet, listening to our talk as if to exotic music. She had the disconcerting habit of staring fixedly at first one, then another of us, as if she were trying to memorize our faces. She would not allow any of the others to come near her but eventually fell asleep against my knees.

The next morning we crossed the Suggredoon at dawn. I had expected it to be difficult, but the hardest part was persuading Dragon to hide with Brydda under his enveloping cloak in back of the cart. Jik, Idris, and Reuvan rode the horses, and Kella and I led Avra aboard the ferry. It took only a few coercive pushes to ensure that our papers and the cart were given the most cursory inspection before the soldierguard turned to the few other passengers. I had found a description of myself and Jik in the soldierguards' minds, as well as a far clearer picture of Brydda, but a coercive push ensured that we did not fit any of those descriptions. Once we had left the ferry on the other side, we took a rutted path straight up the banks of the Suggredoon, which Brydda said would bring us right to the ford. But the road was full of potholes and great stones, so the cart fairly crawled along. Even when the rest of us got out and walked, Avra could not move much more swiftly. Pavo alone remained in the cart, though its jolting must have hurt his poor, weary body.

Brydda grew more silent as the day wore on and seemed increasingly preoccupied. Finally, I asked him if anything was wrong.

"I don't know," he said. "I feel uneasy about my parents. And we're moving so slowly." He looked down at Dragon with mingled pity and frustration.

"Why don't you go ahead?" I suggested. "We can't be more than a few hours away at a fast gallop."

Brydda bit his lip and looked thoughtful. "I think I will. Reuvan can come with me." Thinking of his "knack," I worried that his fears could be well founded.

The triumphant mood of the day occasioned by Dragon's presence evaporated with Brydda's departure. He told us to wait at the ford until he returned to tell us the way was clear. He refused to say what he was afraid of, but his elaborate precautions only served to heighten my apprehension.

As if to mirror my thoughts, a heavy, dark bank of cloud looming on the horizon billowed in to veil the sun near the end of the day, and we reached the ford just as a light rain began to fall.

There was no sign of Brydda or Reuvan, so we decided to make camp behind a copse of trees within sight of the ford. It proved nearly impossible to light a fire with the damp wood, but finally we managed and sat around it shivering in the chilly wind. No one felt like talking. Pavo was nearly blue and shivered constantly, but Kella said these were also symptoms of advanced rotting sickness.

Dragon had reacted to the sight of the Suggredoon with real terror, and it had taken all my strength to reassure her. I was afraid she would run off and be lost. Her reaction to the river and to my submersion seemed to indicate something connected with water had happened to her, but I could not penetrate her mind, and she was unable to explain, only clutching at me in mute plea. In the end, I found myself patting her as I would pet Maruman.

"At least she doesn't stink," Jik said earnestly when I wondered aloud to Kella what might have caused her fear of water. We laughed, but oddly this was true. Dragon smelled like rich, dark dirt after rain. She had not used her remarkable illusory powers since joining us. I hoped she would not tame to the extent of forgetting them altogether.

All at once I heard the drumming of hooves in the distance.

We all stood, the underlying fears that had gnawed at us since Brydda's departure showing clearly in our faces. There was one rider, coming fast. Idris gave a shout of joy as he recognized Brydda's horse, then he fell silent, seeing the rider was Grufyyd, whose face he did not know.

Reining the horse in, Grufyyd dismounted. He looked pale and there were dark shadows in his eyes. After a brief greeting, he urged us to pack up quickly and come with him to the cottage.

The serious note in his voice warned us something was badly wrong.

"Brydda?" Idris began worriedly.

"My lad is fine," he said, then once again urged us to make haste.

Not until we were approaching the great forest of trees at the foot of the mountains did he say, "Soldierguards have been to Rangorn. It was fortunate that ye dinna come sooner, else they would have taken us all."

"They were looking for Brydda?" I asked. But Grufyyd shook his head.

"They said they were looking for seditioners. A small group of young gypsies," he added significantly.

I stared. "But why? How? No one from the Council knew we even existed, and the disguise was all but washed away before we left here."

"Henry Druid an' his folks kenned ye were about," said Grufyyd.

"But how could he . . . ?" I stopped, thinking hard. "They said in the encampment that he has a friend in the Council. Someone influential who sends him all sorts of expensive delicacies. Maybe the Druid told his friend about us." I chewed my lip. "But why go to so much trouble over a few gypsies?"

"Perhaps he no longer believes ye were just gypsies," Grufyyd said. "One of the soldierguards said the gypsy attire might be a disguise and that the seditioners were more dangerous than most."

Uneasily, I remembered that I had been forced to reveal my power in the escape. The gatewarden would have woken with a strange tale of the gypsy girl who had rendered him unconscious with her touch. It had been wishful thinking on my part to assume his testimony would be dismissed as ravings or excuses.

Katlyn met us at the door of the cottage with smiles and talk of a hot meal and warm beds. Despite everything, it was a happy reunion but for Pavo's obvious deterioration.

Wrapped in a blanket and shivering from a chill no fire could abate, he was clearly in great pain. His neck and arms were now covered in bruises, a symptom of tissue degeneration. The slightest bump left a livid mark on his skin. Katlyn did her best for him, feeding him decoctions to numb the pain, but they were only temporary measures. Pavo was dying.

"He is content," Darga sent from where he lay on the hearth. "He is not afraid to die."

After we had eaten, Katlyn managed to do what we had failed and persuaded Dragon to wash.

Jik, Idris, and Reuvan went off with Grufyyd to organize sleeping quarters in the barn, and Kella went to sort out blankets.

I was glad to find myself alone with Brydda, having had no chance to question him about the soldierguards. His first words took my breath away. "I don't suppose you come from Obernewtyn?"

I gaped at him.

He nodded. "It was a thought I had earlier, for I guessed you weren't quite telling the truth when you said you came from the highlands. Then my father said one of the soldierguards had asked about Obernewtyn and everything came together. I had heard the place was near destroyed by a firestorm."

"A lie to keep people away," I admitted. "But useless now."

"I don't think they knew anything for sure."

"They couldn't have managed to connect us and Obernewtyn at all, unless the Druid . . . this confirms he's part of this. We already feared that the Council had been questioning what Rushton was up to. But the Druid is the only one who could have informed them about our disguises." I blanched. "And if he *has* guessed we are not real gypsies, he would question all that I told him about Obernewtyn being in shambles. I must warn Rushton."

Brydda nodded. "It might be safer for your friends to leave Obernewtyn before any investigation. I would be happy to have your people join me. I am sure Bodera will be glad to have you join his rebels."

"Rushton will have to decide that," I said. "He is our leader."

Idris opened the door and asked Brydda to help shift the books from the cart into the shed, because it had begun to rain again. Left alone except for Pavo, I forced myself to accept that he would not survive the journey back.

His eyes fluttered open, and he saw the pity in my face. "Don't be sad for me, Elspeth." His voice was barely audible. "I have lived free in a world where freedom is rare. I have pursued work that I love. I have learned much, and I have had good friends and perilous adventures. What man who lives three times my span can say as much?"

I blinked hard and found I could say nothing without crying. I was glad when everyone trooped back in, laughing and talking. Kella called out that she was warming some fement. This prompted Brydda to sing a rollicking song about a drunken seaman. In the midst of uproarious laughter, the door opened and Katlyn entered with a stranger.

The room fell into an astounded silence. The unknown girl was slender as a willow wand, with creamy pale skin and a thick silken mop of flame-colored curls.

Slowly, it dawned on us who we were looking at.

It was Dragon.

"I don't believe it!" Jik gasped.

I was stunned. Who would have suspected what lay under the dirt? Even clad in a rough hessian shift dress, she was extraordinarily beautiful. And such hair! I had never seen hair that color—like gold and flames entwined. Later, Katlyn told me it had broken her heart to cut it, but it had been so matted and fused with dirt that she'd had no choice.

Dragon's eyes, blue as the summer sky, flickered round uneasily.

"Don't stare at her. She doesn't understand," I said softly.

Though unable to stop looking, the others sank into more natural poses. Beaming with pleasure, Katlyn ushered Dragon around to my side. Reaching out, I tugged at one springing fiery curl.

Dragon took the strand of her hair and pulled it round to her eyes, then she let it loose. She lifted the shift to show the blue underskirt I had given her.

Reuvan burst out laughing. She looked up at him, startled, and bared her teeth. That broke the spell woven by her dramatic transformation. "She may be a girl," Reuvan said, "but she is still dragon-natured and had better keep her name as a warning to anyone who might think otherwise."

Brydda patted his mother's shoulder. "Well, I always knew you were a witch."

Even Pavo smiled at this absurdity.

Over steaming mugs of fement, we talked of ways and means to reach our various destinations. I told Katlyn and Grufyyd the whole story of Obernewtyn, deciding it was better to take them fully into our confidence. If Obernewtyn was under investigation, we would have to leave it anyway. And if not, I had an idea that Katlyn and Grufyyd might be glad of a reason to return to the highlands. The trouble was that the chance of reaching Obernewtyn before the mountain pass froze was dwindling.

"If only the Olden pass had not been poisonous, we might have gone that way and cut off days of traveling time," I sighed.

"Poisonous . . . ?" Brydda began.

Suddenly Darga growled, and Dragon jumped to her feet.

"What is it?" I said, but Brydda hissed. In the silence, we could hear a horse galloping toward the house.

I farsensed the rider and breathed a sigh of relief. "It's Domick," I told the others. There were steps on the porch, and the door was flung open.

"You are here!" cried Kella, leaping up to embrace him.

"Thank Lud you're here," he said, keeping Kella close in his arms. "You must leave tonight, all of you."

"What is it?" Brydda asked sharply, rising to tower over the coercer. Domick's face changed as he noticed Idris, Reuvan, and Dragon.

"It's all right, Domick. They're with us," I said quickly. "They know about Obernewtyn, about everything."

The coercer looked less disapproving than I expected. He glanced at Brydda speculatively. "I guess you must be Brydda Llewellyn, better known as the notorious Black Dog. It is good to meet a man whose name I have heard so many times as one who ferociously opposes the Council."

Brydda met this with a curious look. Domick sighed. "It's a long story, but I'll give you the meat of it."

He threw off his dripping oiled coat. "I first heard the name of Brydda Llewellyn here, but I heard it again before I had even reached Sutrium. Soldierguards were watching the ferry, looking for you. I overheard them saying Brydda Llewellyn's network of seditioners had been exposed, and he was on the run. I wanted to come after you, Elspeth, to warn you, but I knew I couldn't get to you before you reached Aborium." An expression of suppressed agony crossed his face, and I realized what a struggle it had been for him to proceed with his mission.

"The first thing I noticed about Sutrium was the number of Herders about. They seemed to outnumber Councilmen, and there was a definite feeling of fear whenever they were around.

"I mingled with people wherever there were crowds. I had the feeling I was safer that way. I let people understand I was a trading jack whose cart had been burned in a firestorm. That explained my ignorance about customs lowlanders take for granted. And it let me ask questions as I sought work to amass coin enough to replace my cart and tools. I knew I had to get close to the Council, but I couldn't think how.

"Then one night in a drink hall, I overheard two men talking to a third man who was to take up a job at the Councilcourt. They were laughing and warning their friend that his new job was dangerous. The third man was beside himself with fear by the time the other two left. I struck up a conversation with him by offering him a mug and learned that he had come from the highlands to work in Sutrium. He had been recommended by a Herder, and though he neither wanted nor liked the idea of going to Sutrium, he dared not refuse. In the end, I managed to persuade him to let me take the job." Domick flicked a look at me, which told me what sort of persuasion he had used. "I turned up in his place and was accepted at once, since they were expecting someone from the high country.

"At first I heard nothing useful. It was a menial job, and I began to think I would have been better off applying to be a soldierguard. Then I realized I could not have found a better way to spy on the Councilmen. Once my face was familiar, it was as if I were nothing more than a broom or a mop, and they talked quite freely in front of me.

"I heard them talk of a sweeping investigation of the highlands planned for next year, after the first thaw, to flush out traitors and seditioners. I heard enough to make me certain the Council knows the Druid is alive. I also heard much talk about the Black Dog and his efforts to undermine authority and plunge the Land back into chaos. They think of you as a terrible threat, Brydda, and hunger to get hold of you. They were expecting word of your capture from Aborium. My guess is that news has come by now but that it was bad news." He grinned at Brydda.

Domick paused to drink thirstily from a mug Katlyn had given him.

"What about the Druid's friend? Did you learn who he is?" Kella asked.

Domick looked grim. "Almost from the start, I heard talk of a special agent who worked for both the Herder Faction and the Council, getting information to help expose seditioners. He had masterminded the capture of the man who betrayed your network, Brydda. And he forced him to talk when he refused to betray you. The agent was said to be brilliant and completely ruthless."

"Then you heard no talk of Obernewtyn?" I asked.

Domick shook his head. "I had heard no mention of Obernewtyn—until two days ago. I overheard a conversation between two Councilmen about this special agent and his certainty that something was going on at Obernewtyn. One Councilman said he didn't think there was anything in it, and the other reminded him that the agent had seldom led them wrong. I became certain then that this special agent and the Druid's friend were the same person."

"That sounds right to me," I said. "The Druid befriended Rushton at one point, and maybe his agent resented this. It may be why he decided to play Druid for a fool."

But Domick frowned. "That's what I thought, because what other reason would this agent have for wanting Obernewtyn investigated?" He looked so stern, I felt suddenly frightened of what he was about to say.

"I never saw the agent," he went on slowly. "Though I often heard him spoken of, there was never any mention of his name. But I was curious. Someone told me he came only at night to make reports, so I managed to get myself assigned to night duty.

"I was able to catch glimpses of him, but he always wore a hooded cloak that concealed his face. When I heard him talk, I had the strangest feeling I had heard his voice somewhere before. That made me more determined than ever to see what he looked like. Last night, I hid in a cupboard in the meeting room. I watched him through a crack in the door, but he kept his hood on the entire time he talked. I could not see his face, but I could hear him clearly.

"He told the Council he had been torturing more suspected seditioners in Aborium. Most knew nothing, but one seemed to think Brydda had family in Rangorn. A mother and father. Apparently, the poor man had only overheard that, because everyone else believed Brydda an escaped orphan. The agent said soldier-guards had been in the area recently, and their report showed only one couple fitting the description. He wanted Council permission to bring them in for inter-rogation.

"The Council voted to send a troop of guards to Rangorn. They are on their way here now."

Brydda's face was pale and tense. "I did not think anyone knew. I was too careless."

I said nothing. Something in Domick's manner warned me the story was not finished.

"I was desperate to get away to warn you, but I had to wait until the room was empty. At last the meeting ended, and all the Councilmen left but this agent. Only then did he take off his hood, and I saw his face."

"You . . . you recognized him?" Kella guessed.

Domick nodded.

"Ariel," he said. "It was Ariel."

PART III

THE KEN

· 20 ·

WITH SOLDIERGUARDS ON their way, it was too risky to proceed as planned. We decided to hide at the foot of the mountains until the danger was past. No one would guess we would deliberately trap ourselves in a cul-de-sac.

"The soldierguards aren't subtle enough to suspect we would do anything other than the obvious," Brydda said. "When they don't find us here, they'll think we have escaped by going around Glenelg Mor, because that's what they would do in our place."

Brydda knew of an area at the foot of Tor where we could make a safe camp, a narrow valley running into the foot of the hills and concealed by a thick copse of trees. From the other side, no one would suspect the trees continued for just a few steps before reaching the steep mountainside. Brydda had played there as a boy and remembered it well despite his long absence.

We had spent precious time packing Katlyn's invaluable store of dried herbs. Almost everything else had to be left behind, and tears coursed down her face as Brydda threw a flaming torch on the roof of the cottage.

"It is only stone and mud and straw, I know, but all the memories of happy years are in those walls, and now they burn," she sobbed.

Jolting through the darkness and chilled by a damp, blustery wind, I thought bitterly of Domick's news. Obernewtyn was in danger. With Ariel to force the pace, I had no doubt the soldierguards would appear in spring, immediately after the thaw. Ariel, of all people, would know that Obernewtyn was at its most vulnerable then. If we failed to get back in time to warn Rushton, they would be completely unprepared, defenseless against an onslaught of soldierguards.

But it was a matter of days before the pass would be snowed shut. Domick must have known when he came to us that he was losing the last chance of warning Obernewtyn. But if he had not delayed and ridden to warn us, the soldierguards would have taken us all.

I could not imagine how Ariel had survived or what course had brought him to the Council, but I had no doubt that his primary motive was to revenge himself on Obernewtyn and Rushton.

He could not know for sure that the firestorm story had been a lie, but he might have guessed it was a ruse to keep the Council away from Obernewtyn, for he knew that Rushton had befriended me. But how had Ariel inveigled himself with Henry Druid and then the Council? The most obvious likelihood was that he had stumbled into the Druid's men in the White Valley, and he had somehow won the old man's trust. But how had he reached Sutrium from the highlands, and how he had gained the Council's trust?

It did not take us long to reach Brydda's hiding spot. It was as good as he had led us to believe. We could even see the cottage burning in the distance, while we were invisible behind a thick girdle of eben trees. Brydda bade Kella, Jik, and his mother to organize supper in order to occupy the older woman's mind. He asked me to walk with him to collect firewood, leading the way purposefully through the trees. The ground sloped up steeply, offering a sweeping view of the area.

"This is a sight I remember well," Brydda said softly. Over the treetops, I could see the dense darkness of the Blacklands in the moonlight like a shadowy stain across the Land.

Pavo had once said the Blacklands would recede in time, but I could not imagine anything growing on the black, stinking soil. I shuddered, and for a moment, it seemed to me Ariel and the Blacklands were symptoms of the same evil.

Beyond the hills was the silvery rush of the Suggredoon and the huddled village of Rangorn. I could even see the mists that hung above Glenelg Mor. Behind me were the towering bulks of Aran Craggie and Tor. So many ways to go, and none fast enough to get us to Obernewtyn in time.

The wind in the treetops sounded like the whispering ebb and flow of the sea. Brydda stirred as if the same wind had blown through him, ruffling his thoughts like so many leaves. I bent to pick up a stick for kindling, but Brydda touched my arm and drew me aside.

"I want to talk to you alone," he said in a low, serious voice. "I think you should consider coming back to Sutrium with me, all of you, and especially Domick. Very few people have managed to work their way into such a position as he has attained on the Council. He will be valuable to both our causes." He nodded toward Pavo. "He is certainly not up to a hard, long trip to the high mountains. And he needs Kella with him. I can organize a safe journey for you all to Obernewtyn after winter."

I shook my head. "It would be too dangerous to have Jik in Sutrium after what happened in Aborium. Especially if there are as many Herder priests about as Domick said. And Dragon could not be confronted with a city. I would be grateful if you would take Kella and Pavo for the time. But one of us must try to reach Obernewtyn before the pass freezes. I will go and take Dragon and Jik with me."

"Why can't you speak to this Rushton with your mind?" Brydda asked.

"The mountains between the high country and Obernewtyn are badly tainted and thick enough besides to form a barrier that my mind cannot broach," I explained.

"But is it wise or sensible for *you* to go, Elspeth? What about your feet?" Brydda protested.

"My feet will take me where I need to go, and I am better equipped to deal with trouble than any of the others."

To my surprise, Brydda grinned. "If you are so determined, I might have a way to shorten your road back to Obernewtyn. Let's get some wood and go back to camp. I have an idea I want to put to you all."

It was after midnight by the time we had eaten and Brydda laid his plan out. Pavo, Kella, and Domick were to go to Sutrium under Brydda's protection. In exchange for shelter and the setting up of the safe house Rushton wanted, Domick would share all he learned with Brydda, unless the coercer believed it would jeopardize Obernewtyn. "Elspeth, Dragon, Darga, and Jik will travel to the highlands, through the Olden way, and go straight across the White Valley to the mountain pass, being careful to avoid the Druid's encampment," Brydda said.

"The Olden way is poisonous," Domick objected.

In answer, Brydda pointed to Darga. "I grew up in his district, and I know of this pass. It is badly tainted in some parts, but there are parts that are tainted so little as to be harmless. And that is where Darga comes in. I have seen with my own eyes that he can tell poisoned substances from clean ones. Therefore, he will be your guide. Only you have to go on foot. The Older way is passable only on foot."

"If you are right about this pass, it is a good plan, and it may be our only opportunity to reach Obernewtyn in time to warn Rushton before snow closes the pass."

"I'll go," Domick said.

I shook my head. "You have an important job to do. Find out as much as you can of the Council's intentions, but keep out of Ariel's way. If you remember him, you can be sure he'll remember you."

"What about the Druid?" Kella asked.

I grinned. "We know that the settlement is some distance away from the encampment. I will farsense to make sure we do not encounter anyone. And if we find our way blocked, I'll have Dragon frighten anyone away."

The others laughed, including Dragon, who, though she did not understand what we were saying, seemed to find laughter itself funny.

"Rushton will never forgive me for letting you go into danger," Domick groaned.

Ignoring this, I suggested we set off at first light.

Brydda would take us to the start of the Olden way and then he would return to the others and wait until the soldierguards had searched Katlyn and Grufyyd's farmstead before going to Sutrium. Brydda gave me careful instructions about how to contact him in Sutrium, and then we parted in the cold, gray light of the very early morning. It was painful to say goodbye to Pavo, knowing it might be the last time I would see him. I could not hug him, because any sort of pressure was unbearable for him. He was delirious most of the time now, and he blinked at me in a puzzled way, as if his memory were disintegrating.

"He is content," Brydda said gently when we had left the camp behind.

"That's what Darga said. But I'm not content. What a world this is that someone like Pavo has to die so young," I said.

"People will always be dying too young, whether in the Beforetime or now. That is the way of the world."

It took less than an hour to reach the fall of rocks that Brydda said concealed the opening to the Olden way. My feet were already hurting, though we had traveled at an easy pace.

Before leaving Brydda hugged us all tightly. Dragon who liked the big man, cried unself-consciously. Darga wagged his tail slowly. Last of all, Brydda looked at me seriously. "Be careful, little sad eyes; your trials are not yet over. But I expect to see you in the spring."

After he had gone, I straightened myself, determinedly throwing off a wave of depression. I took a deep breath and started to climb, instructing Jik and Dragon to stay close behind Darga. Once we reached the top of the rockfall, I was disheartened to realize we would have to climb down the other side before we could begin the ascent to the pass entrance.

It took us a considerable time to get down to the opening, and we were all dirty, grazed, and exhausted before we reached the narrow slit in the rock, which would barely fit a full-grown man. Thick vines had grown across it like a net, and some sort of spider had made a web in them. It was years since Brydda had last gone there, and I suspected nothing had passed that way since, for the webs were intricate and many layered, and covered in thick dust.

Dragon would not go through until she was certain none of the cobwebby tendrils would touch her.

It was late in the morning when we finally stood inside the Olden way. Darga sniffed, saying he scented no poisons in the vicinity.

Dry reedy grasses made a papery, whispering noise as we made our way up the incline. It was not as steep as the rockfall, but my feet ached with the strain of digging in for purchase. The trees growing in that early section were stunted, with spiky grayish leaves and stonelike buds, but ahead we could see a dark-green belt of trees. On either side of us, the mountains soared straight up, pitted gray walls.

It was an arduous climb to the tree line, and we were all puffing by the time we reached it. I was disappointed to find the ground did not level out—the trees had only given that illusion. It was darker beneath the canopy of entwined branches and leaves, and an eerie silence reigned that reminded me of the Silent Vale, where I had gone to collect whitestick as an orphan.

Jik worked to teach Dragon to say his name as we walked. I listened with only half an ear, preoccupied by a sudden feeling of unease. When we came out of th trees, I noticed the sky had darkened.

After a short distance, the now sparse trees gav way to a high, thick kind of bramble running before u in a solid barrier. It offered no natural paths and wa filled with stinging thorns. That meant we had to us knives to hack our way through. The severed branc ends leaked a defensive odor that made our eyes sting

It took more than an hour to bypass the brambles. O the other side was a narrow, very deep gorge cutting di rectly across our path; at the bottom ran a tumultuou course of water. The stream and the gorge appeared t run all the way from Tor to Aran Craggie. I thought i quite likely the stream was a tributary of the Suggredoor escaping through some crack from inside the mountair It was too wide to jump; the only way to cross was to de scend into the trench and swim the stream.

We wasted another hour trying to find a less stee descent but, in the end, returned to the original spot t climb down. The stream was overhung with a thick trailing fringe of creepers and vines, but the bank o both sides proved treacherously soft. I stared into th water, glumly wondering how we would manage t get across safely. Up close, the water ran very fast, an Dragon eyed it fearfully.

"I will swim with a rope in my teeth," Darga sen "On the other side, I will pass the rope around a tre and hold it tight. Jik can cross first since he weighs little then he can tie it."

I looked at the opposite bank doubtfully. "All righ But I'll tie the rope around you and hold the other en so that I can pull you back if you get into trouble."

At first, Darga disappeared completely beneath th

roaring water. But a moment later, he bobbed to the surface and struck out for the other bank. The current was so strong that he had to swim at an angle that made it look as if he were trying to make his way upstream like a salmon. He crept forward, drawing fractionally nearer the opposite bank.

By the time he reached the edge, he was clearly tiring badly, but the ordeal was not over. I watched in consternation as he tried to scale the soft edges of the bank. Time and again the earth gave way, plunging him back into the raging water.

"Pull him back," Jik cried fearfully. "He's drowning!"

"No," Darga sent, his mind an exhausted whisper. The soft banks were deeply gouged before he managed at last to get a firm footing. I could see his body trembling with weariness as he dragged himself over the lip.

"Darga!" Jik shouted through his tears. Darga flapped his tail weakly twice, then lay like one dead for a long time.

When he had recovered, Darga walked around a tree several times and braced himself. I tugged my own end to test the strength of Brydda's rope, then fastened it to a stout tree trunk, pulling the rope taut.

Jik went across hand over hand. The rope creaked and sagged until he hung waist-deep in the water, but it held. He reached the other side safely and gave a triumphant yell before untying the rope from Darga and fastening it around a rock. I had thought I might have to knock Dragon out and somehow pull her across, but watching Jik seemed to have given her confidence. She was pale but surprisingly calm, and when I saw her cross, I realized it was because she had thought of a way to make sure the water did not touch her. She, too, went across hand over hand but with her legs hooked around the rope, too. She had been less frightened of the crossing than of the water itself.

I went last of all, half sorry I could think of no way to untie the rope. It was the only piece we had and might be needed again.

I was further disheartened at our lack of progress. Unless the way became easier, we were wasting valuable time negotiating endless obstacles. Climbing out of the trench was harder than getting down into it, and at the top, I decided it was time to rest and eat.

Jik lit a small fire, and I set a pot of soup to cook over it. While we waited, Jik softly sang a strange song the Herders had taught him about the Blacklands. He had a remarkably sweet voice and at my request sang songs until the food was hot enough to eat.

Renewed, we went on.

Not far ahead were more trees. The bandages on my feet were filthy, and I suspected the wounds were bleeding again, but the pain was less intense.

We trudged the remainder of the day without stopping. The trees proved less dense than they had been in the first belt, and gradually, the slope became slighter and walking less arduous. Darga assured me we were still some distance from the poisoned region, which was close to the other end of the pass. Obernewtyn still seemed far away. I could hardly believe that in a few days we would be home.

I looked up through the trees at the dim, bleary afternoon fading into a smoky twilight, and shivered, glad of the blankets Brydda had insisted we carry. Winter had begun. It struck me that the first falls of snow would have blanketed the higher mountain valleys. Very soon, snow would fall at Obernewtyn, if it had not already. I shivered again and pulled my cloak around my shoulders. The moon had begun to fatten in its cycle and should have lit our way clearly, but though visible, it produced a wan, strained light, and we were forced to set our torches to flame. We halted momentarily at Darga's warning that we were on the verge of badly poisoned ground.

"Can you find a safe way across it?" I asked him.

He sniffed. "I can smell clean ground ahead," he assured me. We both knew it would be safer to wait until daylight to go on, but I had the queer feeling the delays were bringing us close to some disaster.

I looked over to where Jik was continuing his language lessons with the bemused Dragon. "Ready?" I asked.

Jik looked across at me unsmilingly, and for an instant he looked suddenly old and frail, as near to death as Pavo. Then he smiled, and the impression vanished.

We walked single file from then on, Darga leading the way through a stand of giant trees with monstrously gnarled and misshapen trunks and thick, dark roots writhing up out of the ground. I thought I had seen such trees beyond the compound wall in Matthew's vision and hoped it meant we were nearing the other end of the pass.

At the same time, the ground beneath our feet became wet and soft. Our feet made sucking noises that echoed in the silence. The torchlight flickered on dark, odorous puddles of water that seeped into the slightest depression of earth. There seemed no source for the dampness. The light made a bizarre shadow play on the twisted tree trunks, making them look like the faces of ancient men and women. Dragon eyed them doubtfully as we passed.

After a time, the wind rose, and leaves flapped sluggishly, heavy with moisture. We waded through a thick blanket of them, and the smell of the festering layers of leaves below filled the air with a sweet, rotten scent that made us all gag.

Darga sent a constant dialogue of instructions as the way became more fraught with danger, and I began to regret not stopping. He warned against certain plants, trees, and even areas of bare ground, guiding us through the poisonous labyrinth. Without him, we would have been helpless, for there was scant outward sign of the poisons other than the distorted sizes and shapes of the trees and bushes growing all around us.

In the end, the dog called a halt, saying he needed to rest. We went on until he found a patch of ground relatively clean of taint. My feet no longer gave me any trouble, for an ominous numbness had deprived them of all sensation. I felt I could walk over flames without feeling anything. I did not dare undo the bandages, afraid of what the loss of feeling might mean.

We ate the last of our store of perishable foods and sipped at the meager remnant of water. I had wanted to fill the containers along the way, but Darga had pronounced all water in the pass tainted enough to make a person sick. We would have to ration what was left of the water to make sure it would last us out.

I was drifting into a light, troubled sleep when a terrible, savage growling rent the air around us.

• 21 •

THE GROWLING SEEMED to vibrate in the air, even after it had ceased. Nothing stirred in the silence that followed except for a faint breeze tugging at our blankets.

"What was that?" Jik whispered.

I set my mind loose, searching, hampered by the static given off by the poisons. I found nothing. "Do you know what that was?" I asked Darga.

"Some kind of animal," he suggested unhelpfully.

Dragon was crouched near a tree, her eyes wide with fright. I opened my mouth to reassure her, but another of the blood-chilling growls cut off my words. My skin puckered into gooseflesh.

Again the growl faded, but still there was no sign of the creature that had made it. Neither Jik nor Darga were any more successful at locating the mind pattern of the monster. I encountered a number of barely sentient minor patterns, but these were mere flickers of instinct rather than thought.

We gave up and sat around staring uneasily into the darkness around us.

Five more times the eerie sounds shattered the night, and I began to suspect that it was not, as we had all feared, a signal for attack or a hunting cry. Even so, I could not help thinking that a creature who could make such a noise and conceal its mind might be clever enough to hide its intention to attack.

But there was no attack.

Morning found us bleary-eyed and ill rested, for the sounds had seemed to grow nearer and more frequent as the night wore on. In the end, we decided there was more than one of the creatures, or one was circling us. Either prospect made for uneasy slumber.

To our further dismay, we had not been walking long the next day before the giant stand of trees gave way abruptly to a seemingly endless mire reminiscent of the blighted Berryn Mor. Here the few trees that managed to grow in the sodden ground were thin and sickly looking, bereft of leaf and shrouded in a furry gray mold.

The only reassuring thing about the spindly skeletons looming out of the mist was that they told us the water was quite shallow. The ground lay only a few handspans below the surface and, though soft, was firm enough to walk on. Darga went ahead, warning us to step exactly where he did, since there were holes and trenches all through the swamp. He said the water was tainted but only slightly.

Tired and thirsty, we plodded doggedly after Darga. There was no possibility of resting until we reached dry ground. Soaking through my boots and stockings, the swamp water was tepid. An evil-smelling mist hung low over the surface of the water and swirled about our feet as we passed.

We walked in silence, concentrating on keeping our footing and moving as quickly as we could, until Jik ventured a question.

"If I fell in this water or touched one of those poisoned plants, would I die at once or slowly like Pavo?" he asked gravely.

Repressing a flare of anguish at the thought of Pavo, I said, "I don't know. I guess it depends on how potent it is. If it's strong, it could work quickly. But if weak, like in the places we find whitestick, you have to be exposed to it over long periods of time before it does any harm."

He nodded thoughtfully, his brow furrowed. "What is whitestick, anyway?"

I smiled. "Your guess is as good as anyone's. Pavo says it is what was left by whatever caused the Great White, like ash from a fire. Once cleansed, it's used for everything from starting fires to making medicines. But surely you know that much?"

"I heard that the Herders make a kind of gas with it that makes your skin burn," Jik said.

I looked at him curiously. "I've never heard of that."

He shrugged. "It's a secret. I heard them talk of experiments. A man who they tested it on was said to have gone blind from the gas, and then his skin blistered. It was terrible. I think he died."

The thought of whitestick being used for such a purpose disturbed me deeply. But perhaps it was only a story.

"The Herders told us Lud sent the Great White because the Oldtimers were evil. But the Teknoguilders say the Beforetimers made the Great White happen on their own. Why would they do that?"

I smiled at his insatiable curiosity for taboo subjects. "I doubt anyone meant to cause the Great White," I said. "I believe it was a kind of accident. But no one knows for sure. Not even the Herder Faction, even though they think they know everything."

"Did weapons make the Great White happen? Pavo told me some of the Oldtime weapons and poisons might still be hidden someplace, like the skyscrapers under Tor," Jik said seriously.

I forced myself not to react. "It's possible," I said slowly.

"What would happen if someone found that kind of weapon? Someone like Ariel or the Druid? There might be another accident. . . ." His voice trailed off.

"This is a bad place for such talk," I said.

The water bubbled all around us now, issuing clouds of colored gas. I noticed a greenish vapor first and pointed it out to Darga. He told me it was a poisonous gas but too weak to harm us. One virulent yellow gas was dangerous enough for Darga to give a wide berth, while a sickly blue shade made him backtrack hastily.

The region of gases was narrow but seemed to take hours to negotiate. My nerves felt ragged by the time we left the mists behind. Suddenly, right in front of us, a bluish gas coalesced. Jik almost fell over in his effort to back away from it. I sent a quick command, and he steadied himself. "It's Dragon," I said. "She's mimicking the gases." Jik nodded, staring at the apparition unhappily. Noticing his expression, Dragon's triumphant smile faded and the mist vanished.

"Bad?" she asked contritely.

"Good," I said firmly. "Very good."

"More?" Dragon asked eagerly, waving her hands

to indicate that she would make something huge and mysterious and complex.

"Uh . . . maybe later," Jik said sheepishly.

As soon as the sun set, the dim day gave way to a starless night, and the air resounded again with the mysterious growling noises. They sounded much closer, and I could not get over the feeling that we were being stalked, despite another fruitless mind search.

We were all relieved to stand on solid ground, though the darkness kept us from seeing what sort of land lay ahead. I decided we needed a break, having been unable to stop at all while crossing the swamp. We drank the last of our water with a feeling of recklessness. Already light-headed from lack of food, I prayed we were close to the compound.

Lying with my back against a tree, I heard Darga beside me sniffing delicately, tasting the various scents of the night. I could smell nothing but the noxious swamp gases and my own filth. The dog was proving an invaluable member of our company. I wondered if his presence was the real truth that lay behind the vague futuretelling of Jik's importance.

A slight breeze ruffled my hair, and Darga lifted his head. "A storm comes," he sent.

I nodded impatiently. "But can you smell any funaga yet?"

"I smell them," Darga sent, confirming that we were nearing the end of the pass.

I decided we would rest for a time and leave the pass in the very early morning hours. I slept heavily and dreamlessly. I woke only once to the sound of Jik's laughter echoing in the darkness.

He explained that he had been walking around to keep himself warm and alert on his watch, when he had nearly stepped on a small, lumpy-skinned swamp dweller with bulging eyes. Immediately, the frightened creature's neck had blown up to three times its diminutive size, and it had let out the incredible growling rumble that had so mystified us. We had seen dozens of the creatures since leaving the area of bubbling mists, sitting on logs and blinking sleepily at us, but we had not connected the giant noises with such harmless life-forms.

Jik's suggestion that the dreadful calling was a kind of love song made me laugh until my stomach ached. I lay back to sleep finally, with a smile on my face. It was good to laugh. I had been doubly amused to find that Darga took Jik's guess quite seriously. Beasts lacked only one funaga virtue that I regretted, and that was a sense of humor.

"You may call it a lack," Darga broke into my thoughts. "So might I lack a pain in my head." That made me laugh again.

I had intended to stand last watch, but Jik had not woken me, saying he had felt wide awake and thought I might as well sleep while I could.

I stretched, feeling oddly lethargic. I threw the blanket away from me, realizing it was hot. At once, my feet began to ache with a new pain, and my head and neck felt damp. I looked down at my feet uneasily. Standing carefully, I could not stifle a gasp of pain at the hot fire shooting up my legs.

"What is it?" Jik asked.

"Nothing," I said. "My feet have gone to sleep." It was not easy to lie to an empath, but Jik was young and untrained.

I turned away from him to hide the fear in my eyes. The numbness that had enabled me to climb the Olden way had been too good to be true. I forced myself to face something that I had known for a while. My feet had become infected. Fighting off a dull drowsiness, I roused the others, deliberately isolating the awareness of the pain.

This was a dangerous thing to do, and Roland forbade it in all but the most extreme need. Pain suppressed was pain in waiting. Eventually, it had to be endured, and the longer it was allowed to accumulate, the more devastating its final effect. It was possible to suppress minor pain for so long that the accumulation, when released, could stop one's heart. I knew I would pay dearly for my suppression, but if I could suppress it until we reached home, Roland could have the healers siphon off some of the pain.

Resolutely, I went on, refusing to allow myself to think about the consequences if I failed to reach Obernewtyn before the pass was closed.

We had been walking less than an hour when Darga stopped abruptly, his fur bristling. "Funaga. Just ahead," he sent.

I told the others to wait and limped through the trees. Catching sight of a low wall, I had to fight back tears of relief. This was the last obstacle between us and Obernewtyn.

I peered over the wall warily.

Three or four armsmen stood talking near the diggings. The yellow sky cast an ivory light on their faces, turning their flesh a sickly, sallow hue.

On the other side of the clearing, nearest the gate, an armsman was deep in an argument with a white-robed

Druid acolyte. The acolyte looked angry. A few steps away stood another armsman, leaning on his spear and yawning. There was a lot more open space than I remembered from Matthew's vision and no way of passing over it unnoticed without a diversion.

Jik brought Dragon up to the fence just as a low rumble of thunder sounded in the distance. Dragon shuddered from head to toe, pointing at the sky and gibbering fearfully. I patted her arm, realizing she was afraid of the storm. That was all we needed.

I turned to Darga, who was looking up and sniffing the wind.

"We'll have to go straightaway. Dragon's frightened of the storm, and she might not be able to make a vision if she gets any more agitated."

As if to underline my words, lightning flashed directly overhead, and Dragon cowered to the ground, hands over her ears. I had a sudden impression that time was folding back on itself. My general sense of apprehension had increased to the point where it bordered on premonition, but I knew the suppression of pain could confuse the other senses. And Dragon's growing agitation made it imperative we move at once.

I stroked her face gently, and slowly she relaxed. It took some time to make her understand what was needed, but in the end she nodded.

A moment later, the man leaning on his spear gave a muffled shout, and another man actually screamed with such terror that my hair stood on end. Then chaos broke out across the compound. For a moment, there was a hail of cries and panicked shouts. Peering through a crack in the fence, I could see no sign of any apparition and wondered what Dragon had conjured up. I watched until the clearing was deserted, then hissed at the others to run.

Lightning flashed as we thrust aside the barrier of stakes, but no one cried out. I saw a lone man running frantically for the huts; everyone else was already inside.

Lightning flashed with lurid brilliance, and for a second, our shadows ran before us, elongated and sharp edged, merging with the tree line just before us.

We had reached the White Valley!

Thunder crashed again, and this time the air vibrated with its force.

As soon as we reached the trees, I urged the others to run ahead and slowed to a limping walk. There was no more need to run, and I did not want to aggravate the suppression any further. Preoccupied, I failed to notice a rock in the grass and tripped, sprawling on the ground. Hearing my involuntary cry, Dragon turned as if to help me. Then she froze.

I looked up at her, puzzled, and my heart jerked with sickening force. Her face was a grotesque mask of terror. She began to shriek hysterically. I looked over my shoulder to see what she had seen.

Less than fifty spans away ran a wall of fire, and there was no mistaking the greenish tint of the flames or the blue crackle in the air. I had seen it before—the miscolored sky, the dull, bleared light—but I had not recognized it.

A firestorm, and we were out in the open!

✦ 22 ✦

"GET UP AND run, girl, unless you want to die!" cried a voice.

Wrenched violently to my feet, I found myself half dragged, half carried along by a tall, brown-faced youth. Dragon ran ahead of us, wild with terror.

"That way. There are caves," he shouted, pointing. Dragon swerved the way he indicated, disappearing into the trees. The acrid smoke billowed around us, and dimly, I heard the muffled crash of thunder in the distance. A wave of heat flowed over us. I dared not glance over my shoulder to see how near the flames were. All I could think of was the burning of my mother and father. The screams and the dreadful smell.

"Thank Lud!" the youth said harshly as the trees parted to reveal a rough hill of granite knolls.

"Inside, there," he said, thrusting me unceremoniously into a shallow cave in the side of the steep, stony hillock. "This is not deep enough, but there's no time to search further. Pray the wind changes, or we'll fry." He had to shout over the roar of the flames bearing down on us.

I turned to watch the fire racing across the countryside. Black smoke rose above the trees, blotting out the sun. The youth pressed me into a depression in the deepest section of the cave and forced himself in beside me. Our breathing sounded unnaturally loud.

The wall of fire came to less than a span from the hill before sweeping to the left and away. I found myself trembling from head to foot at the thought of how close I had come to following my parents into the purifying flame.

"That was hellish close," the youth said shakily, wiping sweat from his face. Though we were no longer in immediate danger, the heat was intense, since the firestorm still raged all around us. "If we'd been caught in that, we'd be charcoal now."

"Dragon!" I gasped, starting for the entrance. "Jik and Darga!" My rescuer dragged me back into the cave.

"Are you mad? The girl who was with you came this way. There are many caves she might have taken refuge in," he said.

"You don't understand. There were others—a boy and a dog," I cried.

He shook his head. "Either they found shelter and are safe, or . . ." He looked at the fierce orange glow of the flames, still uncomfortably close.

I sank to my knees, realizing there was nothing I could do until the firestorm ended. Abruptly, the youth leaned down and twisted my face to the firelight.

"You are not from the camp. Who are you?" he demanded in a queer tone. Through a haze of smoke, brown eyes surveyed me from a craggy, tan face. His hair was brown, too, and worn longer than lowland fashion dictated. He was about Rushton's age and wore the unmistakable garb of a Druid armsman.

Recapture by the Druid meant trouble. But that was overshadowed by my fear for Jik, Dragon, and Darga. I tried to farseek them, but the air was filled with static generated by the firestorm.

The young armsman dropped to his knees beside me. "Look at me!" he commanded. "Don't you know me, Elspeth?"

I looked at him properly for the first time and, incredibly, realized I did know his face.

"Daffyd?" I whispered.

He sat back on his heels. "Lud save us, it is you, grown into near womanhood. I met you only that once, yet I never forgot your face."

I sat up too quickly, and the world tilted crazily out of focus. I leaned forward and vomited on the ground, heaving until my stomach ached. Gently, Daffyd wiped my mouth with a piece of cloth. I felt no pain, and the nausea was swallowed up immediately by the suppressing barrier.

"I think you'd better stay still," Daffyd said. "You must have breathed in too much smoke. You're lucky I came along when I did."

I looked at Daffyd searchingly. "You may call it lucky . . . unless you mean to turn us over to the Druid."

He smiled. "Gilaine spoke to me of you and your friends. This is one Druid armsman you need not fear. I was surprised when she called you a gypsy; then I realized you must have escaped from Obernewtyn when it changed hands and had somehow ended up traveling with gypsies."

Daffyd screwed up his eyes, and I was astonished to feel a clumsy probe seeking entrance to my mind. The weakest shield would have held him off. It was like watching a baby trying to walk. He sighed. "I'm not

246

very good at it. Gilaine showed me how to think outside Lidgebaby's net, the way you showed her. It is odd to think we were both Misfits when we met in the Councilcourt that day, though I did not know it then."

He coughed as a thick cloud of smoke blew directly into the cave. "Gilaine and the rest of us thought you were dead. Gilbert saw your raft go into the mountain, but all the same, the Druid had everyone out searching for you when I arrived. He was convinced it was a trick and you too crafty to raft to your deaths." He frowned. "Was it a trick, then? Have you been hidden in the valley all this time?"

"The raft carried us through the mountain and down to the lowlands, though I would not want to take such a passage again. I came back through the Olden way," I said. "It's less poisonous than the Druid thinks. We were trying to cut through the compound when the storm struck. I saw everyone taking cover, but I thought . . . I didn't realize a firestorm was coming."

I looked at the cave opening worriedly. "I hope the others are safe. I pray this firestorm ends quickly." I made to rise, but all the suppression in the world could not make useless limbs work.

Daffyd laid a gentle hand on my arm. "Be patient. Even when the storm front passes, there is the rain. We can't brave that and live."

As if his words were a signal, it began suddenly to rain with great force. For a moment, we both looked outside, watching steam hiss and billow from the dying fires. I bit my lip and hoped Dragon understood the danger of being out in the stinging rains.

The cave we were in was no more than a shallow scoop of erosion, and if the rain had been slanting from the opposite direction, it would have filled the cave. As to the fire, the blackened ground showed that it had come to within a single span of the rocks. I shuddered. The area visible from the cave was devastated, and some of the trees were still aflame with their eerie blue halo. The beat of falling rain was curiously soothing amid the sight and smell of destruction, and my eyes drooped. The suppressing was draining my reserves.

"Elspeth, Gilaine said you were trying to reach the coast. If you did get through the mountain, why did you come back?" Daffyd asked.

Forcing myself to full awareness, I looked at Daffyd squarely. I had always found it hard to trust people, but this time I did not hesitate. My infected feet rendered me useless as a messenger. Providence had brought Daffyd to me.

"The Druid's friend on the Council," I said. "What do you know of him?"

Daffyd looked at me closely as if trying to judge if I were delirious. Then he turned his gaze out at the teeming rain and shrugged. "A couple of years back, a boy stumbled into the camp one winter, more dead than alive. The Druid had him looked after, no doubt hoping for some useful information, or at least another set of hands. When the boy regained consciousness, he claimed to have lost his memory. Eventually, the Druid decided to let him join us.

"Though fair faced, he was not well liked. And yet he had a charm, when he chose to use it. The old man grew fond of him, began to think of him as a son. In the end, he was privy to the armsmen councils. Then he came up with a daring plan to infiltrate the Council and feed information back to us. It was a dangerous proposition, but he is an insidious sort of fellow. If anyone could carry out such an audacious plan, it was he. So he went off to Sutrium." Daffyd shrugged. "A lot of us thought he would disappear as soon as he was out of the Druid's sight, maybe even betray us, but he did as he had promised, supplying us with luxuries and information, working for the day the Druid comes out of hiding to challenge the powers that be."

"Ariel," I murmured, not believing for a minute he had lost his memory or that he truly had the Druid's interests in mind.

"It's strange to hear him named openly," Daffyd said. "The Druid has forbidden us to speak of him by name. How did you come to hear it?"

"We met before he came to the Druid," I said bleakly. "He is a Misfit, from Obernewtyn. You have heard of the seditioners there, Alexi and Madam Vega, once enemies of the Druid? He was their pet creature.

"Daffyd, I did not leave Obernewtyn and fall in with the gypsies. I and my friends came from Obernewtyn *disguised* as gypsies. The new master there, Rushton, has made it a secret haven for Misfits like us. I could not tell Gilaine the truth, but I wanted to return to offer you a place with us at Obernewtyn when Lidgebaby is old enough to leave the Druid encampment."

"Then Obernewtyn was not ruined by a firestorm?" Daffyd said.

"No. It's quite safe—so far."

"But, why are you telling me all this now, if you would not speak of it to Gilaine?" Daffyd asked.

I sighed. "Because I need you to go to Obernewtyn and warn Rushton that Ariel is behind the Council's interest in us, before the pass is closed with snow. Tell him soldierguards will arrive at first thaw, and they will find no firestorm-racked ruins. Maybe Rushton can evacuate, take everyone higher into the mountains. Maybe they'll decide to fight, defend the pass. But if I don't get word to Rushton, they'll be defenseless. Ariel will have won."

Daffyd looked pensive. "Ariel always seemed fanatical about Obernewtyn, now that I think of it. He has convinced the old man that Rushton was a threat to us. He was up here just days ago, and when he heard that a group of gypsies had seen Obernewtyn with their own eyes and then slipped through our fingers . . . Well, he was very interested in you and your friends. He cursed when there was no trace of your bodies and swore you had not died. If not for him, the Druid would have called off the search much sooner. Does he know the truth about Obernewtyn?"

"I'm not sure what he knows, but it seems to me he has guessed that Obernewtyn is undamaged. And he wants revenge," I said bitterly. "He must also realize that Rushton can expose him to the Druid, or to the Council, as a Misfit and a seditioner. Daffyd, will you go to Obernewtyn for me?" I asked, too weak for pretense.

Daffyd's eyes flicked to my legs.

I nodded. "They're badly infected. So far I've been able to block the pain so it wouldn't slow me—one of my more useful Talents. But stopping the pain can't make these legs carry me any farther."

There was a long pause. Finally, Daffyd spoke. "I can do as you ask. But what about you and the girl and boy you spoke of?"

"We'll be fine. Rushton can send help for us. The

storm is interfering with my farseeking, but once it's over, I'll call Dragon and Jik and Darga to me."

I looked out of the cave. There were no more flames, and a gray curtain of firestorm rain obscured the outside world. Carefully, and remembering Daffyd had no love for the Council, I related all that had befallen us in the lowlands. When at last the rain ceased, I urged him to leave at once.

"You must go now—" I began, when an anguished cry shattered the stillness.

It took a moment for me to understand that it was Dragon screaming, the grief in her voice tangible and terrifying. Daffyd gave me one startled look, then plunged out into the open.

Long moments later, he returned carrying the prostrate form of Dragon.

"She's not . . . ," I began, but he shook his head.

"Fainted," he said stiffly as if his lips were frozen. His face was very pale as he laid her on the ground inside the cave and wiped the wetness from her bare skin.

"What is it?" I asked, sensing disaster.

He looked up bleakly. "She had found a body. Burned beyond recognition. It might be one of the people from the compound," he added unconvincingly.

He reached into a pocket. "She was clutching this." He held out a hand, and something glinted dully in his palm. It was the small empath novice token that Dameon gave to new members of his guild.

I felt the suppressing barrier weaken with shock and revulsion.

Jik. It was Jik.

I was filled with a guilt deeper than anything I had ever imagined possible. I was responsible for his terrible death. I might as well have killed him with my own hands. If only I had left him with Brydda. If we had not brought him away from Obernewtyn, had not brought him out of the cloister. My teeth chattered, and I felt dizzy with horror.

Daffyd knelt beside me and made me drink water from a tin jar. "Drink," he said, and his eyes, filled with honest pity and compassion, were my undoing. I wept then, great choking tears that seemed to take pieces of my soul.

Jik's face rose in my mind's eye, sweet and grave with eyes always a little too old for his years. He had hardly joined us before we had set him on a path to this horrible death. And what had bringing him achieved? I was now certain Jik's presence had been necessary on the expedition only because it ensured Darga's. Maryon had admitted her prediction was unfocused. I could not recall any vital action of Jik's, but without Darga, we would never have found Dragon or completed our survey of the library; we could not have come through the Olden way. But even if Obernewtyn was warned in time, was even that enough to justify Jik's death?

"There was no sign of the dog," Daffyd said quietly. "It might have escaped." I shook my head, knowing Darga would never leave Jik in danger by choice.

I wept myself empty of tears.

Daffyd went to bury what remained of Jik's body and returned looking pale and weary.

"Daffyd," I said. "You have to go now, while the pass is still open, or it will be too late. Take Dragon."

"I'll carry you," he said. I shook my head. I would

slow them to no purpose. Not even Roland could help me now. I was sure too much pain had accumulated.

Dragon was less easy to convince when she woke. She only agreed when I told her Daffyd's friends would be coming to help me. Jik had told her about Obernewtyn, and she had built it up in her mind to be a place of endless happiness where everyone was always safe. Her horror at the manner of Jik's death made her vulnerable, and I exploited this shamelessly.

I made them go immediately, maintaining a calm façade for Dragon's sake. I shook Daffyd's hand, pressing my armband into it. "This will make them believe you," I said softly.

"Is there anything . . . anyone . . ." Daffyd hesitated.

I thought of Rushton as I had last seen him, his hand raised to me through the driving rain. There had always been a strange, prickly affection between us, a bond of sorts. It was hard to believe I would not see him again.

I smiled. "Tell him . . . tell them, goodbye . . . ," I said.

When they had gone, I sank gratefully into a black feverish sleep filled with dreams, but I did not release the suppressing. At the end, life and sanity were too sweet to give up voluntarily. I knew it would not be long before the barrier gave way of its own volition.

I dreamed a horse with wings came and carried me to the mountaintops. I dreamed Darga was there and singing to me in Jik's high, sweet voice. I dreamed of Maruman, his fur ruffled by the winds. I dreamed of a voice inside my mind calling and calling.

I dreamed . . . of birds.

✦ 23 ✦

THE SOUND OF a breaking branch in the silence of the devastated valley dragged me from my feverish drowsing. I had imagined myself beyond fear, but the notion came to me that the sound had been made by a predator seeking easy prey in the aftermath of the firestorm.

I stared out of the cave, craning my neck as far as I could to keep from using my legs. I dared not overload my mind with any more pain. Miraculously, the suppressing was still intact, although my vision and hearing seemed distorted.

I could see nothing outside but blackened trees and earth and a drifting haze of smoke. There was no sign of life anywhere, but I felt I was being watched. My scalp prickled, and I groped for a rock to use as a weapon.

"Who's there?" I called, my voice a dry, frightened croak.

Letting my mind loose in desperation, I was surprised to find myself listening to a mental dialogue.

"What do you think it is?" one mind asked.

"A funaga, of course. What else makes such ugly noises?" came the response.

Astonished at the strength of minds that were clearly nonhuman, I projected, farsending my own thoughts. "Who/where are you?"

"It spoke!" came a third mental voice. Younger than the others and less controlled, I thought. There were quick shushing thoughts from the other two, who recognized the significance of my mental questions.

I gathered myself, trying to decide if I was dreaming.

Forcing down a mad urge to giggle hysterically, I made an effort to sound normal. "I know you're out there. There are three of you, and I can hear your thoughts!" Nothing. "Answer me!"

I heard a faint movement and craned my neck, trying to farsense them.

A shudder of branches caught my eye. Squinting, I realized there were birds in the tree. I let my eyes follow the trunk to the ground, thinking the three Talents might well have disturbed them.

No one.

The branches rustled again, and I looked up, wondering what had brought the birds to such a place. Animals generally avoided firestorm-devastated areas for months after, sometimes years. There was no small prey, no insects, and no plant life. No reason—yet there they were, just sitting and staring.

One of the birds extended its wings, and I drew in a sharp breath at the flash of red on its plumage. Guanette birds. I had seen one up close only once, a stuffed trophy. Even dead, the bird had possessed a quality that had enthralled me, a wild sort of nobility.

Looking more carefully, I could tell one of the three was a male, with a straighter beak and smaller body. The two larger, with curved beaks, were female.

I sent a questing probe to the birds. After a moment, the smallest began to fidget, shifting weight from one claw to the other like a sheepish child. I sent a more aggressive inquiry. The male flexed his wings and gave a faint chirrup.

"Will you answer?" I sent directly to him.

There was no response, and I was unsure I had reached the bird. Its mind was oddly opaque, and I felt light-headed and weak. Then I felt a probe in my mind. It had entered with such precise delicacy I had not even been aware of being broached. The finest shield I could create would not bar entrance to such a fine-tuned probe.

"Greetings, funaga," came the thought shyly, but with undeniable grace.

"I am Elspeth," I sent. "What name/shape may I call to you?"

"Do not speak to it!" came a sharp, intrusive probe, no less delicate than the first. I wondered if the infection were somehow weakening my natural defenses.

The first hesitated, then spoke again, its presence the merest cobweb in my thoughts.

"My name is Astyanax," he sent. I heard a brief aside directed to the other mind. "And 'it' is a *she*."

The two females, still side by side on the topmost branch, exchanged a doubtful look, and the effect was so like two old women conferring that I laughed in spite of everything.

All three looked up at the sound of laughter. One of the others addressed me. "Funaga, we of the Agyllians do not give our names lightly. But answer this: Are you a male or a female of your kind? It is not easy to tell your sort of creature apart. You all look so much alike, plucked and naked as an eggling."

"I am female. What are Agyllians?" I sent, wondering why the strange word sounded familiar.

No one seemed ready to answer, and the two females looked at one another for so long, I sensed they were communicating on some unknown level.

Without warning, the silent communion ended, and the largest of the three birds dropped from the tree and glided to land near the cave entrance. The bird was much bigger up close, standing higher than a tall man. I drew back nervously, wondering if Guanette birds were carnivorous.

"Is it the one?" the bird mused, apparently thinking to itself. It eyed me intently with beady black eyes.

"I wouldn't taste very good," I sent uneasily. "My wounds are poisoned."

"Wounds! Did you hear what it said?" sent the other female. I was beginning to be able to tell them apart.

"She is the one," Astyanax sent with sudden certainty. Both females looked at him pointedly; then the first returned to its inspection of my limbs.

"It is dark. . . . Hard to tell," murmured the bird on the ground. It came closer in a curious drunken gait. My fingers closed around a rock.

"Funaga," it sent. "I am Ruatha of the Agyllians, and my companions are Illyx and Astyanax. Do you truthtell about these injuries?"

Bewildered, I nodded. "I was burned a long time ago. The scars have become infected. I'm sure I would taste horrible. I might even be poisonous," I added earnestly.

The bird made a dry croaking noise. "We do not wish to eat you, funaga. Agyllians are not eaters of flesh."

I relaxed slightly but not too much. The bird hopped lopsidedly closer. "Injuries are common after the firestorms. You do not look very important," it added thoughtfully. "But perhaps Astyanax is right, and you are the one we seek."

My involuntary withdrawal had jarred my legs, and I heard this through a red mist of pain. I fought against faintness.

"Are you Innle?" the bird asked.

The mist cleared for a moment in shock at hearing Maruman's old title for me. Innle meant "seeker" in beast symbols. And hadn't I heard that name more recently? The effort of sustaining the suppressing stopped me thinking clearly. I concentrated, shoring up the barrier, and slowly, the tides of pain ebbed.

The bird had not moved, but the other two had flown to the ground and hovered some way back.

"Why do you call me that?" I asked.

"The eldar sent us to find Innle," Astyanax said, "the Seeker, who lay mortally injured in this valley. Many are dead nearby, but the eldar told that you would be alone, wounded and waiting to die. It is hard to know if you are the one. The eldar said there was no time for a mistake."

"What is an eldar?" I asked, fear giving way to puzzlement.

This time Astyanax answered. "Eldar is the name of the high council of the Agyllians. Eldar are the wisest of our kind, and the wisest of the wise is the leader of the council—the Elder."

Now I was sure I was dreaming or delirious with pain. A council of birds? Even the dogs and horses who were organized had not gone that far.

"What is this Seeker?"

"Are you the one we were sent to find?" Illyx demanded with waspish exasperation.

"Peace," Ruatha sent gently. "She cannot know she is the one. We will take her."

I blinked, forcing back a wave of nausea. "What do you mean?"

The bird ignored me. One last searching look from ice-colored eyes, then she thrust her head beneath one wing and appeared to be trying to pick out the feathers there. Instead she withdrew a pouch in her sharp beak, dropped it on the ground, and pecked at it until the woven edges parted. Inside was a net.

"No!" I struggled to maintain the suppressing.

"The Elder cannot leave the Ken, so we will take you there," Ruatha sent calmly, reaching for my leg with one strong claw.

Pain.

More pain.

Darkness.

I fought against consciousness, frightened of what I would find.

"You will not die . . . ," sent a voice, as soft in my mind as a falling leaf.

Slowly, I let myself be drawn, opening my eyes to a sky so pale and clear it was more white than blue. The wind fanned my cheeks with icy fingers, and puffs of cloud burst from my lips and dissolved with each breath exhaled.

Dreaming . . . , I thought vaguely. *All a dream . . . but so real.* Another puff of cloud floated from my mouth. I turned my head slowly to follow it and froze.

I was having one of those horrible dreams where

I seemed to be right on the edge of the highest cliff in the world. Below, visible through a veil of drifting cloud, was a vague grayness that might have been sea or land.

Piercing the cloud rose numerous stone columns; I seemed to be lying atop one. First there had been winged horses, then giant birds that thought more clearly than any human, and now I had been transported to the top of the world. I wondered dizzily if these were the dreams that came to the endless sleep called death.

Guanette birds wheeled and flew and skimmed all about in an intricate airborne dance. It was one of the loveliest sights I had ever seen.

I heard the rustle of wings and turned to see one of the birds come to ground. It was a male.

"You have woken, funaga. Welcome to the Ken. I am of the eldar. My name is Nerat. Among your kind, I would be called a healer." It sent these thoughts past my shield without effort, with the same scything ability the other birds had demonstrated.

He moved closer but slowly, as if his bones were stiff. Just as Ruatha had done, the bird reached under a wing, withdrawing a pouch. Balancing precariously on one foot, it took the pouch into its talons, plucking it open with delicate pecking motions. A few grains of yellowish dust drifted on the wind.

"The infection in your body is bad, but not so bad that Nerat cannot draw it. The real difficulty will be in finding a way to drain off the pain you have allowed to build up behind a mental block. Open your mind to me," he commanded.

I flinched at the hint of strength, for here was a mind easily as powerful as my own.

The bird tilted its head quizzically. "You find it hard to open your mind? Dying would be harder. Understand that there is only so much we can do from without. Your body must be taught to repair itself and build its immunities. That is a simple matter of teaching and can be done even as I drain the mental poisons. But you must open willingly to me. If you resist, the block will crumble. You will die. Let me in and sleep. Trust me."

I swallowed dryly, wondering why even in the midst of a dream, I could not bear the thought of opening my mind completely.

"That is a question you will answer for yourself in time," Nerat sent. "Now, do as I say, before the poison flows too deep. I can do many things, but I cannot bring the dead back to life. And you must not die with so much left undone," he added cryptically.

I saw a sudden vision of Rushton's brooding face and felt the curious ache his memory always evoked.

"He thinks of you, too," Nerat said absently; then he made a choking sound and regurgitated a grayish lump of paste onto the stone.

"This comes from the substance the funaga call *whitestick*," Nerat sent. "We call it *narma*. I have mixed it with various salivas and acids that I have generated to fight the poisons. Narma rose from the ashes of the Great White and is ever a reminder that the poisons now in the earth fade. Next time, there will be no narma."

I shivered, imagining all the world fused smooth as glass, and black.

"That is how it will be, the next time," Nerat sent. He stared into my eyes. "Come now, ElspethInnle, for it is not only your life that hangs in the balance. Open to me, but leave the block in place until I command you to release it."

Slowly, I let my head fall back onto the stone, trying to make my mind a passive vessel.

Nerat's probe was inside then, swift as a snake, smooth as a single strand of silk. "Relax," he sent. "Dream, and I will do my work. I am not interested in the longings and secret thoughts of a funaga."

Once Nerat commanded me to release the suppressing, I drifted between excruciating pain and numbness, burning heat and freezing cold.

And the pain in my legs. The pain. The pain.

For a time, I forgot who I was, and it seemed all my life had been spent in a dream of pain on the top of a mountain.

Occasionally, I was aware of Nerat's mind weaving a pattern in my thoughts as complex and intangible as smoke in the wind. Sometimes I smelled flowers and herbs, and sometimes acrid, choking smoke.

And then I floated for a very long time.

"She wakes," came a thought bound with weariness and satisfaction.

I opened my eyes and found myself looking into pale avian eyes. The bird was so close I could see the fine crack in his beak, thin as a hair. I felt his mind like tenebrous fingers at the edge of my thoughts; then he gave a strangely human bob of his head and hopped away.

I did not move for a long while, waiting to see where

the dream would take me next. Idly, I wondered if I would feel myself plunge into the mindstream when I died. I thought I would like to hear that glorious siren song once more.

Astyanax appeared. "You are well, ElspethInnle. You can get up now. Or do you wish to lie there longer?" he sent with all the politeness of a host not wanting to upset a guest. Urged on by the eager expression in his eyes, I lifted my head carefully.

It is a dream, I told myself. *That is why there is no pain.*

Slowly, I sat upright. I made myself look down my body, prepared to see ruined, evil-smelling flesh and black infection. My legs seemed to rise at me from a dark mist.

Below the skirt they lay before me, pale as cream and utterly without blemish. Even the old childhood scars of skinned knees had vanished.

My heart sounded like a drumbeat as I reached for the laces. They were stiff with congealed blood. The socks were the same, but when I pulled them down, they came away from the skin easily. The flesh beneath was as flawless as that on my calves. Unable to believe my eyes, I reached a hand out. The skin felt smooth beneath my questing fingers. I wriggled my toes experimentally, watching the movement as if it were an exquisite dance.

I laughed, and my laughter seemed to reverberate off the mountains. No one could heal that fast, and I knew enough of healing to know it was impossible to heal poisoned flesh or banish old, deep scarring.

"Well met," Astyanax sent pertly. "You are now to see Atthis—Elder of the eldar."

I climbed warily to my feet and let myself be led across to a cairn of stones and around to face an opening in the other side.

"Greetings, funaga," came a thought from within the cairn, so clear and gentle it was like a song in my mind. There was the sound of shuffling movement, and slowly, a very old female Guanette bird emerged, her feathers less red than dusty brown with bald patches of pink. The end of her beak was broken right off. But strangest of all were her eyes. There was no pupil, and they were white and milkily opaque.

She was blind.

Looking at the ancient bird, a mist of terror crept through my veins at the sudden certainty that I was not dreaming.

The old bird stopped, eyes turned unerringly toward me. The movement reminded me of Dameon's blind grace. "So, now you are come, just as was foreseen. You may call me Atthis, and I will call you ElspethInnle, as does the yelloweyes."

I blinked, startled. Did she mean Maruman? Then something else struck me. This was the voice that had called to me in the old cat's mind.

But I'm dreaming, I thought dazedly.

The old bird stepped closer, and a suffocating odor of dust seemed to surround me.

"Why do you pretend? You know this is no dream."

I felt as if someone had kicked me in the stomach, and I was nauseous and breathless all at once.

"You made Maruman sick!" I said indignantly, remembering what had been said to me inside Maruman's mind.

"It could not be helped," Atthis sent gently. "We could not reach you otherwise, at such a distance."

Something else occurred to me. "You told me I had to go on a journey. Is that why I'm here?" *A dark journey*, she had said.

The bird sent nothing for a long moment, but I had the uncanny feeling she could see from those white orbs.

"I did not know we would meet so soon when first I called to you in my dreamtravels through the yelloweyes' mind. I did not foresee then that the Agyllians would have some other part to play. Even the wise are sometimes pawns."

The old bird came closer, her tattered wing brushing one of my feet. I looked into her blind eyes with faint dread.

"You do not like the look of my sightless eyes? Well, sight is a facile thing," Atthis sent.

It was nearing dusk, and a fleeting final sunbeam bathed the old bird in crimsons for a moment. Beyond the cairn lay the rim of the world. On one side, the sky was night-dark, and on the other, the sun shone its final rays. In the west, the moon was rising flat and bright. I looked back to see that the avian face had not looked away from mine.

"ElspethInnle . . . the Seeker," the old bird sent.

"I don't know why you call me that. It's just a name Maruman made up. I don't call myself by it," I sent.

"Not all names are chosen," Atthis sent. "Some names are bestowed."

"What is this all about?" I sent briskly.

"You know," the bird sent, unperturbed. "Have you

265

not wondered at the coincidences and chances in your life? Have you not felt that there were great forces at work about you—forces for good and for great ill? Have you not felt the purpose in your life burning?"

Unwished, a vision came to me of the black chasm I had glimpsed while being tortured by the Zebkrahn. I thought of Jik asking if it were possible for it to happen again and of the Druid and his insane search for Beforetime weaponmachines, his greed for power and revenge blinding him to all else.

"You know," sent Atthis. "You have always known."

"Who are you?" I whispered.

"You may call me a chronicler and . . . what do your people call it—a futureteller. Long ago, I foresaw that the machines that made the great destruction lie sleeping. I saw that a second and greater destruction would come to the world if these machines were not destroyed. That will be no easy matter, for the machines have a kind of intelligence and will protect themselves. But I dreamed one would be born among the funaga, a Seeker to cross the black wastes and ensure that the deathmachines can never be used again.

"Very recently, I foresaw a faltering in that life—a moment when you might easily die. I saw that you would suffer such mental and physical injuries as only the Agyllians could heal. And so I sent out my egglings to find you."

"I'm grateful," I said. "But why seek the machines at all? If they're so far away—if they're truly in the Blacklands—might they not be useless by the time anyone found them?"

"The machines are beyond the Blacklands, but they have slept without harm for hundreds of lifetimes. The danger of their discovery alone would not be enough to make me act. But I have foreseen that there is another funaga whose destiny is to resurrect the machines. Your paths intersect. You are the Seeker, the other is the Destroyer. If you do not find the machines first . . ."

I felt sick. I wanted to tell myself that it was too ridiculous, that I must be dreaming, that prophecies belonged to stories. But too much had happened. I had seen and felt too much, and in my heart, just as the bird said, I had known for a long time that I would find the chasm from my vision. The burning of the maps on Obernewtyn's doors had only been the beginning.

"Why does it have to be me who finds them?" I asked. "Don't I have any choice?"

"There are always choices."

I shook my head, feeling suddenly bitter. "If what you say is true, then the future is set out, and I *have* no real choice."

"The future is a river whose course is long designed but which a flood or drought might easily alter. Whatever choice you make will have its own consequences. If I had not chosen to interfere and have you healed, your death would have been a kind of choice."

The sun sank, and suddenly it was night, the old bird no more than a dust-scented shadow.

"What do I have to do?" I whispered.

"For now, only live," Atthis sent. "What else comes will come."

"You . . . you brought me here to say that?" I asked, incredulous.

The old bird seemed to sigh. "The time is not yet right for you to travel that black road. You were brought here to be healed, and so you are healed.

Return to your home and friends. Help them in their struggle, for it is worthy and they have need of you. But do not forget that your true path lies away from them and their quests."

"Have you . . . foreseen that I will succeed on that path? Will I destroy the machines if I go on this journey?"

Atthis shifted slightly and dust filled the air. "That, I have not foreseen."

A wave of weariness flowed through me, and a kind of hopelessness. I sensed compassion in the mind of the old bird. "One day, you will learn that it is not always safest to be alone. Until then, happiness will elude you. But perhaps it is best for you to be alone with this secret burden."

"I don't understand," I sent.

"I know. You are tired. Sleep, and while you sleep, my egglings will transport you to a place where one waits to carry you back to the mountain valley of Obernewtyn."

The old bird's eyes stared into mine, and I felt myself falling into them, sinking into the soft whiteness as if it were a feather bed.

◆ 24 ◆

THE COLD WOKE me.

I was freezing, and I wondered if it had snowed in the night. I felt a sharp stab of grief and was puzzled by it. Then I remembered Jik.

I opened my eyes.

It was night. I frowned, wondering at the icy chill of the air. Perhaps winter had come early to the White Valley. Even so, it felt too cold for the highlands. I doubted it had ever been so cold even at Obernewtyn in the dead of winter.

With a shock, I realized something else. The suppressing barrier was gone from my mind, and so was the pain!

The only answer seemed to be that I had slept off the pain somehow, but if that was the case, the infection in my feet would have worsened, being untended. The pain would come, and it would be dreadful. Better lie still.

Then something warm and moist touched my face, and I gasped in fright. Gazing down at me with dark, troubled eyes was a black horse—unmistakably Gahltha.

"It is I, funaga," he sent in answer to my thought

that I was still dreaming. "I am Galta who was once Gahltha."

"Galta?" I echoed stupidly. My eyes drifted past the horse, and questions about his change of name were swept aside in an even greater shock.

I was no longer in the cave in the White Valley, with its pervasive reek of smoke and the blackened skeletons of trees standing outside like silent sentinels.

I was lying on a flat, narrow stone ledge jutting out from a massive cliff face. I had taken the cliff for the wall of the cave, but there were no walls around me and no roof. Running in all directions from the gray-pitted cliff face was a vast, flat plain covered in snow, glittering in the moon's cold bluish light. There was not a single tree or bush in sight. In the distance, I could see the darkly defined shapes of mountain spurs and outcrops of cracked stone.

The ice and snow, the lack of trees, and the incredible brightness of the stars told me I was in the mountains. Except that it was impossible.

I thought fleetingly that the suppressing barrier had shattered, and the accumulated pain had destroyed my mind. Madness seemed the only rational answer. I giggled at the paradox but shivered when the sound echoed.

The black horse watched me patiently, his dark coat almost blending with the pelt of the night.

I opened my mouth to speak, then closed it with an audible snap, thinking of the queer dream I had fallen into after Daffyd had gone. If it had been a dream.

Carefully, I levered myself into a sitting position. There was no pain in my feet or legs. I looked down.

My legs were bare and unscarred. I touched them

reverently, remembering I had done that in the dream. Only it had not been a dream. Thin legs with knobbed knees and rather long feet, but at that moment the most perfect legs in the world.

"Where are we?" I asked my feet.

"In the mountains," the horse answered gently. He looked down at me with grave serenity, and I wondered at the change in him. The last time I had seen him, on the banks of the Suggredoon, he had been almost insane with terror and frustration. The violent impatience and scorching bitterness that had characterized his behavior had disappeared as completely as my own wounds.

"Come," he sent. "If you are too weak to walk, I will carry you. Soon the storm will come, and it must not find us in the open."

I looked up at the cloudless sky, wondering why he thought there was going to be a storm. But I left my doubt unspoken. So much had happened that was impossible to explain that a clear sky might easily hide a storm. I pulled my socks and shoes back on and slid from the ledge, tensing myself for the pain that had been part of my life for so long.

There was a faint jarring but no pain. I stared down at my feet in fresh wonder.

"I have found a place nearby," he explained. "There is wood. You will light a fire for us, and perhaps we will live."

I looked up, startled, and realized with a faint shiver that he was quite serious.

"It will be a bad storm," he sent.

I stepped forward, sinking up to my knees in powdery snow. The black horse went ahead, forging a wide track. I followed in his wake, marveling at the pleasure of walking without pain.

The wind whipped my hair and skirt around now that we were away from the buffer of the cliffs, and the cold stole into my bones long before we reached the shelter. It turned out to be a cave at the end of a narrow cleft. I sighed, thinking I was in danger of becoming accustomed to living in caves; I had seen the inside of so many. This one was quite big, dry, and surprisingly warm, being cut off from the wind by its awkward position in the wedge-shaped cleft.

"We must block the mouth or the coldwhite will come in," the horse sent.

Under his direction, I labored for more than an hour, piling stones at the mouth of the cave, shivering in my light dress and coat. When I had finished, there was nothing but a narrow slit I could barely squeeze through.

"Now the fire," Galta instructed.

Fortunately, I still had my hand flint, and there was a pile of wood and twigs. I managed to burn myself twice before setting them alight. I crouched over the flames, trying to warm my fingers as smoke curled up to the roof of the cave. Outside, the wind had reached a shrieking intensity, and snow fell in a dense curtain. I looked at Galta searchingly, but he only stared into the flames as if mesmerized. "How long do you think the storm will last?" I asked humbly.

He answered simply that he did not know.

I bit my lip. "How did you get here?" *Never mind about me*, I thought.

The horse looked up. "The funaga must know everything," he sent, but without his old contempt. He

272

looked into the fire as if it were a window, and miniature flames leaped in his eyes.

"I spent many days in the place where the mountain ate you. I thought you must be dead, and I was tortured by my cowardice. I believed then that I did not care what happened to me, but when the funaga tried to trap me with their nets, I fought them and ran away. I did not go to Obernewtyn, but higher, to the fields where I once ran with Avra. But I could not stay there. I went on and on to the high places where the old equines go to die. I meant to abase myself before their spirits. I hoped I would die myself, that they would demand it of me.

"I did not eat or drink, as is the custom among equines seeking a vision. I waited and day after day, there was no answer. I thought the old ones were deaf to me and had cast me out. I called myself Galta—nothing.

"Then one night I slept, and in my dream I saw a vision of a high mountain valley, where a lake lay yet unfrozen in the midst of ice and snow. A voice told me to find that place. It promised that I would find absolution there. When I woke, I began to search.

"It was hard, and many times I despaired and thought of giving up. But every night in my sleep, the voice came, reassuring me, urging me higher, promising an answer to the pain in my heart and a purpose for my life. It told me many things for my ears alone, and a blackness, one that had been inside me all my life, began to melt as easily as coldwhite before the sun. I could have gone back to Obernewtyn then, for I understood that pride and arrogance, rather than true grief, had kept me away. But the voice urged me always to go on.

273

"At last, I found this valley. Then the voice came again, telling me I had been drawn to the mountains to take part in a quest whose end would concern not only equine and funaga, but all living creatures. This was to be my life's most important work, above any other glory I had imagined." I could feel the faint sense of awe that marked his thoughts.

"The voice told me a funaga would be brought here, one whom I must keep safe. One day, this funaga would fight a great and perilous battle whose outcome was unknown even to the wisest of the wise but which might mean the destruction of all life on the earth forever. I must carry this funaga wherever it wishes to go and protect it with my own life if it were needed.

"It was strange and ironic that I, who had so despised the funaga, should find myself bound to such a task. There was a time when I would have refused, believing your kind to be a blight on the world. But the voice had helped me see that no life-form is greater than another and that all are bound up in an intricate and delicately balanced pattern of coexistence.

"In the daylight, I found this cave. And then I waited. Many weeks passed, yet always the voice told me to wait. So I waited. Two moons passed, and still I waited, wondering if it was my punishment to wait forever in these cold lands for one who would never come," he sent bleakly.

"Two moons?" I whispered incredulously. I remembered how I had imagined time passing in my sleep. If he was right, winter was near ended. I felt a stab of despair at the thought that Obernewtyn was yet unwarned, unless Daffyd had got there in time.

"Then I found you, lying on the ledge. At first I

ould not believe you were the funaga the voice had poken of. But why else would you be there? And how ould you have come there, when there was not a single ootprint in all the untouched snow? Then I thought ou were dead, for your skin was like ice. But your heart was beating, and you woke."

There was a long silence in the wake of his strange ale. Outside, the storm winds howled derisively, and iny whirlwinds of snow blew through the cave opening, falling in a white drift against the stones. The fire's orange light danced silently upon the walls.

"Only someone insane could believe your story. Or nine," I said softly, but my words sounded hollow. I had fallen asleep, half-dead, in the highlands and had woken completely healed, sixty days and thousands of spans distant, on the highest and loneliest of mountain peaks.

I felt a ghostly echo of the dangerous weight of pain that had pressed against the feebly erected barrier in my mind. I shuddered.

The fire crackled, and I turned my face to the glowing embers, drinking in the warmth.

"When this storm is over, we will go back to Obernewtyn," I said.

But outside, the storm winds shrieked.

⋆ 25 ⋆

Hᴏᴘɪɴɢ ᴛʜᴇ sᴜᴅᴅᴇɴ silence was not merely a lull, used a stick to clear the snow and rocks from the entrance of the cave. We had lost count of time, and the firewood was nearly exhausted.

Coming out of the narrow crevice, I was cold and hungry, but I forgot physical discomfort in the dazzling sight that met my eyes. The world was blanketed in pristine white, reflecting the sunshine with painful intensity. A delicate lace of icicles hung from the ledge on which I had slept until I'd been found by Gahltha—for that, I'd decided, was a far more appropriate name for the formidable black horse than "Galta" could ever be.

Unaccountably, I remembered sitting at the Kinraide orphan home with Maruman, dreaming of the fabled world of the Snow Queen, a forbidden Oldtime tale my mother had told us.

"It is a hard trek to Obernewtyn," Gahltha warned. "It will not be safe to go too quickly. The coldwhite will hide crevices and rocks. We will have to put our feet down carefully."

"Life has always been a matter of putting one's feet down carefully," I said. Even the prospect of a long hard trek through frostbitten country with an empty belly and scant clothes could not quell my joy.

We left at once, for there were no preparations to be made. Gahltha led, forging a path; even so, my shoes and legs were quickly soaked. I was glad to walk, since the exertion kept me warmer than the dazzling sunlight could on its own.

Gahltha warned me to shade my eyes with a piece of cloth to avoid being snow-blinded.

I looked back once at the mountain in whose skirts we had sheltered. It sloped backward, outjutting rocks and drifts of snow adhering to the flat surfaces, making it look like the stern face of a very old man. The slant made it impossible to see the top, and I wondered if that was where the Ken of the Agyllians lay.

We traveled across the ice lake, and the land beyond seemed to go right to the horizon. This puzzled me until Gahltha said the distance was an illusion. We were on a large, flat plateau and would shortly reach its edge.

The wind, which had howled for days and nights, seemed to have exhausted itself, and the air was clear and still. The only sounds to break the silence were those of our footsteps and breathing. We could have been the only beings alive in all the Land. I felt as if the air were a kind of fement that one might become drunk on, and hunger increased the heady feeling. At the same time, I felt I could understand anything and everything very easily there on the roof of the world.

It was nearing dusk when we reached the edge of the plateau. I was within a single handspan of the edge before I realized. Only a sharp warning from Gahltha stopped me walking off the edge. I looked over, and a cold, freshening gust of air blew up into my face. What I saw below took my breath away.

Clouds were strung out across the sky like skeins of wool—below my feet!

Seen from above, the clouds were fluffy mounds of cream or sea foam shot with glorious sunset colors—a fairy realm. The Land was barely visible through the woolly curtain. And between the Land and the plateau there were rank upon rank of mountains, jagged as upturned teeth, streaked with snow and lacking the slightest touch of color or softness.

Some of the mountains were dense and dark, unmistakably Blacklands. Few dared travel through mountainous terrain, because a snowfall could hide lethal poisonous ground. Yet Gahltha seemed unperturbed, saying only that the voices had told him where to walk safely.

I had often gazed at the distant mountains, but I had never had any real idea of the sheer size and barrenness of them. Gahltha's lone trek to the heights had been an incredible act of faith.

Something glistened on the far horizon. Squinting, I realized I was looking at the great sea. For a moment I seemed to smell the salty wetness of waves on the shore. All the world lay spread at my feet. The one thing I could not see was a way down. The plateau stood apart from the other plains and mountains. I looked at the black horse and found him watching me inscrutably.

"I brought you here to see the world, funaga. I wondered if it would move you as it once moved a proud and bitter equine. It was here I saw my own smallness and understood how stupid and arrogant I had let pride and hatred make me," he sent.

"Not many could see this and be unchanged," I sent gently. "But you haven't said how we can get down."

"Patience," Gahltha sent.

He made for the opposite side of the plateau, and there I looked out, aghast. Again the plateau was high, but there were no clouds to hide the dreadful vision from us.

Stretched out like a charred skin were hundreds of spans of Blacklands, lifeless and still. I had thought the snowy slopes barren, but this was a terrible stretch of obsidian, flecked here and there with dark, gleaming pools reflecting a tarnished sky. A stretch of mountains, breaking away from the main mass, ran across the nightmarish terrain and out of sight. It was the Land, dead and without hope of life. Looking at that, it was impossible to share Pavo's assurance that the Blacklands would not last forever.

Even as I watched, night crept like a dark shadow across the bleak plains, and though the heights were still bathed in sunlight, I felt strangely cold. I had wondered why the Agyllians left me in the mountains when it would have been so easy for them to carry me down to Obernewtyn. Now I thought I understood.

"I did not know it went on so far. So much land poisoned . . . ," I whispered.

"Perhaps there are many lessons to be learned in the mountains," Gahltha sent gravely.

I could not take my eyes away.

I thought of the Oldtimers and wondered whether they would have built their weaponmachines if they could have foreseen what would come to pass. And why create machines that would outlast a hundred lives? Had they been so enamored of war and destruction that they had to make it immortal?

For the first time, I felt I could understand the original Councilmen and their tyrannous rule. Farmers and children of the Oldtimers, they had seen firsthand the will to destroy and the hunger for power that knew no boundaries. Perhaps they had even known the death-machines existed and had hoped to ensure no one would ever use them again. No wonder they had forbidden delving into the past.

They had been afraid.

Unfortunately, the repressive philosophies had become a different sort of threat. I doubted the present Council understood the real dangers any better than those who had made the weaponmachines in the first place. I had only to think of Henry Druid and Alexi to know there would always be men and women prepared to pay any price for power. Even our own Teknoguild would risk agonizing death to revive the knowledge of a lost age.

The Elder was right. It was inevitable the machines would someday be unearthed and used. And Atthis had said I was the only one with any chance of destroying them. If that made me the Seeker, it was a responsibility I was finally ready to accept.

Resolutely, I thrust the machines and the Agyllians from my mind and looked at Gahltha. "I will be glad to go from this place and its foreboding lessons."

He blew air from flared nostrils. "I did not bring you here for lessons. See, there is where we will go down."

I followed his gaze and saw a natural stone path leading unevenly to the next plateau, cleaving to the edge of the slope. The path began not far from where we stood, moving this way, then that, ever lower, across the face of the cliff.

Gahltha looked at me. "You are weak still. Ride on my back and we will travel more quickly."

I looked at him curiously. "You want me to ride?" I asked.

"One warrior will carry another, if the strength of one proves greater. Each has his own strength but also his own weakness." He spoke with the air of repeating a well-learned lesson.

"Wise words," I said simply. "I am glad to ride on your back if it will help us move more quickly."

We traveled that day and the next through the monotonous snowbound terrain of the high mountains, and on the third day, we came upon a few scant green shoots, thrusting their tips through the snow. "It will be more dangerous now that the thaw has begun," Gahltha said. "But I think tomorrow we will reach the valley of the barud." *Barud* was the equine word symbol for "home"—it seemed Gahltha had come to miss Obernewtyn.

Snow clouds gathered overhead, and with the bleak afternoon came unexpected doubts. I began to fear Obernewtyn had changed and that I would find there was no longer a place for me there. My whole life had been spent as an outsider, and even at Obernewtyn, I had felt misplaced until the journey to the coast. Ironic if I discovered too late where my own barud lay.

Just at dusk, for the first time, we encountered another creature. A wolf.

The wolves that frequented the mountains were

savage, pale-eyed wraiths with coats the color of mist and snow. They were nearly impossible to spot deliberately, and it was sheer luck that I saw this one. I had been plodding along, shivering and staring aimlessly into the distance, when the landscape appeared to shift fractionally. I realized I had been staring right at a wolf without seeing it. It had been watching us, but now it turned, melting back into the white landscape.

Later I heard several desolate calls in the distance. I was tempted to try communicating, but the wild keening calls across the frozen wastes made a desolate song of the night and did not invite a response.

The calls went on for hours, then abruptly ceased.

I was glad of the respite, but Gahltha seemed more disturbed by the silence than by the bloodcurdling howls. I was too tired to worry and slept leaning against his warm flank. Gradually, I felt him relax, too. Exhausted and half-starved as we were, we needed sleep. Initial hunger pains had long since given way to an empty ache that was easier to bear. If sleep was all the comfort that remained for us, then that would have to be enough to get us home.

Suddenly Gahltha stiffened, and I was jerked awake. Dense clouds obscured the moon. I looked around in the pitch darkness fearfully.

"What is it?" I sent.

"The Brildane," Gahltha responded.

I laid a gentle hand across his back, wondering if there was danger.

"What or who are Brildane?" I asked.

"I do not know what name is given them by the funaga, but Brildane is the name they call themselves. We call them gehdra, because they are invisible. They have no time for any creature but their own kind. But they hate the funaga, because your kind trap and slay their young."

"Are they hungry?" I asked, trying to understand what sort of animal it could be.

"If they were, we would already be dead," Gahltha sent. "You heard their calls throughout the night? The mountain equines know a little of their strange speech. Their calls concerned us. They wonder what we are doing here. The gehdra claim the high mountains as their own world. Here we are intruders."

"Wolves! The Brildane are wolves!" I cried. I looked at Gahltha. "Are you telling me they're just curious?" I asked.

"The curiosity of the gehdra is as savage as its hunger," Gahltha sent quellingly.

I looked around uneasily, wondering how he had known of their presence. I had heard not a sound. And even now, I could sense no minds but our own. The wolves must have some ability to cloak their minds.

"Would it help if I sent a greeting?" I suggested.

"No!" Gahltha sent urgently, as if he expected me to leap up and rush into the night with a cry of greeting on my lips. "It is impossible to predict what they will do. Speaking to them would not stop them eating us, if that was their desire. And if they wanted to confront us, they would have done it. But I think they came to look, not to feed or speak. Better to do nothing. With the gehdra, that is always safest."

Gahltha's warnings were underlined by a sense of tangible fear. Bleakly, I realized these may be the very wolves Ariel had hunted and trapped. He had driven them mad to ensure their ferocity and had used them to

guard the grounds, hunting and killing runaways. We
had hoped to heal the beasts once Ariel had gone, bu
his sadistic treatment had made it impossible. In the
end, the best we could do was give the wolves back
their freedom.

I dared not stir a limb until Gahltha reported tha
they had gone, fading back into the night as mysteri
ously as they had appeared.

"Are you sure you didn't imagine them?" I asked.

"In the morning you will see," was all he would say

It was hard to go back to sleep, but after a while I fel
into a light, troubled slumber. I dreamed of Ariel as he
had been, a boy with almost unearthly beauty and a
sadistic turn of mind that delighted in causing pain.
woke disquieted. The night grew steadily colder, and
even Gahltha's considerable body heat could not keep
me warm. Eventually, I gave up trying to sleep and lay
waiting for the horse to wake.

With relief, I felt Gahltha stir at dawn. It was barely
light before we were off but light enough to see tha
Gahltha had been right the night before. The snow al
around us was covered in paw prints, some a mere
handspan from where my feet had lain.

The Brildane.

I shivered, and suddenly it began to snow. Just a
few flakes at first, but blown with stinging force into
our faces by a hard, icy wind. The snow was already
thick underfoot and made walking tiring. Gahltha of
fered to carry me again, but he could only walk a little
faster than I and was easily as tired, so I refused. I knew
neither of us could go much farther without proper res
and food.

Near to dropping, I was trying to remember how long it had been since I had eaten when Gahltha neighed loudly. Squinting against the wind and flying snow, I realized he had rounded a spur of rock and was out of sight. Forcing weary limbs to hurry, I caught up.

"What is it?" I sent, wondering if I had strength enough left to deal with another obstacle.

"We have reached the valley of the barud."

I blinked stupidly. Barud? "Obernewtyn!"

All weariness fell away from me then. I was close enough to send a questing probe, but something kept me from it, a desire to have my first glimpse of Obernewtyn unhampered by greetings and explanations.

I had just begun to recognize some of the hills and stone hummocks when the wind fell away and the snow stopped, making our first glimpse of Obernewtyn clear and unmistakable.

A cry of happiness died in my throat, stillborn. I stumbled to a halt, unable to believe my eyes.

All that remained of Obernewtyn was a charred ruin.

✦ 26 ✦

ONLY A FIRESTORM could have done so much damage.

Little remained of Obernewtyn but rubble. The walls of the main building were no more than jagged, blackened stumps of stone. The windblown snow adhered to the crevices, and a rambling kind of thorn brush thrust its roots deep into the cracked rubble.

It looked like a ruin of years rather than moons. How had it degenerated so quickly? I blinked, for when I stared hard, I seemed to see the ghostly shape of Obernewtyn as it had been.

Tears blurred my vision, and the wind froze them before they could fall. It was bitter cold on the hillside, but I scarcely felt the chill. To have traveled so long and far only to find Obernewtyn destroyed was beyond a nightmare.

"Come," Gahltha sent.

I stared at him incredulously.

He asked doubtfully, "Do you not want to go to the barud? I am sworn to take you wherever you will."

I shook my head, disturbed by his lack of emotion. Perhaps he had changed less than I realized and welcomed the downfall of any funaga institution. I looked back at the wreckage and wondered whether any had escaped the firestorm. What a tragic irony that the lie hat had protected us for so long had come so horribly rue.

Stumbling forward, I prayed I would find some clue is to where everyone had gone. The ground was sodden from the melting snow, and fresh flakes fell soft as ashes on the dark, wet earth.

Abruptly, I stopped and stared, squinting against he cold wind blustering across the valley. I thought I had seen a smudge of smoke.

It had come from somewhere on the far side of the valley, near the pass to the highlands. My heart beat faster as I made out a number of dark shapes that might be buildings. It seemed to me I was looking at a small settlement.

Gahltha offered to carry me, though he seemed puzzled at my instruction not to pass too close to Obernewtyn. It occurred to me that equines might not know that a poisonous residue was left behind by a firestorm.

Some obscure instinct of caution stopped me riding directly into the camp. I asked Gahltha to take us into a clump of trees a short distance away. With the mountains behind and on one side and the ruins of Obernewtyn on the other, we were safe from detection.

Peering through the greenery, I could see several roughly constructed stone-and-thatch huts, set in a circle and surrounded by a wall of stripling branches. Even at a distance, it was clearly a poor settlement, and an air of hopeless dilapidation hung over it.

Two men emerged from one of the hovels. I bit my lip. Soldierguards!

They could only have come through the pass. That meant the thaw had already opened the way. Bleakly, I reflected that at least the Council would have no more cause to doubt Rushton's word . . . if he had survived the firestorm. A strange feeling of despair filled me a the realization that he might be dead.

I felt Gahltha's restive movements and looked a him. "Perhaps we should go to Obernewtyn to find ou what has passed here," he suggested.

I shook my head impatiently. "What good will tha do? Besides, it would be dangerous to go there now. want to get a better look at that camp. The soldier guards can't have built those huts. I want to know who did. We'll go back the way we came and right around to the other side."

Before I could mount, Gahltha sent a warning tha someone approached.

To my horror, it was three soldierguards. Fortu nately, they stopped in a clearing several spans from where we were hidden. Grumbling about the cold, they sat on logs, rubbing their hands and faces.

"I tell you, I am weary of this hellish place," said one man resentfully. " 'Get wood,' the captain orders, but what is the use of it? Quick as the fire warms you, the wind chills you to the bone."

"That fellow Rushton does nowt seem to feel th cold," said a big burly man with a highland accent, and I was glad to hear Rushton's name despite the circum stances. "It whistles through th' holes in his clothes an' he nary shows a shiver. His blood must be as cold as th' snow."

"There is a madness in him," said the first. "No sane man could wish to stay up here, yet the fool claims he will rebuild Obernewtyn once the taint is faded."

The big man nodded. "I heard he was offered a billet in th' lowlands but chose to come back here."

"He is proud enough to want his inheritance rebuilt," said the first speaker, rising and stamping his feet. "But what does any of this matter to the Council? I swear this is a fool's errand. Three suns have risen on this barren valley since we came here. And why?"

"Why indeed?" asked the third man, who had not spoken yet. He had an unpleasant hissing sort of voice and quick, sly eyes. "We are to find out if Obernewtyn is truly destroyed and if there is truth in rumors of sedition here."

"One look answered those questions," said the first man.

"Did it?" asked the third in an insinuating tone. His two companions eyed him curiously.

"Do ye say there is sedition here? I have seen no sign of it," said the big highlander at length.

"I say neither yes nor no to it. But the captain is no fool. He would not stay here for pleasure. Perhaps he knows something we do not."

"What do ye mean?" asked the highlander.

"Just this—captains, as a rule, are told more than rank-and-file soldierguards. I heard he had his orders direct from the Council's agent. Who knows what information he has," said the hissing man.

"There *is* somethin' strange about these mountain folk," opined the highlander after a moment of thought. "I dinna know what it is, but when I am among them, my skin creeps."

"Mine too," said the first man. "Ariel spoke certain of sedition, and he's seldom wrong."

"Call him not by name!" snarled the third man, glancing about as if he feared immediate reprisal.

"His name is not so secret," sneered the first.

"Well, then call him by it when next you see him, fool. *There* is one to make a man's skin crawl."

"I say we mun just as soon kill them all, miserable creatures," the big highlander pronounced. "Then we need not trouble ourselves with findin' out if they be seditioners."

"Usually, we are told to bring back prisoners alive. But I have heard it whispered the Council's agent wants none to come alive from the mountains. I wonder if it is true, and why," pondered the first man.

"Indeed. I wonder what he suspects . . . or fears," said the third soldierguard.

After a long pause, the highlander shook himself like an ox. "I wonder only how long before my head rests on a real bed an' my tongue tastes a sweet fement," he sighed plaintively.

"Never, if I catch you idling again when I have given an order!" came a new voice, so close my heart skipped a beat. Cautiously, I moved and saw that two more men had entered the clearing. From the markings on his collar, the tall, sallow-faced newcomer was the captain.

But the person behind him was no soldierguard. I stifled a gasp at the sight of Rushton!

Clad in shabby trousers and a ragged jumper, he was grim-faced and gaunt. The wild, dark gleam in his eyes told me why the soldierguards had judged him mad. He looked like a man possessed, and deep lines of suffering and despair made him appear far older than he was. There was a bitter twist to his lips that I had never seen before, and I was filled with pity at the thought of what the destruction of Obernewtyn had meant to him. He must have loved it more than life for its demise to mark him so.

As if he sensed my scrutiny, his head turned; he seemed to stare straight into my eyes. I shuddered at the emptiness in his face and was glad when he turned aside to follow the captain and his men from the clearing.

I slumped back, aching all over from tension. I could not forget Rushton's face, for it warned me worse might have happened than I could even imagine.

I went afoot as we made our way back along the valley, but this time we went more warily and stayed close to the walls of Obernewtyn where trees grew thickly, offering shelter. I noticed fumes of faint blue smoke rising from the ruins and was struck by the feeling that I had seen them before.

"Elspeth?" came a voice from behind. I whirled in fright and found myself looking into the astounded face of Daffyd. Gahltha, who did not know him, moved aggressively between us, until I reassured him.

Daffyd came forward slowly, as if he thought I would disappear. "By Lud, it *is* you!" he cried. "I thought I was dreaming with my eyes open. We thought you dead. Your feet . . ." He looked down.

"Are healed," I said firmly. "I coerced you to think them worse than they were, because I knew I could not make it back to the mountains before the pass closed. But what has happened here? Was Obernewtyn like this when you arrived? Were any hurt in the firestorm? And when did the soldierguards come?"

Daffyd burst into laughter. "It must be a powerful

illusion if it fools even the guildmistress of the farseekers. But they do say little Dragon is as strong as you were . . . are," he added ruefully.

I felt my mouth drop open, and a great joy welled up in me. "Then . . . this"—I waved a trembling hand at the ruins—"this is all an illusion?"

"Of course," Daffyd said.

I sank to my knees, weak with relief. "No wonder Gahltha behaved so oddly. Dragon's illusions do not work on animals." I sent an explanation to Gahltha, who still looked puzzled.

"Then everyone is inside?" I asked.

Daffyd shook his head. "Rushton thought that too much risk. We are using the Teknoguild cave network as a base. Only a few live in the camp, for appearance's sake. Rushton, of course, and Ceirwan, Dameon, and most others trained in farseeking and empathy."

"Not coercers?" I wondered.

"They are in another hidden camp very near the pass," Daffyd explained. "They are our insurance, in case this sleight of hand fails to deceive the soldierguards and open battle is needed to stop them carrying tales to the Council." He frowned. "But how is it they did not see you come through the pass just now?"

I shrugged, realizing it would suit me to have everyone think I had come from the highlands, rather than from the high mountains. "I came very stealthily. And I have some coercive Talent. The soldierguards didn't see me either, but I saw them. And I fear we might have to fight despite this illusion." I told Daffyd what I had overheard.

"It is true the soldierguards have stayed longer than we hoped," Daffyd said worriedly. "Tonight Rushton

vill come here, and you can tell him this news." He
;ave me a quick look. "He will be amazed to see you
.ere. I think your death was a grievous thing to him."

I nodded absently. "I heard one of the soldierguards
ay they have been here for three days. How is it
)ragon can sustain an illusion so long?"

"She has practiced all wintertime," Daffyd said.
Even so, it is a strain, and she does not maintain it in
he dark hours. Luck has made them come in the wan-
ng of the moon. The blue fumes are an added touch to
;ive credence to Rushton's story that the ruins are con-
aminated. That stops the soldierguards wanting a
loser look." He glanced at the ruin pensively. "I won-
ler what keeps the captain suspicious."

"From what I heard, it has to do with Ariel's insis-
ence."

"You were seemingly right about his haste for revenge. As you feared, the soldierguards arrived the
moment the pass thawed," Daffyd said. "We have kept
)ragon out of their sight. It is easier for her to hold the
llusion away from the distraction of people. Matthew
tays with her to protect her during the day. At night,
ve three camp not far from here, for no one would dare
ome so close to Obernewtyn. They will be back soon.
n the meantime, what about some food?"

"I'm starving," I said fervently. "And so is Gahltha."

As we walked to the campsite, I explained to the
)lack horse all that I'd learned. It did not take Daffyd
ong to make a small fire and warm some stew. Gahltha
)referred grass to the bags of horse feed. I sat gratefully
)y the fire and accepted a cup of strong fement once I
.ad eaten.

"I meant to go back down to the Druid camp after

delivering Dragon and your message, but that very night, snow fell thick and closed the pass," Daffyd said sitting beside me.

"I suppose you're worried about Gilaine and the others . . . ," I began, then faltered, seeing the grim look on the armsman's face.

"I don't know if they're still there. One of the soldierguards said the firestorm had all but burned out the White Valley."

"Oh, Daffyd," I said, aghast.

Again he shook his head. "I don't believe they are dead. Rushton has pledged Obernewtyn's help to find them when the soldierguards are gone." He sipped his drink as if it held a bitter draft.

We both froze at the sound of running feet. The brush parted, and Roland burst into the open. "Where's Matthew?" he cried. "We need him to farseek the camp. Something has gone wrong. All contact has been severed, but we dare not go down there with the soldier guards . . ." He stopped dead, catching sight of me. "Elspeth?"

"Yes, it's me," I said impatiently. "I'll see what's happened."

"But you . . . ," he said, dazed.

I waved him to silence, closing my eyes to concentrate. I sent my mind flying toward the makeshift camp, seeking out any familiar pattern. It was as if all there slept.

At last I located a weak consciousness. Focusing in, discovered it was Ceirwan.

"Who . . . who is that?" he sent groggily, barely discernible.

"It is Elspeth," I sent. "What has happened there?"

There was a pause. "Elspeth . . . impossible."

I felt his grief but could waste no time on it. "I did not die. Now you must focus. I can hardly understand you. What has happened?"

I sensed his struggle to concentrate. "I . . . They drugged us. The soldierguards think we hide evidence of sedition in the ruins. You must stop them from getting to Obernewtyn . . . get coercers . . ." He faded out again, and this time it was impossible to recall him.

I opened my eyes. "They're okay, but they all sleep," I said. "The soldierguards have drugged them and are about to go and examine the ruins firsthand."

"We'll have to fight," Daffyd said.

I shook my head. "I have a better idea, Daffyd. One less likely to escalate into violence. You ride Gahltha and bring back one of the coercers. The guildmaster, Gevan, if you can. Also, get a group of them to go down to the camp as soon as the soldierguards leave." I outlined my plan quickly.

"It might just work," Roland said.

"And it would explain why Rushton was so anxious to keep them away from the ruins. But will the captain react as you expect?" Daffyd asked.

"It's my guess they'll prove a craven lot, more worried about their own skins than their duty. But if not, Gevan is a coercer, and so am I, at need."

"You, a coercer?" Roland asked sharply. I ignored him, giving Daffyd a leg up onto Gahltha. The black horse allowed Daffyd to mount, then sped off, keeping close to the tree line.

"Come. We'll meet Gevan in front of Obernewtyn,"

I told the Healer guildmaster. "We'll have to make sure they don't come too close to the buildings. Now describe to me the symptoms. . . ."

It was dusk when the soldierguards appeared, riding along the entrance road leading up to Obernewtyn. Catching sight of Gevan and me, the captain reined his horse.

"Who are you, girl? I've not seen you before. What trickery is here?" he shouted harshly.

When I did not answer, he ordered one of his men to bind us. The man dismounted, but he paused when he was close enough to see my face clearly.

"Captain . . . I think there's something wrong with her . . . ," he called uneasily.

I lurched toward him, and he backed away hastily. "Help me!" I moaned. "Help me. I am ill."

The captain dismounted, staring at me suspiciously. "Ill? What do you mean? I won't stand for . . ." He stopped, having come close enough to see the black blisters on my lips. Gevan moaned loudly, making the man jump. His face changed, contorting with horror, and he spun away. "Lud's curse! These creatures have the plague!"

The soldierguards murmured in dismay.

"Shut up and let me think!" the captain snarled, mounting his horse. The other soldierguards did the same.

"What are we goin' to do, Captain? We won't be allowed to live if anyone finds out we've been in contact with the plague!" said one soldierguard.

"We can't stay here. I don't want to die of plague!" wailed another man.

"We won't," said the captain tightly. "Now listen to me, all of you. It will take closed mouths and a tight story to save us from being burned. We will tell the Council all was as Rushton had claimed—Obernewtyn a poor ruin, the valley tainted. We will tell them we found no one here. No one must ever know there was plague here. Even a whisper would be enough to see us dead."

The men nodded, ashen faced.

"But are we not already infected?" asked one of the men.

"Thank Lud we made our own camp and did not sup or dally with these wretched people. 'Tis said plague spreads by close living. We should be safe if we leave at once."

"What about these two and the people in the camp? We can't leave them here alive," said another of the soldierguards.

The captain shook his head grimly. "There must be no witnesses. If anyone ever does come up here, it must be exactly as we have said. Do not bother with these half-dead wretches. The wolves will finish them. But while the others are drugged, we will burn the camp. Now let's ride. I want to be quit of this cursed valley as soon as possible."

It was growing dark when the soldierguards torched the camp.

As I had hoped, they did not trouble to make sure their victims were inside, else they would have found the settlement deserted. The coercers had carried all the unconscious out and set them under the trees.

From the distance, we watched the huts blaze.

Silhouetted in orange light, the soldierguards let out a hoarse cheer before mounting and riding out of the valley. None looked behind him.

"Are they all right?" Gevan asked, watching Roland lift Rushton's eyelid.

He nodded in satisfaction. "Only drugged, though I have not seen this kind of drug before." He moved to look at Ceirwan.

I leaned over Rushton and stared into his ravaged face. In repose, he looked so terribly sad.

Unexpectedly, his eyes fluttered open, flamed with longing; then he shook his head and groaned. "Ah, Elspeth, love," he sighed; then his eyes fell shut.

I stared down at him in wonder.

✦ 27 ✦

"I am the Master of Obernewtyn. Who among you will choose a guild this night?" Rushton asked.

Those prepared crossed to stand in line facing him. "We choose our places," they spoke in unison.

Rushton handed each of the candidates a candle and then lit them all from his own, the flame guttering slightly. Fortunately, the wind was low. "May you choose well," he murmured.

"I am Merrett. I choose the Coercer guild," said the first, a thin, dark-eyed girl.

There was a predictable buzz of surprise, since her mother was a healer. Merrett crossed to the table and set her candle amidst the Coercer token.

Zarak, grinning with pride, held up his own candle. "I am Zarak, of the Beastspeaking guild. With permission, I choose anew: the Farseeker guild." There was a burst of applause as he crossed to the Farseeker table, and I smiled inwardly at the success of Ceirwan's negotiations.

There were no other surprises, and when all had chosen, the newly guilded led a toast to Obernewtyn.

Able to escape momentarily from his affectionate guilders, Dameon came to sit beside me. I was amused and flattered to hear some children sing an idealized version of my own first journey to Obernewtyn.

"I had no idea how brave and wise I was," I laughed.

Dameon smiled. "I think they are already at work on the epic of your journey to the coast. But I doubt anyone will ever sing the complete story."

I looked at him. Dameon had always been able to see more than most people. Like Atthis, his judgment lay in some keener place than his eyes. I had not told anyone what had happened in the mountains, but for a moment, I was tempted to confess to the empath. Such a secret burden made me feel lonely, even in the midst of my friends. Then I remembered Atthis's warning that I must tell no one of what I was to do.

Behind my seat, Gahltha stirred, as if he, too, heard an echo of the voice that had changed his life. The black horse had become my shadow whenever I moved outside Obernewtyn's halls, regarding himself as my special guardian. Fortunately, this was not too noticeably odd, since he and Avra had become the first animals to attend guildmerge. Rushton had decided to make use of the direct entrance from the outside that had once been a secret passage; the horses used it proudly.

Dameon patted my hand. "Some secrets are safer kept."

I smiled wanly. "I'm glad to be home, but I can't help worrying about what will happen next."

Dameon shrugged. "The battle is won, but the war goes on. Do not dwell too much on yesterday's struggles. Take things as they come. Today is a day for singing and celebration." He laughed. "Do you suppose

Kella and Domick will bond before they go back to the safe house in Sutrium?"

I stared at the empath. "They told you?"

Dameon smiled. "I am an empath master, but the greenest novice might guess as easily. They might as well announce it and get it over with."

I grinned. "They're working up courage. It will rock their two guilds on their heels. Merrett's choosing will be nothing to that."

"It is well done. Such divisions are not good for Obernewtyn," Dameon said approvingly.

"I hear Dragon is doing well as an empath novice," I said, catching sight of the red-haired beauty.

Dameon shook his head. "She is a handful, that one. I do not envy Matthew her violent affections. Yet I would like to know more about her past."

Lina ran up, grinning. "Dance with me, master?" she cried, taking his hands. I opened my mouth to rebuke her, but to my surprise, Dameon let himself be coaxed to his feet. As if sensing my surprise, he cast a smile over one shoulder. "Remember, today is for dancing, not worrying about the future."

I sat back in my seat. So much had changed subtly at Obernewtyn, as if winning one battle, even if by trickery, had given everyone bolder hopes.

It was spring, and the choosing ceremony had been the high point of our own moon fair. It was the wrong season and the moon had waned, but the brief, lovely season and an increasing feeling of hope for the future ensured its success. There had been a merry feast. After the choosing, there were tests of skill between the coercers, a vision demonstration by Dragon, and various entertainments by the other guilds as the musicians played their instruments.

Daffyd appeared beside me with a mug of fement. I motioned him to sit as the musicians tuned between songs, and strains of discordant music filled the air.

Daffyd smiled, but his eyes were sad. "Gilaine would love this," he said wistfully.

"Is there any news of them?"

He shrugged. "Nothing definite. You might remember Gilbert, the leader of the armsmen? He devised a plan some time back in case there was a need to evacuate the camp in a hurry. It was meant to be used in case of soldierguard attack, but it would have served well in the firestorm. If Gilbert survived to put it into operation, he would have kept the survivors together."

"Have you spoken to Maryon? She might be able to help pinpoint them."

"The Futuretell guildmistress thinks they're alive, but 'tis hard for her to get a definite reading, because she dinna know them." Daffyd was sunk in thought for a minute. "I mean to leave when Domick, Kella, and the others go. I'll travel with them as far as Sutrium and then . . . well, I'll keep lookin'. Rushton has offered help, but until I find some clue as to where they are, I'm better working alone."

I felt a shadow touch my heart at the thought that each had his own deeds to do, his own battles and quests. Mine lay in a dark chasm across endless Blackland plains.

I caught sight of Rushton deep in conversation with Brydda and Gevan, apparently oblivious to the music and laughter. As ever, he treated the festivities as yet another guildmerge, going from one group to the next in his effort to have everything organized before his departure. He was going down to the lowlands with Domick and Kella when they returned to Sutrium with Brydda. The big lowlander had been vastly impressed with all he had seen at Obernewtyn, and he and Rushton had taken an instant liking to one another. Brydda was eager to have Rushton meet his allies.

Addressing a guildmerge, Brydda had made it clear that though he had no prejudices about Misfits, he could not speak for his allies. But he was certain that, in time, the book I had found about mind powers would convince them that our Talents were not evil or mutations caused by the Great White but were a natural development of human abilities that had existed in the Beforetime.

Brydda had brought Katlyn and Grufyyd to Obernewtyn to stay. His parents had hated the city and had been only too glad to be invited to live at Obernewtyn. Katlyn had already begun to replant her collection of herbs, much to Roland's delight.

The news of Pavo's death had saddened me, though I had expected it, and the Teknoguild, still mourning his loss, had mounted an expedition to the city under Tor in his memory. I felt the loss of Jik even more keenly.

Maryon had told me she'd foreseen his death soon after we had departed, though not Darga's. "It is true the predictions focused on the boy, but I think the dog would not have gone without him," she explained. "Futuretelling is inexact at the best of times, and I regret that. But there is no sense blaming ourselves for Jik's death. Who knows what would have happened to him if he had not left the cloister or if he had not gone on your expedition and Obernewtyn had fallen. Dwell not on this death, but on his last happy days with us."

Brydda whirled Kella past me in a dance, rousing me from my memories. I smiled, already regretting that Brydda had to leave. He had a heartening manner and a cheery way of making everything seem possible.

As with all coming and going at Obernewtyn, they would travel across the now barren White Valley and down the Olden way. Few dogs were as sensitive to poisonous taints as Darga, but with care, it would be possible to find a suitable path, retracing our own journey. It was no longer safe to come openly along the main way, as our mountain valley was supposed to be deserted and barren. Domick had gleefully informed us that this was the report made by the soldierguards. It had been accepted by the Council, and Ariel had lost some credibility over the matter. With this and the disappearance of the Druid and his people, Ariel was no longer in a position to threaten us.

From the corner of my eye, I watched Rushton. No emotion showed on his features. It struck me suddenly that he had spent a lifetime hiding his thoughts and feelings.

The memory of his words as he lay dazed after being drugged by the soldierguards came back to me with a queer thrill. No one had heard those words but me, and it was clear from Rushton's behavior afterward that he did not remember having said them. Yet, in the light of them, many things seemed suddenly clear: Kella's cryptic scolding about my inability to see the truth of things, for one, and Rushton's reluctance to let me join the expedition to the lowlands.

I turned to find Rushton standing beside me and

flushed at my thoughts, glad he had no ability to deep-probe.

"You are always alone, even when there are people about you," he observed.

I shrugged. "Matthew tells me I'm too gloomy. But I find it hard to forget all the bad things. All this is wonderful . . . but sometimes it seems like a pleasant dream that can't last. So many have died. And Jik was so young. It's a high price we pay for our place in the world."

"If we did not fight, there would still be deaths, because Misfits will continue to be born. We want to stop the killing, and that means fighting."

"War to end war? It doesn't sound very sensible," I said. We stared at the dancers for a moment in silence; then I felt his eyes on me.

"I could scarcely believe it when I heard you were alive," he said remotely. I did not know what to say. When I looked up, embarrassed by the long silence between us, his expression was stern and unsmiling.

"It will take much to convince me to let you go away again," he said gravely. "Yet I sense you don't really belong to us or to Obernewtyn. There is something in you that holds you ever apart. You are like a piece of smoke in my hand."

"I am glad to be home," I said, not knowing what else to say.

A wintry smile lit his dark features. "Home? This is the first time I have heard you call Obernewtyn that."

I smiled. "You would be astonished at how often I thought of it that way and longed to be here. What is that saying Louis has?"

"The greenest grass is home grass . . . something like

that." He gave me a long look. "You are a strange one, Elspeth. Everything you do is mysterious and unexpected. Roland is sadly puzzled over the healing of your feet. He tells me even the scars have disappeared—something he assures me is impossible. The coercers talk of nothing but your ability to coerce as well as Gevan, and the healers praise your miraculous healing of Maruman. Not to mention the change in Gahltha. And what of your sudden appearance when we had thought you dead? How much more is there about you that you choose to keep hidden? I would swear you tell more to Gahltha and that cat than to any of us."

I suppressed an urge to smooth the frown from Rushton's forehead. I had never imagined loving anyone, and I had always believed Rushton incapable of doing so. Perhaps I was wrong in both cases. But something stayed my hand and tongue.

My life would not be fully my own until I had fulfilled my vow to destroy the weaponmachines. Until that was done, I could not truly belong anywhere or to anyone; I had no right to think of Rushton as anything but the Master of Obernewtyn while my dark quest lay before me. That secret set a tiny chasm between us. And until that was gone, I did not belong even to myself.

"Tomorrow you go to the lowlands," I said, wanting to distract him.

He looked out beyond the walls of Obernewtyn. "Maryon said the time to take our stand is not far away. I want to meet Brydda's friends and see how they regard Misfits. There is no good our making allies of bigots, and despite his optimism, I think not all his friends will welcome us with open arms."

"What about Ariel? Domick said he has taken vows to become a Herder," I mused.

Rushton shrugged. "We have nothing to fear from those dabblers in dresses. But Ariel has much to fear from me. I'll deal with him once I have dealt with the Council."

I looked at him, hoping he was right.

"We have come far, but the road is not yet ended," Rushton said.

I sighed. "Don't you think of anything but fighting battles and winning? There must be more to life than that."

"More? Perhaps," Rushton said. "But life is a battle just the same, whether you fight it with weapons or with words. You have to fight for what you believe in and for the things you want."

Abruptly, he held out a hand. "Dance with me."

I stared at him, astonished. I had never seen Rushton dance, and I did not dance myself. I opened my mouth to say so, but the words died on my lips.

His arms went about me, lightly and impersonally as one might hold a piece of soap.

"I have always fought for what I want," Rushton said with calm determination.

✦ EPILOGUE ✦

IT WAS RAINING.

"Soon the coldwhite will come again," Maruman sent.

I looked down at him, marveling again at his recovery. His appearance was as disreputable as ever, but his eyes shone with their old stringent light. We were in the Futuretell hall, waiting for Maryon.

"The time of cold is the time when Obernewtyn is safest, secure behind a barrier of snow and ice," I sent.

"There are some things no barrier can hold away," Maruman sent.

I stared at him, suddenly uneasy. "What do you mean?"

"When the others come, it will be time to make the dark journey," he sent.

I shivered, knowing at once what he meant, though we had barely spoken of it since the day I had returned from the mountains. "What others?" I sent.

"You will not go alone," Maruman responded. "The oldOne has promised." I received a vague mental picture from Maruman of what looked like many dogs. One, I knew.

"Darga?" I whispered, wondering if it was really

possible Darga had survived and, if so, where he was. And what did he have to do with my quest?

"He will come, and when he returns, it will be time. Best to forget until then," Maruman sent.

I dared not ask him to explain. Maruman had only ever told what he wanted and no more. Besides, I thought morosely, I would know soon enough if what he said was true.

If Darga returned . . .

I wondered suddenly if this had anything to do with Maryon's request for me to call on her. I was aware she was more likely than anyone else to see what lay ahead for me. Already I had appeared in her dreams, but as yet she had not fathomed the meaning.

Abruptly, I felt cold with premonition. Unlike Maryon and those of the Futuretell guild, my ability to see the future was restricted and infrequent. Most often, my premonitions were no more than a strong feeling of danger, but I had become accustomed to trusting them.

Sensing my mood, Maruman looked at me, his yellow eyes gleaming in the dull evening light. "Fear or no, you must do what must be done. You are the Seeker."

"That's what scares me most," I sent. "If I fail . . ." Strangely, Rushton's face and his words on the day of our moon fair came into my thoughts.

Life is a battle. You have to fight for what you believe in. . . .

"Even the funaga have their times of wisdom, rare though these come," Maruman sent with oblique humor.

I laughed.

✦ ABOUT THE AUTHOR ✦

ISOBELLE CARMODY began the first of her highly acclaimed Obernewtyn Chronicles while still in high school. She continued writing while completing a Bachelor of Arts and a journalism cadetship. This series and her short stories have established her at the forefront of fantasy writing in Australia and abroad.

She is the award-winning author of several novels and many series for young readers, including The Legend of Little Fur, the Gateway Trilogy, and the Obernewtyn Chronicles.

She lives with her family, and they divide their time between homes in Australia and the Czech Republic.

What will come of the Misfits' alliance with the rebel forces?

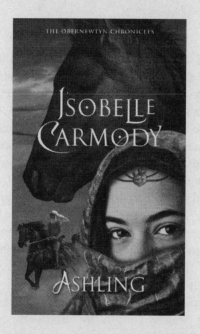

THE OBERNEWTYN CHRONICLES

ISOBELLE CARMODY

ASHLING

Turn the page for a sneak preview of Elspeth's journey to Sutrium—available now!

Excerpt copyright © 1995 by Isobelle Carmody
Published in 2008 by Random House Children's Books,
a division of Random House, Inc., New York.

WE HAD REACHED the outer rim of the labyrinth of narrow streets that was the city center of Sutrium.

We came around the corner and groaned at the sight of the sea, a seething gray mass in the rain. "We should have turned left back there," I said. My senses detected powerful static from the direction of the water. There had to be something nearby tainted with holocaust poisons, I thought.

I opened my mouth to speak to Matthew and almost bit my tongue off when Gahltha leapt forward and galloped at a breakneck pace back along the lane. I managed to keep my seat, but I almost flew straight over his head onto the cobbles when he halted abruptly and swung sideways.

"What are you doing?" I demanded. Then I faltered, feeling the panicky shift in my mind that could mean only one thing. Someone was tampering with my thoughts!

The alien probe sensed my awareness and fled from my mind, at which point I saw what I had been prevented from seeing sooner.

Crouched in the alley was Dragon, dripping wet and staring up at me with defiance and fear.